GAME ON

JUSTIN FOX

Printed in Australia

Cover by Melinda Childs @studioorchard

Internal design by Coven Press www.covenpress.com.au

First printing: December 2025

RICHFOX BOOKS Pty Ltd

www.justinfoxauthor.com

Paperback ISBN 978-1-7637492-4-5

eBook ISBN 978-1-7637492-3-8

Hardback ISBN 978-1-7637492-5-2

Distributed by RICHFOX Books

RICHFOX BOOKS acknowledges the traditional owners of the land and pays respects to the Elders, past, present and future.

A catalogue record for this work is available from the National Library of Australia

Also by Justin Fox

The Fallen
Quietly Waiting

Author's Note

Game On is actually my first attempt at a novel and precedes *Quietly Waiting*, which was released first in 2024 and my novella *The Fallen*, also released in 2024. The first draft was written between the 25th November and 31st December, 2018. This final draft, completed in 2025, is vastly different to the first one, though the foundation of the story remains the same. The events in this book take place between August 1978 and October 1980, the month before the US Presidential Election.

I hope you enjoy it.

-JRF

For Grant, a great and true friend.

For my wife Meg and children Nicholas, Hayley and Charli.

Special thanks to Peter Richmond, an unwavering pillar of support,

my mother, Evelyn Fox, who encouraged me to write,

my editor, Samantha Elley, whose brilliant insights turn good into great,

Alana Lambert for the incredible formatting,

Melinda Childs for another incredible cover design.

1

I T WAS 1978 and Rory watched the flames slowly shrinking, through the car's rear vision mirror, as it sped into the blackness. There was something hauntingly beautiful about the way they danced across the narrow glass that momentarily distracted him. It was only when his friend went into convulsions, that he was jolted back to reality. Rory fought to hold onto his friend, as the bottom half of his body bucked off the rear seat and into the air. Rory stroked his hair as his face contorted and he frothed at the mouth, sweat breaking across his brow.

The convulsions seemed to increase the flow of blood that was covering both of them, soaking their clothes, seeping through to the white upholstery beneath. A memory came to him from the distant recesses of his mind. Whether it was something he had read, watched or been told was lost to him, he wasn't sure but only that it was now screaming at him to be acknowledged. He called to one of the others, without naming anyone in particular.

'We need to stem the flow of blood, one of you reach across from the front while I hold him. We need to fashion a tourniquet.'

One of the boys leaned back over the seat, uncertain what to do.

'Take off your belt, run it around his leg, then tighten it.'

He removed his belt and was thrown sideways as the car went sliding around a corner, the sound of the engine roaring, tyres screeching. His eyes shifted down the blood-soaked torso, to the waist and then the right thigh where he spotted a hole in Johnny's jeans. This is where the blood was pouring from. He held his belt, hovering over the prostrate young man.

'What's the hold up?'

'I need something to act as a bandage.'

'Here use this.'

Another young man appeared, bare chested, brandishing a white t-shirt.

'Fold it over.'

With a lot of effort, the three of them managed to get the torniquet in place. The blood soaked through the white material at first then, as pressure was applied, gradually began to slow.

'Has the bleeding stopped?' Rory yelled, panicked, as seconds felt like hours.

'No but it's slowed.'

Rory let out a sigh. Every one of the five occupants of the car was pushed beyond their limits. None of them was equipped to deal with the situation which they currently faced. They desperately needed someone to take charge. Rory had begun to, only to stop once the torniquet was in position. The three men in the front seat were younger. Apart from the frantic, shallow breathing emanating from the back seat, there was silence. They were looking to the back seat for guidance, but Rory had nothing left. Johnny, who normally filled that role, was bleeding to death.

As Rory sat paralysed, unable to act, an argument erupted over what to do next. Rory felt it all slipping away. He looked down into his friend's eyes and saw he was in so much pain. Then for an instant, Johnny opened his eyes, fixing them on his friend. They said one thing, more than any words.

"Help me."

Digging deep, Rory found his last remaining energy, balled it up in his stomach then screamed at the top of his lungs.

'Shut the fuck up!'

The three sitting in the front seat looked around in shock. Rory's voice echoed throughout the tight confines of the car. It was followed, not by a suggestion but, by a command.

'Drive us to the university hospital!'

Without another word, the car accelerated through the deserted streets, towards its goal, leaving some of the tension in its wake. Light rain began to fall, and Johnny retreated into unconsciousness as Rory shed a tear.

2

TOMMY NERVOUSLY LOOKED over his shoulder. Seeing nothing, he snapped back around, eyes darting in every direction, scanning the shadows for danger. Moving quickly, the desire to run was overwhelming. He focused on his breathing; in through the nose, out through the mouth, 1, in 2,3,4,5,6, out, 2,3,4,5,6 repeat. It worked. After a few rounds he felt calmer; his discipline held. His brain, on fire and flooded with endorphins, began to slow. He needed to rest, needed time, time to think. That was impossible, not yet. Be calm, keep on moving, was the order he issued.

The muscles in his legs ached. He was no longer used to this. He dragged himself along. Something, call it instinct, drew him towards the beach. He battled his way towards the ocean, when he heard the waves breaking, there was relief. He could hide here; there were plenty of places. Here he could blend into the surroundings, either on the beach itself or beneath one of the piers. Salvation was at hand. He strode quickly along empty bike paths. Soon he was walking on sand, there wasn't a soul to be seen. Light rain began to fall as he set out for the nearest pier.

Walking across the sand was difficult, his breathing becoming laboured. Anxiety returned. Sweating, despite the increasing rain.

The pier, seemingly out of reach as he battled towards it. Slowly he trudged on, relentlessly, one step at a time. He was beginning to crack when, looking up, he found himself just a few feet from it. Hesitating for a moment at the entrance to the cavernous underbelly, he checked the beach again. It was still empty. He looked underneath the pier; if there was anyone in there, they were well hidden in the blackness. The rain continued to intensify. Setting aside his misgivings, he headed underneath.

The pier was made of concrete. Although it provided excellent protection from the weather, the sound of the waves breaking was amplified in the tomb-like space beneath it. Tommy wondered how far the tide might rise. Perhaps there was a reason people didn't take shelter beneath it. He reasoned that, for now, it was far enough away not to worry him.

He kept walking until he reached what he reckoned to be the middle. There was no light. He judged his position by the light at either end. An uneasy feeling followed him. It was irrational, he told himself, bending down he picked up a hand full of sand which was dry. He removed the knapsack he was carrying then sat down, his back resting against a stonewall. He had a torch but dared not take it out. Tommy collected his thoughts, replaying the events that had led him into hiding beneath the pier.

How long could he stay there, or more to the point how long should he stay? The mantra began again; keep moving. He silenced it, keep moving but where? There was also the problem of the gun.

With a jolt and a sickening feeling in his gut, he realised the gun in his knapsack was currently his biggest problem. Disposing of it could greatly improve his chances of escape. With a burst of energy, he removed it, along with a small torch that he very carefully switched on. Lifting himself onto his knees, he turned to face the stonewall, shielding the light. Tommy studied it. The stones were stacked on top of one another. Testing a few with his hand, he found some were loose. He began working these back and forward until he could remove them, leaving a gap. Quickly, he wiped down the gun with a rag, then wrapped it in another one, before carefully sliding it into the hole he had made. He then replaced the stones, taking a quick moment to observe his handiwork, before plunging himself back into darkness, turning, then slumping against the wall.

After a few minutes, he gathered his things then made his way to the other side of the pier, emerging into the same rain that continued falling. It was then he realised he still had a box of cartridges in his bag. That would be difficult to explain if he was searched. Climbing up onto the boardwalk he began to walk out to the end of the pier. Mercifully, there was nobody there. He took the box out then, stopping every few paces, he threw them into the swirling ocean below. He stopped for a few moments at the end of the pier to look out, before retracing his steps and continuing into the night.

3

THE UNIVERSITY HOSPITAL was little more than a teaching clinic. It was a place for students to find their feet, to play at being doctors and nurses and added some prestige to the institution. They treated students and a few members of the community, all at no or little cost, though their offerings were limited. The emergency department treated sporting injuries, cuts, bruises, sprains and the odd broken limb.

A knee specialist was in high demand during football season for injuries of a very minor nature. Other operations performed included appendectomies and tonsillectomies. There had once been plans for a larger facility, for research; grand plans that were never realised. The teaching faculty was small but experienced, if not distinguished. The students were carefully monitored, watching, more than doing. It was somewhere to begin, before moving on to something more real. They certainly were not used to dealing with situations like the one that was about to unfold.

The car containing Johnny turned into the hospital's driveway, coming to a stop with a screech of brakes outside the emergency room door. The boys in the front seat jumped out as the car was still moving. Two of them ran inside for help, while the third tentatively opened the back door. The sight of so much blood shocked him. Awkwardly, he reached inside, taking hold of Johnny's legs and helping Rory carry him out.

The emergency door burst open. A student in green scrubs emerged, took one look, then set off at a run. He returned a few minutes later with a middle-aged woman and a stretcher. They carefully placed Johnny onto it, while he moaned loudly. Nurse Schroder had begun her career at a dreary hospital in downtown Chicago and was no stranger to sights like this. She took charge.

'Now, everyone calm down. The most important thing in situations like this is not to panic. You're going to be fine son, just fine.'

With the assistance of the student and two wardsmen, they wheeled Johnny into the emergency department.

As a veteran of the Korean war, Doctor Cortez was no stranger to gunshot wounds. He strode into the emergency department and, like Nurse Schroder, he was calm, decisive. He examined the wound. The amount of blood was concerning but no great worry; he would check the artery for damage.

'Piece of cake. He's lost a lot of blood, but he'll be okay. Prep him.'

The surgery went as the doctor had predicted. The bullet came out easily, the artery was fine. There would be a scar but the doctor felt that within days the patient would be walking around. A few weeks after that, it would be nothing more than a memory. After changing out of his scrubs, he went to see the young man's friends.

He found them spread around the waiting room. As he entered, all eyes followed him.

'Your friend will be fine; he's resting right now.' There were visible signs of relief, amongst them. 'So, tell me what happened.'

They shared glances, worried glances. One of the young men, covered in blood, raised his hand to speak. He introduced himself as Rory.

'Our friend, Johnny, was showing us his grandfather's pistol, when it went off,' he said.

The young man's eyes avoided the doctor while he was speaking. *Is he lying,* the doctor thought? *Why would he?*

'I thought that it might be something like that. Where's the gun now?' asked the doctor.

'Is that important?' asked Rory.

'The police will want to see it.'

'The police?'

'Yes, not to worry though, accidents like this happen all the time.'

More nervous glances. Rory continued, 'That might not please the governor.'

'The governor?'

'Johnny, our friend, who you treated, he's Governor Hollingworth's son.'

The doctor considered this. Governor Hollingsworth was a benefactor of the university.

'Okay, you had better come to my office and call him.'

4

RORY SAT IN the doctor's office, staring at the phone. He had tried ringing Johnny's father, the governor, only to have to settle for the butler, who said he would pass on the message at once. He was dreading his arrival. *How had it come to this*? he wondered. Johnny and his games. What was he going to tell him? That his son, the class president, the bright, star of the football field, also liked to play other games; games that more closely mirrored his dark and psychotic nature.

It had begun innocently enough. Rory remembered the first game they had played three years earlier. It was not long after he had arrived at Barker University, he was young and naïve, the winner of the Bell-Montague scholarship, a kid from less fortunate circumstances who had gotten lucky. He arrived on a bus, with a single suitcase. Johnny, in contrast, arrived in a new, black Pontiac Trans Am, following the family limo, laden with the bare essentials to begin university life. Tradition dictated that all freshman students were allocated their room and roommates by way of a lottery, drawn by the residence hall director. Round wooden tokens with painted numbers, handmade by the director, were placed into a box; two tokens for every room. Then, with great ceremony, they were drawn. Johnny and Rory both had number six called. They were lucky, room six was prime accommodation on the second floor that overlooked the garden of the historic, whitewashed, redbrick building.

He saw little of Johnny in those first few days. His belongings had been placed in their room, then unpacked for him, but after a week he had not stayed a single night there. Then on Saturday, he had arrived and announced they were going out to get to know one another. Along with three other muscle carloads of fellow students, they headed to a party in the Hollywood Hills. Rory wandered around, staring in wonder at the sheer opulence that surrounded him, when Johnny called them all together.

'Gentlemen,' he proclaimed, 'in order to better get to know one another and to make the evening even more fun, I suggest a game of tag.'

They had all looked at each other and at Johnny. One of the boys, Rory couldn't remember his name, asked the question on behalf of the group.

'The game we played as kids, where we chase someone?'

'No, my version of tag,' Johnny replied, 'I'll choose a girl, one who is single. When I pick her, I'll touch her, tagging her, then the game is on. I'll withdraw, then whoever can land the girl before midnight wins and, to make it interesting, we each throw in 10 bucks. I'll throw in 50, because it's my idea. Winner takes all.'

They looked at one another.

'Come on fellas what do you say?'

Each of them reached into their pockets and offered Johnny the money.

'Rory, you hold it,' said Johnny.

'I'm not sure I can affor-'

'Don't worry, I'll cover you. You can owe me.'

Rory remembered how he wasn't sure.

'C'mon, we're roomies. It'll be fun.'

'Okay.'

Rory remembered Johnny handing over the money. He could not

ever remember another time, up until then, when he held $130 at once. For the next hour, everywhere Johnny went, the eyes of all the boys followed until, ever so slightly, after speaking to an attractive brunette, he touched her on the left arm as he walked away. And so, the first game began.

All night, one after the other, each of the boys tried and failed to get anywhere with the girl whose name was Gwen. Rory, who had always felt nervous around members of the opposite sex, waited until Johnny, who was the last to try, before swallowing hard and making an attempt of his own. As he approached her, she smiled at him. This gave him some encouragement. At the same moment, someone turned up the stereo, so their voices couldn't be heard above the music.

Gwen leaned close to his ear. 'This music is too loud, let's go for a walk.'

Without waiting for a reply, Gwen took him by the hand, leading him through the maze of people and rooms, out onto the patio. Her skin was soft, her touch warm.

'What did you say your name was?'

'Rory.'

'Where do you go to school, you're a student aren't you?'

'Barker.'

She looked him up and down, he couldn't tell if she was impressed or not.

'What about you?' Rory asked, with a confidence that surprised even him.

'Carter.'

'Nice.'

'Tell me, you're a scholarship kid, right?'

'Yes, that's right, how could you tell?'

She smiled.

'Because you're not an arrogant asshole.'

He laughed. 'Is that a problem?'

'Why would it be? No, anyway, I'm a scholarship kid myself.'

'Boise, Idaho.'

'Lincoln, Nebraska.'

They shared a smile. A voice came from the shadows.

'Gwen, it's time to leave.'

She looked at him and shrugged.

'Sorry.'

Gwen started to walk past him, then turned, stood on tip toes and kissed him on the lips. Rory, taken by surprise at first, soon warmed to the idea and gripped her firmly around the waist. They were both enjoying the kiss when the voice returned.

'Come on Gwen, or we'll leave without you.'

She broke off the kiss.

'Got to go. Call me, Aphrodite sorority.'

And she was gone. Just after she had left, Johnny stepped from the shadows.

'Well done,' he said as he noticed Rory blush with embarrassment. 'No need to be embarrassed.'

The other boys stepped out onto the patio.

'We have our winner, boys. Rory has proved quite the Valentino.'

'Hurrah.' There were continual cheers and punches on the arm, all in good humour.

'Now let's get a beer,' grinned Johnny, slapping Rory on the back.

With that, they all headed back inside to celebrate. Over the next six months, Rory went on a few dates with Gwen but they never went beyond that. The game had been innocent, pure, a little fun. Nobody got hurt, but it had set them on the road that led them here.

<h1 style="text-align:center">5</h1>

TOMMY CONTINUED WALKING until the dawn sun had fully risen. Although he had put miles between himself and the events of the previous night, his problems were following close behind, chasing him down. His mind was racing again. Due to fatigue and under the heavy weight of anxiety and paranoia, it was collapsing. It was time to rest, properly rest; he could go no further. Searching for somewhere, he spied a café, another sanctuary. Sitting down at a table gave him great relief. He spoiled himself, ordering too much food: pancakes, toast, coffee.

Tommy's mood improved with every mouthful but now he needed sleep. He asked his waitress, who tipped him off that there was a motel, a short walk down the street. He found it, paid cash for two nights and registered under an alias. He was now in shutdown mode. He barely made it to the room, yawning all the way. Quickly undressing, he fell onto the bed and was asleep in seconds.

When he woke, it was afternoon. He didn't know where he was at first; it took a few seconds to clear away the fog. His first impulse was to keep running, to pack his things, then hit the road. It was perhaps even time to consider getting out of the country: Mexico, Canada, maybe permanently. He managed to calm himself down enough to take a shower. After washing away the grime, he felt more human. He talked himself into returning to the café for a late lunch. Changing into fresh clothes, he carefully opened the door. After a few moments of doubt, shielding his eyes, he ventured out into the world.

The café wasn't busy. He flirted with the same waitress from breakfast, while she took his order. She brought him a newspaper and coffee, while he waited for his food. Opening the paper, Tommy wasn't paying much attention, sneaking glances at the waitress, until he reached page four. Halfway down the page was a story that sent shivers down his spine, pushing him straight back into the dark places. He was re-reading it when she returned with his food. Fully engrossed, he ignored her.

'Are you okay, honey?'

Tommy looked at her, confused, glanced back at the paper and spotted the food. Remembering where he was, he tried to smile.

'Umm, yes, yes fine, thank you.'

She smiled, leaving him with a slight look of concern.

He ate with no joy, going through the motions as the dark thoughts continued to grow. The air around him grew heavier. Losing his appetite, he put the food aside, returning his attention to the paper. Time stood still; he could hear his heart beating, his lungs dried up and sweat broke across his brow.

'You okay, hon?'

She was back, asking again, her voice showing genuine concern.

She liked the look of this man. She felt there was some mutual attraction. She had even considered asking him to join her for a drink when she finished her shift. When he didn't move, she became concerned. After an eternity, Tommy looked up at her, snapping out of his stupor.

'I'll be okay I just need a minute.'

'Can I get you something?'

'No, I just read something that affected me. I'll be fine.'

'I'm just about to finish my shift, would you like to join me for a drink? You look like you could use one.'

Tommy was surprised at the offer.

'Sure,' Tommy said, rallying a little.

'Great, there's a place right down the street, the Camelot Lounge. Give me ten minutes to change.'

Tommy followed her with his eyes as she walked away.

'Wait, your name is Louise, right?'

She stopped.

'That's what it says.' She pointed to her name tag. 'What's yours?'

'Tommy.'

'Nice to meet you, Tommy, I'll see you in a few minutes, then we'll go for that drink.'

She gave him another nice smile and a wink.

6

SLEEP HAD LATELY been hard to come by for Governor Hollingsworth. There was too much going on. He had taken to laying down on the leather sofa in his home office for a few hours each night, so as not to disturb his wife. Sometimes he managed to drop off, mostly he just lay there with his eyes closed, trying not to think. On this night, he must've fallen asleep at some point, because the next thing he could remember there was a knocking at his office door. It was their butler, Saunders. He opened the door to a grave faced man wearing a dressing gown. There were no greetings.

'Sorry to disturb you, Sir. It seems that there has been an accident involving Johnny.'

'What happened?'

'The caller didn't say, only that he is alright and currently a patient at the university hospital.'

He sighed. Instinctively, he knew this wasn't good. He loved Johnny, loved all of his children but Johnny was a problem.

'Thank you, Saunders, could you bring the coupe around? I'll drive myself to the hospital.'

He crossed the room to his desk and picked up the phone; it was answered on the 3rd ring.

'Randle, it's me.'

There was a pause.

'What is it?'

'Johnny's had an accident.'

'Where is he?' came the reply, in a tone of annoyance.

'The hospital at the university.'

'What happened?'

'I don't know yet?'

Another pause.

'I'll meet you there.'

With a click, Randle was gone.

The governor, James Hollingsworth, reflected as he drove through the empty streets towards the hospital. Johnny had always been a troubled child. Now, as an adult, he was becoming a liability. A problem right at a time when he needed to have no problems of this nature. It was no secret that he was favourite to be the Republican Presidential candidate for the upcoming election. The last thing he needed was a scandal involving his youngest child.

There had always been a dark side to Johnny. They had noted it from a very young age; it scared both him and his wife. Although he had yet to learn the details of this particular incident, knowing his son's history, his knack for getting into trouble, it would not be your regular, run of the mill situation.

Randle, his trusted advisor, met him at the hospital door.

'Any details?'

'None. Saunders took the call, only that it's an accident, that he's okay.'

Randle sighed. The governor put on his friendly public persona, as they approached the reception desk, where a young nurse was stationed.

'Good evening, I'm here to see my son, Johnny Hollingsworth. I believe he was admitted earlier.'

The young woman looked him up and down, she recognised him. He offered his broadest smile. She returned it.

'We've been expecting you. Professor Cortez is waiting, please follow me.'

She led them through a series of corridors to the professor's office. The governor, always one with a wandering eye, enjoyed the view following her from behind. The professor stood when he spotted them, greeting them at the door. He offered his hand as the nurse stood aside

'Thank you for coming Governor Hollingsworth, I'm sorry to meet you under the circumstances.'

'That's quite understandable, please call me James.'

'John Cortez, I operated on your son earlier.'

'Thank you, Doctor. How is Johnny?'

'He's fine, he's in recovery; he was sleeping the last time I checked.'

'That's a great relief. Are you able to share the nature of his accident? We are yet to learn any details. Forgive me, this is my chief advisor, Randle.'

'Pleased to meet you.'

The doctor shook Randle's hand then looked at the nurse.

'Nurse, could you please bring the patient's friends in to see us?'

'Yes, Doctor.'

'Please, gentlemen, come in, take a seat.'

'Thank you.'

The office was small, plain, just a desk, two chairs, some filing cabinets and a potted plant. When they were settled, he continued.

'This may come as something of a shock. Earlier this evening, I treated your son for a gunshot wound to his upper right thigh.'

He paused as Randle and the governor exchanged glances.

'A gunshot wound?' repeated the governor. 'Do you know how my son came to be the victim of a gunshot wound?'

'He arrived here with some friends of his.' The professor leaned forward on his desk, hands clasped. 'They told us that it was an accident, something about an accidental discharge when he was showing them a gun he had borrowed. Here they are, you can ask them yourselves.'

Randle and the governor turned around to find four young men, one the Governor recognised as his son's friend, Rory, standing sheepishly outside the door. Rory's clothing appeared to be covered in something. *My god,* he thought, *that's dried blood.* He regained his composure, offering one of his campaign smiles.

'Gentlemen, sounds like you've had quite the evening.'

'Boys, come on in. Please tell the governor what you told me earlier.' Doctor Cortez said, in a calm, encouraging tone.

The governor offered another smile as they shuffled into the cramped space. With much hesitation, Rory repeated the story he had told earlier, constantly looking to the others for encouragement. He was met with eyes cast down at the floor. By the time he had finished, the governor's smile had somewhat wilted.

'Gentlemen, there is no blame here,' he finally responded. 'My family and I are grateful for the help that you have given to Johnny. You have our complete support; there is no question of that. Please, is there anything that you have left out that we need to know? Anything at all?'

The smile returned as he said this. He was met with silence, so he tried to push harder.

'I understand in times like these, we want to protect the people we care about, you are all good friends of Johnny's. You want to protect your friend.' He paced back and forward in front of them as he said this, all their eyes carefully following him. 'Only now is not the time for that. In order for us all to help Johnny, you boys must tell us everything, no matter how difficult that is. I know that you all look up to Johnny, I also know he is no angel. Hell, I love the boy.' He chuckled, looking down for a moment, as if remembering some childhood mischief. 'This isn't the first jam we have had to pull him out of, so is there anything that you haven't shared with us or been completely honest about?'

A knock at the door. The nurse had returned.

'Excuse me, Doctor, the patient has woken up.'

'Thank you, Nurse.'

The doctor wanted to escape what was becoming an awkward

situation. The governor seemed bent on cross-examining the boys. Politely, he excused himself. Taking one last look at the boys, who looked like prisoners standing in line, he took pity on them.

'Governor, might I suggest you accompany me to visit your son. We can continue this discussion later.'

Smiling, the governor stood then, with Randle, followed the doctor out into the hallway, while the boys remained.

7

THE CAMELOT LOUNGE was only a short walk from the café. It was bar, come night club, with a stage at one end of the room, surrounded by tables and a long bar with bar stools at the other. It was clean and a little classier than Tommy had imagined. Louise knew the barman and introduced him, when they ordered drinks.

'This is nice, do you come here often?'

'I've become a regular. It doesn't look like much but it's a nice, clean place, people are friendly, it's close to my apartment, the food is good, the music is great.'

He smiled. It had been a long time since a member of the opposite sex had shown any interest in him. He was enjoying it.

'What's your story, Tommy? What brings you here?'

'I'm from back east, divorced. I decided that it was time for a change of scenery, I have no children, no ties, so I decided to come west. A good friend is out here, he's always telling me to make the move, the timing was right and I thought, *why not.*'

'Welcome to sunny California,' Louise said raising her glass.

He clinked her glass with his and they each took a drink. He wanted to ask her a question or two, however, he was feeling shy. Louise kept the conversation moving.

'What is it that you do?'

'Law enforcement, that's what I've been doing since I left the army.'

'That's interesting,' Louise smiled.

'I'm ready to try something new. My friend has a law practice and said he will help me find something.'

'I used to see a lot of law enforcement people in my last job.'

'What job was that.'

'I used to be a nurse.'

'Now that's interesting.'

'Not really as glamourous as it sounds. I'm on an extended break from it. I started in the military too, five years.'

'Another drink?'

Without waiting for a reply Tommy headed to the bar. When he returned, he steered the conversation into more general areas of interest: sporting teams, movies, TV shows, books each had read. It turned out they had a lot in common. The time passed quickly, the bar began to fill as evening gave way to the approaching night and he felt the pangs of hunger returning,

'Would you like to get something to eat?'

A band began to play.

'Yes, but not here,' said Louise, nodding towards the band, 'it's too loud. There's a Chinese place down the street.'

The soft, warm California air welcomed them as they stepped back out into the street. Emboldened by the alcohol, he took her hand and Louise led him to the restaurant, where they feasted, enjoying one another's company. Tommy managed to leave his problems behind, focusing on Louise.

When they were finished, he walked Louise home. They stood outside of her building, holding hands. Louise dropped her eyes as Tommy leaned in to kiss her. It had been a long time since he had kissed anyone. When their lips met, he felt the passion rise and placing his hands on her waist, he drew her closer to him. The desire was powerful as it started coursing through their bodies.

When they broke the kiss, he held onto her, looking into her eyes.

'Come upstairs?' Louise said softly. 'We have tomorrow.'

Louise had the day off. They had agreed to spend it together. She looked into his eyes but he could not be persuaded. Tommy knew that he wasn't ready. She let him go, smiled turned and walked inside.

8

THE GOVERNOR LEARNED an important lesson the night of Johnny's accident. Regardless of your feelings towards them, the frustrations and trouble they caused you, when you walked into a hospital room and saw one of your children with tubes coming out of them, helpless, it simply broke.your.heart. Fighting to keep control of his emotions, he stood staring, unable to get the image of the innocent little boy, who used to run to greet him whenever he returned home, out of his head. He wanted to cry one moment, then became angry the next, wondering how his son could be so dumb, fooling around with a loaded gun.

'Rest now my boy, rest.'

The feelings of helplessness were overwhelming. Doctor Cortez moved in and began looking Johnny over. The governor retreated next to Randle who was standing alone, just inside the doorway. Randle's ability to detach himself emotionally was legendary.

'How do you read this, Randle?'

'Boyhood hi jinx. So long as they have been truthful, we can easily hush it up.'

'Truthful?'

'Well, if they are lying and there is more to it, such as...'

'Such as what?'

'Such as, a police investigation or a body in a morgue somewhere, that can be connected to them, then we have a serious problem. Right now, all we are dealing with is some drunk young men, fooling around with a gun.'

'Do you think one of the other boys may have shot him accidentally?'

Randle shrugged. 'It's possible, then what they told us is also plausible. Johnny has never been very bright in situations where he is showing off, especially when he has been drinking.'

'Perhaps we should grill the boys a little harder, make sure they are telling us the truth.'

Randle nodded his agreement. They found them in a waiting room, looking lost. They didn't spare them, wasting no time in getting to the point, Randle leading the way. He had no problem playing the role of the bad cop.

'Look boys,' he started, 'it's not that we don't believe your account of events, it's just that we need to be certain that we haven't missed anything.'

Rory, having had the time to come up with an alternate truth, one that contained some facts, gathered all his courage, looked the governor in the eye and lied.

'Well, I suppose we need to come clean,' he said, 'we had been drinking all day, an unofficial back to school party that just grew a little out of hand. We ran out of beer. Timmy,' he pointed towards one of the boys, 'was the only one of us sober enough to drive, so we ventured out to buy more. On our way out of the liquor store, a man, a homeless man asked Johnny for some money. An argument began that escalated quickly. Johnny was drunk, the man began to fight and then another man appeared.'

He paused, wondering if they were believing his story; they were both very hard to read. The governor encouraged him, 'Please continue.'

'As I was saying, another man appeared out of nowhere. He had a gun. We backed away. The man fired. That's when Johnny was hit.'

For reasons he didn't fully understand, saying this brought his emotions to the surface. The horribleness of the night descended upon him with full force. Rory began to weep uncontrollably. None of them knew what to do. Sheepishly, the governor approached Rory, placing his arm around him, despite the dried blood of his own son still covering his clothes.

Speaking softly while the others stood staring, 'It's okay, it's okay, we will get through this together.'

The unbridled release of emotion gave validity to his story. The governor and Randle exchanged glances. This changed things, changed them drastically. They were both thinking the same thing and they waited for Rory to regain some composure before continuing.

'I'll need the location of the liquor store, and the approximate time. Timmy, was it your car you were driving?' asked Randle.

Timmy replied without confidence, 'Yes, it's parked right outside, It's a mess.'

'Not to worry. We will take care of that. If it can't be cleaned, we will replace it.'

Timmy nodded, Randle paused for a moment before continuing, 'Now boys, I want you to listen very carefully to what I'm going to say. For now, what happened tonight never happened, do you understand?'

They all nodded.

'Good. Tell nobody. No parents, girlfriends, teachers, not a soul. You have all been through quite the ordeal. We will send you all for a two-week mid-term vacation to somewhere nice, so you can forget all of this and have some fun. Somewhere in Mexico, perhaps. Don't worry about school, we will speak to the dean, then when you return it will be as if you had never been gone. Is that agreeable?'

Rory looked at the others. It seemed agreeable. The sombre nature of the occasion prevented them from showing much enthusiasm.

'Sorry, I should have mentioned, there were more of us there, when the shooting took place,' Rory said.

'How many?' asked Randle.

'I'm not certain.'

Timmy intervened.

'Three carloads. Us five and another eight.'

'Okay, then you are all going to Mexico. You boys gather the others. Here's my card, call my secretary and she will arrange everything. Also, that's the number you call if the police or anybody else comes to talk about what happened.' He handed them all a card each. 'Timmy, leave us your keys. Here's $50, take a cab back to the fraternity, get changed, enjoy your vacation. We will be in touch, thank you boys.'

Randle needed a phone. Both he and James traced their way back to the doctor's office, which was empty. He took out the small address book that accompanied him everywhere then dialled the number of a police detective who was friendly. It took three separate calls before he answered. Randle was effusive in expressing his gratitude for answering the phone in the middle of the night, though he did not apologise for calling. Very calmly, he went about explaining the situation, careful not to give any incriminating details. The detective promised to come back to him as soon as possible.

'Now we wait,' he said.

James, who suddenly looked tired, shrugged. 'Can't be helped let's get out of here.'

'What about Johnny?'

'They'll contact us when he is ready for visitors. For now, he is well cared for.'

Randle looked at James. He knew he cared about Johnny in his own way. *I mean*, he thought, *we are here, aren't we?* Still, at times, he was left to wonder.

'Should we move him to a private clinic?'

'I suppose so.'

'I'll add it to the list. We need to see the dean.'

'That won't be a problem, he will want to help us, we're old friends. Our family considers him to be a highly honourable man.'

Randle understood immediately. Somewhere in the past, either the dean or his father or perhaps grandfather, had come to the old man for help. Such things were not forgotten. Their world was built upon being able to ask favours of one's friends.

'What about the staff here?'

'Reward them. We need to ensure their cooperation. Make a list of everyone on duty tonight. We need to keep this out of the papers and off the TV screens.'

'I'll take care of it.'

9

L OUISE HAD IMAGINED many different scenarios that might have taken place on the following day after her date with Tommy, as she fell asleep alone in her bed the night before. Back then, she was in the afterglow of having met a nice man, enjoying his company, then sharing a passionate good night kiss. Louise had been a little disappointed at how the night had ended, a little rejected when he hadn't wanted to come upstairs. After all, she was a child of the summer of love, without the hangups about sex that plagued previous generations. At the same time, it was romantic, chivalrous, another reason to like him.

No, the day was not turning out as she had envisaged. Not for the first time she asked herself, what the hell she was doing there? Why she hadn't simply called for an ambulance, then left?

She arrived at the motel at the agreed time. When there had been no response to her knocks at the door, she thought he had overslept. A sympathetic maid offered to check for $5. No sooner had she entered the room, she called Louise in, where she found a catatonic naked man, lying on the floor. The maid had abandoned her to her fate. Louise had spent the rest of the day, whispering to him, trying to get through to Tommy who was there physically but seemed miles away mentally.

When she wasn't doing that, she was trying to phone his friend, having found what she prayed was the number next to the phone. She had almost given up, when she tried one more time just after 6pm. On the third ring, it was answered, Louise swallowed.

'Hello?'

'Hello, my name is Louise, are you Tommy's friend?'

There was silence.

'Yes, my name's Jack.'

'You don't know me; this may sound a bit strange,' she paused, gathering her thoughts. 'How do you know Tommy?'

There was a pause on the other end of the line.

'We were in the army together.'

'And he was coming out to stay with you?'

'Yes, I've been expecting him to call me.'

'My name's Louise, I recently met Tommy. He's unwell. I didn't know who else to call but he had mentioned a friend and I found your number.'

'What do you need me to do?'

Louise felt relieved. Tommy's friend's willingness to help lightened her load considerably.

'It might be easier if you came to his motel. I think he needs to see a doctor, maybe a psychiatrist. I could better explain in person and you could see for yourself.'

'Louise, was it?

'Yes, that's right.'

'It's very nice of you to look after him like this, I appreciate it. Where is the motel?'

'It's The Three Lanterns Motel, room seven. Do you know it?'

'No but I can find it. I'll leave in five minutes and be there as soon as I can.'

'Thank you.'

Louise put down the phone. She felt better now that help was on the way. She walked back over to where Tommy lay, staring up at the ceiling. Reaching down, she held his hand and waited.

No sooner had Jack hung up the phone, he picked it up again dialling the number of his secretary, Maria.

'Maria, it's Jack, I'm sorry to call you at home, I need your help with something.'

'That's okay, what do you need?'

'That doctor, the psychiatrist who did some work for us a few months back, what was his name?'

Maria recalled from memory, 'Doctor Feldman.'

'That's it. Is there any way you could contact him tonight? A friend of mine needs someone in his line of work. I could really use his help.'

'I can try; he owes us a favour. We took care of that thing for his nephew, free of charge.'

'That's right, I remember now. Could you call him and ask him to be on standby, explain the situation and that I'll call if I need him?'

'Sure thing, where can I contact you?'

'I'll be at the Three Lanterns Motel, room 7. I should be there in an hour; someone is already there, her name is Louise you can leave a message with her,' he said and added, 'Thanks Maria, you deserve a raise.'

'My boss is too stingy,' she replied cheekily.

Jack had one more call to make. He dialled the number of his friend, Marcus, a doctor.

'Marcus.'

'Jack, to what do I owe the privilege?'

'Where do I stand in the favour stakes?'

Marcus laughed.

'Anything within my power to grant you.'

'A friend of mine needs some help. I'm about to go and see him at a motel. I was wondering if you would come along, in your capacity as a doctor and for moral support?'

'Gee I'd love to help you out, only that gallery thing is on tonight and I promised to attend. I don't want to let Elanor down.'

Elanor was a mutual friend who owned an art gallery.

'You're right, I completely forgot. I promised to go also. Tell you what, it's only early, I'll make sure we make it there. We can do both.'

The line went quiet as Marcus considered the proposal.

'If you promise that we will make it, I'll come.'

'Thanks, you got it, I'll pick you up in five.'

10

THERE WAS LITTLE conversation in the car on the drive to the motel. It wasn't that Jack didn't appreciate Marcus for coming with him, on the contrary, he was happy he had been able to convince him to. It was just that he had no idea what awaited them and this was causing Jack no end of anxiety. Marcus, while disappointed in the lack of conversation, understood. He had never been in the army, had never tasted battle, had never known the bond that developed between men who relied on one another for survival, men who they owed their lives to. Neither man was able to express themselves, so they continued in silence.

Before they knew it, they spotted the motel. Jack turned into the driveway. They both approached the door to room 7 with trepidation. Jack looked at the closed door, sensing, that trouble lay behind it.

'Ready Marcus?'

Marcus nodded and Jack knocked on the door. Louise was quick to open it. They looked at each other for a moment.

'Louise, is it?' Jack asked, his voice grave.

'Yes, please come in,' she replied.

Both he and Marcus noticed a tinge of fatigue in her voice. They stepped into the room and saw the only light was coming from a lamp next to the bed.

'I'm Jack, we spoke on the phone. This is my friend Marcus. He's a doctor and I thought he might be able to help.'

'Louise, what can you tell us?' Marcus asked in a calm voice.

'His vital signs are all okay, his pulse has been fluctuating a little, his temperature is okay. I have noticed his breathing, at times to be a little irregular, though nothing I would worry too much about.'

'You sound like you know your stuff,' Marcus said, impressed.

'I'm a nurse. Apart from his vitals, he is as you see him: curled up in a foetal position incoherent. He's been like that since I arrived this morning. I was about to call for an ambulance when I found your number.'

'I'll give him a quick once over,' Marcus said, leaving them as he crossed the room to examine Tommy.

'I was about to give up when you answered,' Louise said. 'I'm sorry about that, busy day at the office,' Jack replied. He looked across to where his friend was lying, what he saw sent chills through him.

Marcus came back to where they were standing.

'I can confirm what Louise said, there's nothing wrong with him physically. He needs the help of a specialist, someone who works on the mental side of things.'

Marcus' tone was serious. He raised his hand to his chin, deep in thought.

'I'd call that psychiatrist friend of yours, I don't mind admitting I'm out of my depth. I suspected something like that. Sometimes in Vietnam, they would bring in boys like that.

'Battle fatigue, they called it,' Louise added.

'I'll give him a call,' said Jack.

Marcus went to find them something to drink and they sat largely in silence as the they waited for Dr Feldman to arrive. Doctor Feldman was friendly; he conveyed an air of confidence.

The first thing he said when he entered the motel room was, 'Well, what do we have here, nothing that can't be put right I'll bet.'

He warmly shook hands with everyone, taking time to introduce himself. He left Tommy until last and the others retreated outside, while he conducted his initial assessment. The doctor's demeanour had not changed when he eventually joined them.

'Your friend in there is a lucky man,' said Dr Feldman.

'Why do you say that?' Jack asked.

'Well, how many people have friends like you three? People who would care enough about them that they would be here, at this time of the day, that would use their contacts to have someone like me visit out of hours. I'd say that made him pretty lucky, wouldn't you?'

'Yes, I hadn't thought about it like that,' said Jack.

'What's your diagnosis?' Marcus asked.

'He has reached a crossroads in his life,' said Dr Feldman, 'Something has brought on this particular episode but this is something that has been brewing for a long time. A ticking time bomb of sorts. I don't know what the root cause is, I don't know exactly what triggered this episode. I do know, however, that if it's left untreated it will manifest until he breaks down completely.'

'What do you recommend, Doctor?'

Louise was touched by Jack's concern for his friend.

'If he will agree to it and we can find a way to pay for it, I would like him to be admitted for an extended stay, for treatment at a private clinic that I work at, there he will get the care and support that he needs, under my direct supervision.'

'I'll cover the cost, no problem there,' Jack quickly offered.

'And I can help give, emotional support,' said Louise, an offer that surprised even her.

'Well then, that sounds fine, if he agrees. I can take him there myself right now, get him settled in, then in a few days, time, you can begin visiting.'

'Thank you, Doctor. Whatever he needs, just bill me directly,' said Jack, shaking the doctor's hand.

11

RANDLE'S POLICE CONTACT was Ray Kent, a senior detective in the LAPD and a 20-year veteran. He was a similar age to Randle, tall, with the build of a heavyweight boxer, a no-nonsense street man, who didn't mind getting his hands dirty. Over the years, Randle had met far more senior people, yet none of them could be relied upon like he could. Ray didn't mind stepping across the line for a friend. He wasn't cheap. His loyalty came at a price but he had never let them down. They met in a small coffeeshop downtown, sitting in a booth far away from prying ears.

'Thanks for coming at such short notice. I appreciate it. I know how busy you are,' said Randle, shaking the man's large, club-like hand.

'No problem, it's been a while,' said Senior Detective Kent.

'How's the wife and family?'

'No complaints.'

'What have you got for me?' said Randle, getting straight to business.

'Not much. Only one call last night matches some of the details that you shared. At 23:30 hours, a unit responded to a call for assistance; officers arrived to find a homeless man, badly injured with first degree burns to 95% of his body. There was one witness, a drifter. He was asleep but heard the man screaming, came to his aid, accompanied him in the ambulance to hospital. Officers were called away to another emergency but when they returned to the hospital to take his statement, the man was gone. The victim passed away from his injuries and the case sits in limbo.'

He watched Randle for a reaction but there was none. He was playing his cards very tightly.

'Interested?'

'Possibly, who was the man?'

'The victim is well known in the area. He was something of a local celebrity, kept to himself, a war hero. The press has been digging into it. His nickname was the General and his belongings have been recovered. They are being held as he had documents and the body is yet to be formally identified. They are trying to chase down a next of kin, poor guy. I guess the world just forgot about him.'

'Any idea how it happened?'

'Nope, evidence points towards an accident. These old guys make fires on the cooler nights to keep warm, maybe he just got to close to it. The drifter is the only witness to come forward so far, now he's gone. Maybe we'll never know.'

'Any ID on the drifter?'

'No, he wasn't known hence the nickname. One minute he was there, the next he was gone. Nobody is really looking, there are potentially other witnesses but nobody's looking very hard though. Looks like it may be open and shut.'

'Other witnesses?'

'Yeah, somebody called it in for starters, somebody other than the drifter. Then there may be others. It was late, there's always other homeless people down there, they probably took off when they saw us arrive. You know how it is. Why so interested?'

Randle just smiled. His friend understood, he didn't pry. This cup of coffee was worth five grand.

'They'll probably call for witnesses to come forward. There's press interest so they have to make it look good. There's an election coming. Oh, is that why we are here?'

Randle shrugged.

'The governor cares for all members of the community.'

'It might just disappear. There's nothing suspicious, an accident, everyone is real sorry, we should do more for veterans. Might be some votes in it for you.'

Randle nodded, then slid an envelope across the table. Without a word, the detective put it into his jacket pocket.

'Keep me informed,' said Randle, 'let me know the moment you hear anything. This issue is important to the governor so there's plenty more where that came from.'

'Sure thing.'

As he drove away from the meeting, Randle turned things over in his mind. On the surface, there didn't seem to be anything to worry about. No mention of a shooting, that was in a way a relief. The boys' version of events didn't match what he had just been told. There were many red flags, inconsistencies, things that didn't make sense.

He didn't have any answers. Randle decided to visit the scene. The remnants of what had happened were still evident. He found the pavement, scorched black by the fire. Continuing his investigation, he found the blood stains and followed them back to where he supposed the boys had parked. Had the police investigation team done the same? Or had they thought that it was blood from the victim? The biggest hole in the story so far was that there was no liquor store. None anywhere in sight. The way the boys had told it, there was one person and he had been the attacker. If he, as the boys had reported, shot Johnny, then at what point did he catch fire?

An eery chill ran down Randle's spine. His years of experience gave him a vision of what may have happened. He prayed it wasn't the case, that he was wrong, only intuition told him, with near certainty, that he wasn't.

He arrived at the governor's personal residence in Beverly Hills. The governor was sitting out by the pool. It was a pleasant setting, only the governor was working. A telephone lead snaked its way out of the cabana, connecting the phone onto a table covered in files and notebooks. One of his secretaries retreated as Randle approached.

'Randle, good to see you. Come join me.'

As always, the governor was at his charming best, his casual dress of light blue slacks, deck shoes and white cotton polo shirt, belying the heavy work load he was undertaking.

'I've just left a meeting with our detective friend.'

'Oh, anything interesting?'

He asked this with the air of a man without a care in the world. Randle was about to spoil his mood.

'A few complications.'

'Complications?'

'I'm afraid to report that the boys have not been completely honest with us.'

The governor's expression began to change; he removed his reading glasses then began rubbing his eyes.

'What makes you say that?' he finally asked.

'An old man is deceased, there is a witness, a drifter who has disappeared. The police aren't suspicious. So far, they think it's an accident, only that may change if this man, this drifter reappears.'

'Are you concerned?'

'Very. I have a suspicion that, the boys did something to the old man, something terrible, then this other man intervenes. Now he's out there, doing who knows what.'

The governor raised his hands.

'Hold on for a minute, have you confirmed any of this?'

Randle eyed the governor carefully.

'No, not yet but why would somebody shoot Johnny? Think back to what the boys told us. This old man was a war veteran, a hero from World War Two. From what I have been told, experienced, battle-hardened. Why would he allow things to escalate that quickly? Sure, he might pull out the gun to warn them off, if he felt threatened, but why would he shoot one of them over a minor incident? It makes no sense.'

'What do you base that on?'

'Johnny still being alive.'

These chilling words stopped the conversation dead. After a long pause he continued, 'Johnny was shot in the leg. It was a warning shot, a shot to stop them from doing whatever it was they were doing. Whoever could make that shot, could have just as easily taken off his head!'

The governor had heard enough. He would face this as he had faced so many other problems.

'What should we do?' he asked.

'Speak to the boys, speak to Johnny. Discover the truth, plan our next move.'

Governor Hollingsworth threw up his hands in surrender.

12

J ACK WAS IN a far better mood on the drive back from the motel. He was still thinking about his friend, only now he was determined to keep the promise to his other friend; after dropping off Louise, it was full steam ahead to the gallery of their friend Elanor.

When they arrived, there was a sizeable crowd in attendance and the party was in full swing. Elanor was happy to see them, greeting them warmly by hugging them both.

'I didn't think you boys were going to show?'

Jack apologised for the both of them.

'It was my fault. Sorry we missed the start.'

'Looks like it's going well,' Marcus said, gesturing around the room.

'Better than expected.'

Jack had become distracted by someone on the other side of the room. He was looking at a woman, who was exquisitely beautiful. She wore a sleeveless, short, pale blue dress, that was elegant and unassuming, though something of a throwback to the dresses women wore 10 years earlier when fashion was daring. Even from across the room, her skin shone like burnished copper. It was a beautiful tone and he tried to pick her nationality. Was she South American or European? He couldn't decide. Her hair was long, black and free flowing. Her red high heels made her look even more elegant. He was instantly enchanted; she was stunning.

'Is everything okay buddy?' Marcus asked. Jack ignored him.

'Elanor, who's that?' Jack asked, his usually confident voice, reduced to a whisper. Both Marcus and Elanor's eyes followed his pointing finger.

'Who, the woman in the blue dress?'

'Yes.'

'That's Cindy, one of the artists. Her work is really stunning, unique. She's from Mexico, come with me and I'll introduce you.'

Jack crossed the room on shaky legs to where Cindy was standing. She turned around as Elanor said her name.

'Cindy, I'd like you to introduce you to a good friend of mine, Jack. Jack, this is Cindy.'

Cindy offered Jack her hand. For him, sparks flew as their skin touched, his heart raced. Jack stared at her smile. It was a beautiful moment; one he would remember and replay for the remainder of his life. Elanor noticed, suppressing a giggle; she looked for an excuse to leave them alone.

'Jack's rich, has a big new house, lots of empty wall space. We need to turn him into a collector, show him some of your work, Cindy. You have your cheque book with you, don't you, Jack?'

He was still thinking of Cindy's beautiful smile that she flashed once more. He would have agreed to anything.

'Um yeah sure, somewhere here.' He patted his jacket pocket.

'Good, I'll leave you both to it.'

Elanor winked at Cindy, then departed, Jack looked lost but she reasoned that he would survive.

'Becoming a collector, Jack? That's exciting.' Cindy's voice did nothing to break him out of his new state. To hear it was wondrous, like an angel. He tried to place the accent. It was subtle, adding mystery and accelerated his growing attraction.

'Yes, I'm interested in filling the house with beautiful things.'

This made Cindy smile and she began guiding him around the gallery. Stopping in front of a large painting of a woman dancing, she gestured subtly toward it with her hand. Jack stood motionless, entranced, his eyes moving up and down the canvas. It was a painting of a woman standing in a bar. She was wearing a white dress with pink flowers, black stockings and brown shoes. Her hair was tightly pulled back in a bun and between her teeth she was holding a white rose. The colours were raw, they caught his eye, the pink flower on the sleeve of her dress, drew attention to her expression that was intense serious, she was standing side on, no she was spinning and was caught in motion, mid-way around. The more he looked, the more he saw and the more he liked it. The mood was dark. There was smoke in the air; the woman, while spinning, was causing it to swirl around. Jack raised his hand in front of his face, palm facing towards the painting, as if seeking permission to ask it something.

'Tell me about it,' he said calmly, without breaking his trance, his hand still raised.

'It's part of a series of four, named The Dancer. I painted each one in a different style. Slightly abstract, they were all painted in a small cantina back home in Mexico. The cantina was only open at night, so I was able to convince the owner to let me work there during the day. Some of the dancers were willing to pose as models for me. These girls spend their nights dancing with lonely strangers for money, very small amounts, less than $2 a dance. Some of them are hoping that one day a man will come along, who will fall in love with them and rescue them. Their Prince Charming. Some have no hope, resigned to dancing like this until they can do it no longer.

'In between dancing with the customers, they perform traditional Spanish and Mexican dances in the flamenco style to entertain the customers. Some of them are very talented. I found their performances amazing; they really know how to captivate the audience. There are many great artists there. It's moving watching them as they give so much of themselves while performing. Then reality returns, as they return to dancing with strangers, shuffling around the floor for a few pesos. I found it difficult to accept their having to exist in this way. I felt their pain, the slow destruction of these beautiful artists' souls. I cried often there. The owner of this cantina is a mostly good man. He serves as a surrogate father, taking care of them, yet he exploits them also, so it is, well, a little complex. Still, when you consider the alternatives, a life in one of the brothels, this doesn't seem too bad.

'They all live together in the floors above the cantina and they have rules. They don't work Sundays, for example. The other three paintings in the series were sold. This one I had trouble finishing; I restarted it twice. I wanted all four to stay together but it was not to be. When I finally finished it, the collector didn't want it so, here it is. If you would like to buy it, it's yours.'

Cindy's explanation made the painting even more exquisite. Now, not only did he see, he felt the emotions also. These senses combined to bring a powerful force from within that, like the smoke, went swirling around inside him. Did he want it? How could he say no? The desire to own it was overpowering. The next painting Cindy showed him was just a few paces along and smaller in size to The Dancer.

Captivated, Jack found that although it may have been smaller, there was so much within. On a sunny beach, an older lady was playing with a group of children. Cindy waited, allowing Jack time to view the painting, before speaking. Jack took his time. As he looked more deeply, each time he felt he was unlocking more of the painting's secrets. The older lady was smiling. The joy of playing with the children was so evident; it radiated out from her face, surrounding them. The children's bathing costumes were bright colours, then he realised their colour was further enhanced by the sun. His eye was attracted to a green towel, a yellow bucket and spade in front of a half-built sandcastle. Cindy interrupted his thoughts to speak.

'This one is a memory from my childhood. It's very personal. The old lady is my grandmother, the girl on the left is me and the other three are my cousins. My grandmother loved the beach, loved the ocean, she always took us there on holidays. After I finished it, I started to question the authenticity of the memory as it's my recollection of a day spent together. My cousins have no memory of this. I think now it is more likely that it's pure fantasy, nothing more than an idyllic daydream. It's all from my head, no models, no setting; that's the second problem, nobody has a recollection of the location. I've visited the beach my grandmother took us to and it bears no resemblance to the one in the picture. Was it my ideal of a beach?' She shrugged. 'I have no idea, hence my decision to part with it.'

'It's, well it's very...' he tailed off, leaving the thought hanging.

With every glance, Cindy was becoming more beautiful in his eyes. Now, just as with the paintings, with every passing moment, he was noticing something new about her. She guided him around the rest of her paintings, explaining her work as they went.

They stood awkwardly when the final viewing was completed, Cindy smiling, Jack not knowing what to say. Elanor saved the day, arriving just when she was needed, champagne flute in her hand.

'Find anything that you like?'

Jack turned to face her. Without saying anything, he turned back to Cindy, then back to Elanor, amidst the confusion he addressed them both at the same time.

'I would like to buy the first two that you showed me: The Dancer and the beach scene.'

Cindy smiled. 'What do you like about them?'

He wasn't expecting this. *What was he expecting?* he wondered. Some fantasy about her falling gratefully into his arms, flashed across his mind.

'I like them, very impressive.'

Elanor intervened. 'I think Cindy was asking, what particularly draws you to these two pieces of work? What aspects motivate your interest in purchasing them?'

She smiled at Jack, waiting for his reply. That was not forthcoming. After what was an unusually long, uncomfortable silence, the penny dropped.

'Well, your use of the...' He stopped. They were staring at him.

Closing his eyes, he searched for the words to express that he genuinely liked them; they must be there somewhere inside his head.

'When I looked at them closely, I saw so many things; things I had never seen before when looking at a painting. Then as you explained each of them too me, they came alive in my imagination,' he said, 'I liked both of them straight away but when you described them to me, I fell in love with each, for different reasons. I immediately connected with the first story, about the women dancing with strangers. When you described it, all of a sudden, I could see their sorrow then, I found, when you spoke about their emotions, not only could I see, I could also feel these things in what you had painted. In the second painting, as you described your feelings of the inaccuracy of the memory, I was flooded with thoughts of a similar nature. Where I had remembered something, something special, only to be disappointed at the realisation that this memory, so perfect, so special in my mind, was simply untrue.'

It was Cindy's turn to be moved and she looked at him for the first time with different eyes.

'Thank you,' she said simply.

Elanor brought things to a close.

'Thank you, Jack, we appreciate your support. Cindy, perhaps you could exchange numbers and show Jack some more of your work on another occasion?'

Cindy smiled. 'I'd be happy to.'

Jack was emboldened; he continued speaking without thinking.

'How about dinner tomorrow night?'

'Sorry?'

'Have dinner with me tomorrow night. We can make plans for you to show me more of your work?"

Cindy rolled the invitation over in her mind.

'How could I say no.'

'Jack, come with me, we can finalise your purchases,' said Elanor.

Jack, a little reluctantly, followed Elanor. Later, when they were alone, packing up after the showing, Elanor spoke to Cindy.

'You look happy.'

'Why wouldn't I? I just sold two paintings.'

Elanor looked bemused.

'Strictly business then?'

'It's always exciting, when you sell your work.'

'I see, I'm impressed with your ability to stay detached.'

'He seemed nice but I don't fall for every handsome man who comes my way, tell me about him.'

Elanor gave her a look of complicity.

'So, you think he is handsome?'

'He has a certain something, I'm not certain that he is my type, even if he is an emerging art lover.'

Cindy's Mexican accent, usually very slight, was more pronounced as she said this.

'I see, well, I have known Jack for quite some time. He's a friend as we were at school together,' said Elanor nonchalantly, as she was checking over the books. 'He's single, has his own law firm, does very well for himself. His clients are all celebrities, actors, musicians, athletes, writers. He's carved out a real niche for himself. He has offices in New York and London or he's opening them or something. He recently bought a big house just up the road a way.'

'Have you ever dated him?'

Elanor giggled, 'Jack? Are you kidding?'

'Why not?'

'Perhaps but answer the question.' Cindy said this with a smile.

'I've never dated Jack; I was just never interested in him in that way. We have seen each other naked though. So, if you do date him, you will have to live with that.'

'When did you see him naked?'

What is this, the Spanish Inquisition? It was years ago, we were staying with other friends at a house out in the desert, Palm Springs. It was too hot to swim during the day so, one evening, late after too many drinks, we all decided to go skinny dipping.' Elanor blushed at the memory.

'Tell me, Elanor, do you think he might be interested?'

'Think it's a pretty safe bet.'

'Do you think it was his primary motivation to buy my paintings?'

Elanor placed a hand on Cindy's shoulder.

'No, I don't think so.'

Cindy smiled, taking Elanor's hand then squeezing it. *But it helped*, Elanor thought as she looked beyond Cindy's shoulder at the paintings hanging on the other side of the room.

13

CLAIRE HAD KNOWN Rory for three years. She was Johnny's first cousin on his mother's side. She had gotten to know him at various family functions and vacations over the years and from this, a friendship had developed. Johnny, wanting to make Rory more than a friend, had played matchmaker, encouraging both of them to become more romantic in their feelings. They began dating and a romance blossomed. They had been going steady for the past six months and were now crazy about each other.

Johnny had also worked toward securing a future for them. Through careful politicking, he had introduced Rory to key people at the family's bank, which led to an internship the previous summer that had impressed everyone. When word reached the old man, Johnny's grandfather, of the favourable reports of his granddaughter's beau, he had personally become involved in the young man's development, offering advice and support. As they were both in their final year of university, the family was expecting a happy announcement sometime soon. Johnny had done a better job in creating a future for Rory than he had done for himself.

It was only a day since the incident with Johnny. Rory needed to see Claire. He badly needed her company after all that had happened. He had already decided that he would not bring up what happened, unless she did, then he would lie just as he had been instructed to by the lawyers. He was overly sensitive, during their hello hug, holding onto her a lot longer than usual, kissing her with a lingering intensity.

'What's gotten into you?' she asked.

'I just miss you.'

'It's only been a week, you would think I hadn't seen you for a year. Maybe we should skip dinner?'

Rory was tempted but he wasn't certain he could be intimate in his current state of mind. *Hopefully later,* he thought, so he made a joke of it.

'I'm more hungry for food.'

'Typical, I should have known. It's not fair to get a girl all excited then disappoint her.'

She playfully punched him on the arm, before they walked to Rory's car. To Rory's relief, there was no mention of Johnny on their way to Madame Cho's, Claire's favourite restaurant. She waited until they were eating dessert, when he was relaxed, least expecting it, then casually said, 'What do you know about Johnny, being in the hospital?'

It took Rory by surprise. Claire noted his reaction and kept talking.

'You know my friend, Jenny?' Rory shrugged, non-committal. 'You remember? The blond girl plays tennis all the time. Well, anyway, she was playing tennis and sprained her ankle. She was in the hospital and somebody told her that the governor's son was there. Had some kind of emergency.'

'How did the person know it was Johnny?'

'Are you kidding, tell me someone at the university who doesn't know Johnny.'

He could think of one. Dr Cortez hadn't recognised him.

'I was wondering if you knew anything. I tried calling him earlier, the person who answered the phone said he was out,' Claire continued.

Rory didn't want to lie to Claire. He loved her and didn't want things to come between them, didn't want to start life in that way. His own parents had hated one another and he didn't want to live life in that way. With that in mind, he spoke.

'Johnny was shot in an accident. He's still in the hospital but he's okay.'

'And you're only telling me this now?'

'His father's lawyer told us not to say anything. I wanted to tell you, believe me.'

Claire looked hurt. She pushed what remained of her dessert, away. Rory, who was already experiencing the ups and downs of a hundred different emotions, took a deep breath

'I'm not hungry anymore, I think we should leave.'

Rory nodded, then called for the bill. They skipped the movie and were halfway home before another word was said.

'Should we go by the hospital?' Claire asked.

'The lawyer said he would be in contact, when visiting was possible,' replied Rory.

'The lawyer said. The lawyer said,' Claire used a mocking tone. 'I'm so tired of what the lawyers think we should do, aren't you?'

'In this case, I think that it might be for the best.'

'Why? What happened in this accident that was so sensitive that the lawyers became involved?'

Rory sighed. He pulled the car into a quiet street, parking opposite an empty playground.

'He was showing us an old gun. He was drunk, really drunk and it went off.'

Claire eyed him suspiciously.

'Did the lawyer make that up?'

Rory shook his head.

'No, that one was ours. We weren't thinking, it all happened so quickly.'

Claire was becoming impatient.

'You know, I don't even really care. Stuff like this happens to Johnny, he's been creating drama like this his entire life. He loves being the centre of attention. What I care about, is you putting my family over me.'

With this, Claire burst into tears. He spent the next half hour consoling her. Claire barely spoke on the remainder of the journey back to the university. He was expecting the cold shoulder but when they arrived, she surprised him.

'So, Mr Grumpy, are you going to sneak me up into your room?'

'You mean you still want to, after all that's happened?'

'I love you Rory, I love my family, but you come first. Be careful of my uncle and cousin, they can be ruthless, they can be kind. Remember always, they didn't get to where they are by accident.'

They were laying entangled on his bed. Rory was lost in the afterglow as he had needed this: the intimacy, to feel her touch, the softness of her skin.

'Are you going to tell me what really happened?' Claire whispered in his ear.

He had enough of this. He was going to come clean. What was the worst that could happen? She was Johnny's cousin, after all, but he would sanitise it. Johnny was already a villain in her eyes; he didn't want her to think any less of him.

'We had been drinking all day long,' started Rory, 'We were wasted but we had run out of beer. One of the guys was sober enough to drive, so we went searching. We couldn't find any and then Johnny spots this homeless guy. I don't know exactly what happened but the next thing I know, he's attacking the guy. A fire starts, then this other man appears out of nowhere, shoots Johnny. We grabbed him, loaded him into the car then high tailed it out of there.'

'That wasn't so hard, was it?' Claire said, moving so she was looking at him in the dark.

'No.'

'Doesn't it feel better now that you told me?'

'Yes.'

She rolled over, their soft moans escaping into the night. The next morning, she repeated it all in her uncle's study. Both her Uncle James and Randle listened intently. Claire finished with a warning.

'Make sure he doesn't find out that I told you, I intend to marry this man.'

'Thank you for telling us, Claire. Please understand what made this so necessary was, the boys haven't been very forthcoming. Believe me, we are only here to help,' said her uncle.

'He was only protecting his friend. That kind of loyalty is what makes him so dear to me.'

'You don't have to worry, he won't find out it came from you. I'll tell them that we have been informed by the police that another man was involved. That should get them talking,' Randle added.

'You've been a great help, Claire,' said the governor.

'I want a ring on my finger, Uncle. I helped you, now I need you to help me seal the deal, you know our motto, "Family First".'

'And you will have it, don't worry about it, leave everything to Randle and me.'

When she left the governor turned to Randle.

'You were right.'

Randle sighed. 'This Rory kid, what's your real opinion? Is he nephew material?'

'A hundred percent,' said the governor. 'Look at the loyalty he has shown my son. He's ambitious, extremely intelligent, good looking. He will be a great asset to our family.'

'I'm not convinced.'

'It's a good thing that you don't have to be.'

'Now, we had better get to work.'

Randle could foresee that the road ahead was going to be a long and difficult one. All the same, he started down it.

14

J ACK SPENT THE day in a state of tortured excitement. He should have been preparing for a case that was about to go to trial, however, very little work was done. He left the office early, then spent the afternoon trying to remain calm, which proved impossible, teetering on becoming a nervous wreck. He left his house too early and was forced to drive around aimlessly for 30 minutes, before pulling up in front of Elanor's home, where Cindy was staying, arriving at the front exactly at the agreed time. He was disappointed when Elanor, not Cindy, opened it.

'Hello Jack, Cindy will be right down.'

They stood awkwardly, both unable to come up with any small talk. When he saw Cindy coming down the stairs behind her, he felt his heart begin to beat faster.

'Hello,' she almost whispered.

She was wearing a short, white dress, that highlighted her soft, brown skin and her long, black hair which was free and flowing. Jack stood mute.

'Have fun you two,' Elanor called, stepping out of the way to let Cindy past.

Cindy turned toward her friend and winked. 'Don't wait up.'

Elanor giggled. She found the transformation of the strong, confident lawyer into the man in the early throes of love, amusing. She watched them as he fumbled with the car door. When she saw that Cindy was safely inside, she closed the front door and left them to it.

Jack closed Cindy's door then, awkwardly, walked around and climbed into the driver's side. Despite his nervousness, he managed to put the key into the ignition and start the car.

'I booked us a table, at Domenico's on Santa Monica Boulevarde, it's an Italian place,' he said.

'Sounds nice,' she replied.

They lurched away from the kerb.

'Nice car.'

Jack smiled. He glanced down to change gear and caught sight of Cindy's legs and failed to change it properly. There was a grinding sound.

'Thanks,' he replied.

'How has your day been?' Cindy asked, making small talk, in an attempt to calm him down.

'Oh, you know, what can I say? A lot of distractions, it was one of those days where you just never seem to get anything done. How was yours?'

'I didn't do much, just sat around Elanor's pool. I went for a walk in the afternoon, then wrote a letter to a friend.'

It was only a short drive to the restaurant. Jack pulled up in front. He raced around to her side but was beaten by the valet who, not only opened the door, but helped her climb out. He stood wounded until Cindy, smiling, offered her hand. They were seated and started reading the menus when the awkwardness returned, but this time, Cindy was ready for it.

'Elanor was telling me that you're a lawyer. How did you come to be doing that?'

'It's a long story, I have always had an interest in the law, going back to childhood, for as long as I can remember. I had never been very academic, though. In high school I was in a military program called the ROTC. I wanted to attend the military academy, West Point, only my grades were never good enough. When I finished high school, I went to college and continued the ROTC training. After two years, I had an associate's degree in prelaw and accounting. As part of the ROTC, I had completed several courses in the army, during summer breaks. There was a shortage of officers, so I underwent some accelerated training and was commissioned as a second lieutenant.'

'You were a soldier?'

'Yes.'

'Were you in the war?'

'I was. In many ways, it made me. I gained a lot of confidence there. I realised I could do anything if I put my mind to it. Towards the end of my career as a soldier, I decided to become a lawyer and I had an inner belief that I would find a way.'

The waiter returned with drinks and to take their orders. When he had gone Jack was happy to leave the conversation alone. Cindy made him continue.

'Are you going to finish your story?'

'Sorry, I thought I was boring you.'

Christ, she thought, *he was actually starting to loosen up.*

'No, far from it.'

'I decided to try life here in California. I'm not from here originally, I grew up back east. A great-aunt left me some money and I bought an apartment in Venice Beach and started studying law under the GI bill of rights, at UCLA. I found some part time work in a pizza joint. After I graduated, I worked for a while in a firm that had some celebrity clients and came to realise that a lot of these clients were being exploited. I gained a reputation for treating them honestly, for being their advocate. Championing their rights. I took a chance and opened my own practice. I specialise in celebrity clients: film stars, writers, musicians, sports stars. I represent a real diverse portfolio of people.'

Their food arrived.

'Do you have any famous movie stars on your books?'

'A few, plus a few rock stars, baseball and football players, couple of golfers.'

'Any artists?'

'Not so far, would you like to be the first?'

Cindy laughed.

'When I need a lawyer, I'll call you.'

'What about you, what's your story?'

Thank God, she thought, *he was starting to relax.*

Subtly, she studied him, his facial expressions. She used her mind to dissect him, peeling back the layers, slowly learning about him. Almost as if he were a subject she wanted to capture on canvas. Ultimately, she wished to gain a peak at what was inside, a glimpse into his soul. That was a way off yet and would be difficult; he was so uptight.

She considered her answer carefully. An expert at seeing people as they really were, she gave little when it came to herself. Overly cautious, she usually only gave out tiny pieces about her, though he had been honest with her and she did find him attractive.

'My family is originally from Spain; we came to Mexico in 1780. We have connections to the Spanish royal family. My ancestors were given large land holdings here in California and in Mexico. We also still have a large villa and other property in Spain; property that has been in the family for hundreds of years. I had what you might call, a privileged upbringing.'

'How long have you been an artist?'

'All of my life.'

The answer surprised him.

'I love art, love being creative, painting is my passion. I've never considered doing anything else, it's a part of my life,' she continued.

'Did you study?'

'Yes, I was at art school, back home in Mexico.'

'How do you know Elanor?'

'We have known each other for a while now. She visited an exhibition of mine in Mexico and we became friends. When she opened this new gallery, she invited me to exhibit, offered to put me up at her house so how could I refuse?' She leaned in. 'How do you know her?'

Cindy was curious to see what he said, for she had already asked Elanor. They seemed close and Cindy suspected they had once been lovers.

'We met at university; I was dating her roommate.' Jack said without thinking and immediately he felt embarrassed.

'Her father is a client now; you know he has the detective show on TV?'

'Yes, I've met him, he's a very nice man.'

Jack smiled. Elanor's father was very suave, charming man. A former supporting star of the big screen, he had successfully transformed himself into a producer at the advent of television. His most successful production, The Detective, had been running for more than a decade. This, along with several other hits and some astute investing, had made him a very wealthy man, one of the most powerful in the business. He had been divorced from Elanor's mother since she turned 10, dating a string of beautiful women half his age. He doted on his only child, though. There was a rumour that one of the biggest studios was eager to buy him out.

'Your friend, Marcus, was he also at university?'

'Yes, he and Elanor are part of my west coast friends. They were in high school together. He's a doctor and has his own practice here in Santa Monica. His parents were both actors, his father is a producer now, same as Elanor's. His mother still works but they are not clients.'

'Interesting, I always wondered what it would be like to grow up the child of a movie star.'

'I asked him once, why he chose medicine. He told me that he wanted a stable life where he could do some good.'

'Ah, think of all the joy and happiness his parents have created for the world,' laughed Cindy. 'He's very handsome, don't you think?'

This cut through Jack like a knife; he felt an icy chill followed by the heat of anger, along with pangs of jealousy. Cindy, who missed little, noticed but Jack quickly recovered.

'That may be so. He certainly could have attempted to go down that path if he wanted. His grandfather gave him a toy medical kit when he was a child. He said from then on, he never wanted to do anything else.'

'Then it was meant to be. Is he popular with the ladies?'

Jack laughed.

'His longest relationship could be measured in days.'

They both laughed, Jack wanted to move the conversation away from potential rivals. He was struggling to think of anything, then, in a light bulb moment, he thought of something.

'Where do you base yourself, Mexico?'

'Yes, in the capital, Mexico City. We have a large home there. My parents tend to stay more in New Mexico nowadays. They have a large estate in a private enclave there. I have an apartment in New York but I'm more of a nomad. I go wherever the wind takes me.'

Making small talk had never been Jack's strong point. Crippled by anxiety and of the belief he was talking pure rubbish, he was unable to keep coming up with things to say. He wondered if there was the slightest attraction on her side. If he could convince himself of this, then things would become easier, then Jack had a thought.

'Why don't we get out of here, it's still early. Let's go take a walk along the beach.' Cindy smiled. For Jack, it was a glimmer of hope.

Parking the car near the beach, Jack took Cindy's hand. They walked along the ocean front walk. *This was better*, he thought, *far more natural*.

'Let's get off of this concrete, take off our shoes and walk along the sand.'

Without waiting for an answer, he led her down onto the sand, kicked off his shoes, then went down on one knee helping Cindy remove hers. They wandered down to the water's edge. The air was warm; the waves broke softly against the shore. Cindy was thinking that this was all very nice. Jack was planning something dramatic when Cindy took over. She stopped, squeezed his hand, let it go and pointed out to sea.

'Look at the sky, isn't it beautiful? See how the clouds dance.'

Jack stared at the sky, taking it in.

'It's beautiful,' he said, turning to face her. Gently, she placed her hand on his shoulders, turning him back out towards the ocean.

'Don't talk, just take it in, live in the moment.'

They watched together in silence.

When the moment passed, they continued walking along the sand, at the water's edge, just enjoying being together. When it was time to leave, he leant in, giving Cindy a simple kiss on the lips.

15

OMMY SPENT THE next few days drifting in and out of reality. Unable to latch onto anything, he floated along as if meandering down a river on a raft. Time passed differently in this private world, at times even seemed to stop! He was aware of the nurses, visits from Doctor Feldman, however, they appeared as ghosts on the periphery.

Slowly, things started to make sense again. As he became more self-aware, Tommy felt embarrassed by the entire episode at the motel, was racked with guilt for the trouble he had caused to his friend, dreading the inevitable visits from one of the people who cared about him the most. Doctor Feldman's daily visits became more welcome, with the passing of time. It took a while until Tommy warmed towards him. The doctor liked to discuss the night that they first met. It made Tommy cringe. He was far from comfortable talking about himself. Although the doctor said they were making progress, Tommy couldn't see it.

At times, Tommy wanted to run away from it all, pack up his things and just go. But that would not be fair. The only thing that was keeping him there was Louise. Louise had been a godsend; Doctor Feldman had been forced to change his no visitor rule in the initial stages to accommodate her. She had changed her hours at the diner so she could visit him.

Tommy had confided in her, his intention to run away but Louise had made him promise he would stay for at least another month, that he would discuss any escape plans with her before leaving. Tommy loved the way Louise listened to him, never passing judgement, patient, taking everything in, rather than waiting for a chance to speak. In private, Louise was hard on herself. *What on earth was she getting herself into?* she would wonder repeatedly, then she would see him and all of those thoughts would disappear. For whatever reason, at this moment in her life, he needed her and she needed him. For now, she would reassure herself, that was good enough. He gave her life purpose and, although she tended to dream into the future, she kept her reality in check, knowing there was a long road ahead and, in all likelihood, they would never make it.

Louise was careful about what she said. She wanted to take him into her arms, hold him, reassure him that this dark period in his life would pass, that everything would be okay. She wanted to say this even if it wasn't true, for she wasn't certain that it was. Perhaps there was no way back, perhaps the rest of his life would be spent in places like this or, if he did run away, a life of hardship, isolation and misery, for however long that it lasted. She realised that her desire to say these things was to make him feel better, to make her feel better, to make Dr Feldman feel that things were on the improve.

Jack phoned her for regular updates. She kept this from Tommy as she understood his embarrassment, understood that his pride was hurting. While he lay there, his friend, a person he loved, was out living, leading a very successful life from what she could gather.

It hadn't always been that way. They had been equals once. That was the problem, in his mind only, perhaps, but still. Equal in status, equal in worth. That had shifted. It was a crazy thought, but Louise understood, knew that it bothered him. She knew that he wanted Jack to see him how he had been, not how he now was. She could see he feared that it would always be like this, that he would never recover. She knew, he felt Jack, who was on an upswing in life, would look down upon him, that even if he loved him, he would pity him. That he would never again be his friend's equal.

Louise knew that the very thought was pure insanity. That Jack, a person she barely knew, would never look upon him like this. But there it was, the elephant in the room. Were these unavoidable? Was it not normal to feel this way? Louise did not judge, she simply understood, so she sat, being careful, when she wanted, desired and longed for more. Instead, she tried to convey these feelings with gestures, with kindness, with the look of her eyes and the tone of her voice.

Dr Feldman had taken a slowly, slowly approach to Tommy's treatment. They had reached a stage now, though, where he felt comfortable pushing a little harder. When the doctor visited, Louise would take a walk around the garden. It was a very serene place. She enjoyed sitting on a bench in the shade and the beautiful gardens were therapeutic. At times, she found herself wondering what it might be like to work here. Back in his room, Doctor Feldman and Tommy sat in comfortable armchairs. They were positioned next to each other at a slight angle. This was so that, although you could see the person you were talking to, you were not looking directly at them. A small table sat between the two chairs. Doctor Feldman placed two newspapers on it.

'Tommy, what do you remember about these newspapers? They were on the table of your motel room?'

Tommy reached over and picked them up; he spent several minutes looking at them.

'I remember buying them. No wait, I bought one, I think Louise gave me the other. I remember reading them in the coffee shop and back at the motel.' Tommy paused, as those memories returned, overwhelming him.

He drifted off on his own for a moment. Doctor Feldman, sensing something, pressed on with the conversation.

'Do they hold any special significance for you?'

'Yes, very much so.'

'In what way?'

'They are reminders of something painful, something in which I was involved.'

'What emotions do they arouse in you.'

'Anger, frustration, inadequacy.'

The doctor took a moment for them both to absorb this.

'Why do they make you feel that way?'

'We live in an unjust world. People can be incredibly cruel; the world is incredibly unjust. I feel that way because I could not stop what happened then, when it happened, I could not stand up to what had happened, be honest about it, pursue justice.'

He was talking in riddles, Doctor Feldman thought, giving just snippets.

'Do you feel ready to discuss the details?'

'Not yet, I am perhaps ready to face them.'

'Then that's a start. Tell me, do you remember exactly what you were doing prior to your incident at the motel?'

Doctor Feldman was careful here; it was dangerous ground; the chance of a relapse was very real.

'There's still many things that are not very clear to me,' Tommy started, 'I recall being at the dinner, remember arranging the date for the following day with Louise, then everything is distant, like I am viewing it through out of focus film footage.'

'Is there a chance, that you were reading or re-reading these newspapers?'

The memory came flooding back.

'Tommy, when you begin to face things, that is when the real work will begin. There is no hiding from what has happened, I can't make anything go away. What I can do, is help you learn how to deal with it. I can teach you ways to acknowledge these feelings and emotions, ways to avoid becoming overwhelmed by them. For this to work though, it's up to you. You must accept this help and commit yourself to the treatment. We can only do so much. The desire to get well and learn to live with this must come primarily from you. I can help establish the foundation but the building must come from you!'

These were powerful words. They resonated deep within Tommy. He sat contemplating carefully, for a long time, all that Doctor Feldman had said. When he finally spoke, it was with some nervous trepidation.

'Doctor, I was reading these newspapers when it happened. I put them down, took off my clothes, then laid down on the floor.'

Doctor Feldman smiled. 'Good luck to you Tommy, I'm sure you will succeed.'

'Doctor tell me, is there a time frame for how long this usually takes?'

'No, in your case, however, time is on your side. You have a good support network, access to excellent care. All the help that you need is available to you. You can take as long as you need, as long as it takes. We can all work together until you are feeling well enough to cope on your own. Even then, we will have regular sessions, perhaps for a long time. We are at the beginning but, by doing things properly, not rushing things and taking our time, we are giving ourselves the best possible chance for recovery.'

Tommy offered a rare smile, the doctor left him. Not long after, Louise returned. He was lost in his thoughts for the remainder of the afternoon. A few hours later, he asked Louise, who was reading, to call Jack and ask him to visit.

Louise noticed a small change in him that afternoon, a positive one. He wanted to get on with things, to start down the road that would get him out of the clinic, back into the real world. She was pleased. He had been avoiding his friend, now he wanted to see him. There was an urgency in his voice when he made the request. Jack had not been expecting Louise's call but there was something in her voice that compelled him to go. When he arrived, he found Tommy and Louise sitting calmly together. He did not embrace Tommy or even shake hands, it was awkward. Louise quickly excused herself, leaving them to talk. Jack sat down in the chair previously occupied by Louise and, earlier, by Doctor Feldman.

'How are you feeling, Tommy?'

'You, know, the sun keeps on rising.'

Tommy had no desire to get hung up with small talk. He wasted no time getting straight to the point.

'Firstly, are you my lawyer?'

Tommy knew from TV and his years in law enforcement that this was important. Jack wondered where this was coming from. He took a moment to consider it before responding, 'Do you have a dollar bill on you?'

Tommy stood up, then walked over to the drawers next to his bed, then returned, handing Jack a crisp one-dollar bill.

'Now I'm your lawyer,' Jack said, taking the money.

'Good, I've made a big mistake, I need your help.'

Jack looked around to make sure that they were alone, not knowing what to think.

'I thought we were already doing that?'

'Yes, let me rephrase that, what I mean is, I have made another mistake and you're the only one who can help me.'

'Okay, flatter me with some details.'

Tommy stared straight ahead, taking his time. He had no choice, he had said too much to change his mind now. It didn't make it any easier to say but, very slowly, he recounted the events of that night, how he had been sleeping in a doorway when he heard the commotion. How he had taken the pistol out of his knapsack; how they had set the old man on fire; how he had shot the young man. He left out nothing: the chaos, the confusion. How he had snuck out of the hospital, making his escape. Jack had heard some tales in his time. This one left him stunned and there was still more to come.

'I... I was confused. I was wandering down by the ocean and went beneath a pier. I stashed something there and I need you to go there and retrieve it. That is, if it's still there.'

'What is it that you left there?'

'My pistol. I need you to go and get it, to keep it safe for me.'

'I don't know, Tommy, I could get into trouble. You're asking me to commit a felony. What happens if I pick it up and get caught by the police?'

'You say that you were retrieving it for a client.'

Jack was nervous. He didn't want to say no to his friend.

'It's a hell of a thing to ask someone.'

They sat in silence for the longest time; it was a battle of wills. In the end, Jack was the one who conceded.

'Write down the details, I'll try to go get it.'

A million questions were on the tip of his tongue but he said nothing. They spoke about little else. When Louise returned, he was the one to excuse himself. To say that he was annoyed, was the understatement of a lifetime. *To think,* he thought, *I come all this way and leave with some crazy job, an illegal one at that.* He pictured himself standing before a judge, then in front of the bar review panel, trying to plead his case.

At one point, he decided to tell Tommy he couldn't find it. The next, he was pulling into a gas station to buy a torch. Still later, he was fumbling around beneath one of the piers, as the waves crept ever closer and a couple of rats scurried away at the flash of the torch's light. He hadn't sweated like this since he had been laying booby traps in the middle of the night in the jungle.

Tommy's instructions proved accurate. Very accurate, unfortunately. Finally, dripping in sweat, he made it home, locked the gun in his safe then sat in the dark with a cold beer. Not for the first time, wondering what on earth he had gotten himself into.

16

THE GAMES JOHNNY introduced them to the first year, followed along the same lines as tag. They were simple and fun derivatives of games they had played as children and teenagers. They were chase games, where you had to follow a series of clues to pursue someone across the city, truth or dare games, make out games, including spin the bottle variants, that had as their prize, kisses, shots of liquor or having to suffer humiliations through hazing, all in the name of fun. Time passed and the boys grew older, maturing. Some dropped away, feeling the stigma of the games' childish nature. They were college men now and serious.

The dynamic dramatically shifted when they moved from the student residence into the fraternities. Eight of them, their core group of friends, joined the same fraternity as Johnny, who was emerging as a campus leader. He was also the unofficial leader of their group, where he moved secretly to build his following.

Rory, with nowhere to go, had begun spending the holidays as a guest of the Hollingsworths. This led to him accompanying Johnny as a companion on a journey through Europe at the end of their first year in school. It had been a mix of traveling in buses, camping, staying in hostels, to first class tickets and five-star hotels, depending on Johnny's mood. In Spain, they had witnessed a bull fight. Rory watched on in horror, turning away when the final blows were delivered, while Johnny became excited, sent by the scene into a frenzy of excitement. For reasons Rory never understood, it was while they were in Spain, on a bus from Barcelona, that he had asked Johnny about the games, inadvertently, while speaking about the bull fight, a new favourite topic of Johnny's.

'It was like poetry. Did you not see the elegance in which the bullfighter moved around the ring? It had all of the grace of a ballet dancer,' said Johnny.

'I found it brutal, horrible. There was nothing magical there for me,' replied Rory.

'It was the ultimate game, the excitement, the danger.'

'Danger for who? The bull was the only participant in danger, from my point of view.'

'How can you say that? A slight misjudgement by the bull fighter, a movement to the left or the right, could see his guts spilled onto the ground. At any second, his life could end.'

'And that's what makes it so special?'

'It's the risk that makes it the spectacle that it is. Without that, what are you left with? Honestly Rory, you become more like one of my family's accountants every day.'

Rory was uncomfortable at this suggestion, probably because it was true. He sat silent for a moment.

'This makes me wonder what it must have been like to be a spectator at the colosseum,' said Johnny. 'Imagine watching as two gladiators battled, giving their all. Imagine witnessing a contest like that, where there can be only one winner, where the loser, loses everything. Imagine every last drop of their strength would be used; the adrenaline would kick in, fighting with limbs hanging off. You really see who wants it more. More so, imagine what it's like to participate in such a contest. Imagine a football game where the losing side is put to death just like the Aztecs used to do to the losers of that ball game they played!'

'It would be a tough discussion, with the parents afterwards.'

'Or would they be honoured?'

'Somehow I doubt it.'

'Okay what about that car race we saw in France, the Grand Prix. Look at the crowd, they are there solely because off the risk. Remember the reaction when the Italian spun out his car catching fire? The crowd went wild, the element of death is what drove 100,000 people there to watch, the thrill of what might happen.'

Johnny was right, motor racing was a blood sport. Johnny was not the only one who had been worked into a frenzy at the bull fight, either. Yet, there were others there, curious, like him, who had been appalled. Those people, unlike himself, would not go again.

'You know, I've been thinking, what if we could introduce the same elements into the games we play,' said Johnny thoughtfully.

'I'm not sure you will find much support for death ball.' The sarcasm was thick in Rory's comment.

'Perhaps, but consider it, the finality of a game where life hangs in the balance.'

'Who's life?'

'Not necessarily one of us and not to the bitter end. Only, what if there was a slim chance one of the participants might perish. What would that be like to witness?'

'I don't know.'

'Ponder it, Rory. Let your imagination run wild. After all, what is it they say? We are closest to life when we are nearest to death.'

It was a chilling pronouncement. Rory remembered it clearly and he had done so. He let his imagination run wild, harboured darker and darker thoughts, thoughts that would lead to where they currently had arrived, thoughts that left him desperately searching.

For a way out!

17

JACK WAS ATTEMPTING to review a case, one that required his urgent attention but, as had become usual of late, he was having trouble focusing. Cindy was taking over his life, consuming him. Not that he minded. Their relationship had been developing slowly since their initial awkward first date, although they hadn't progressed much beyond the kissing stage. Cindy had proved to be cautious, taking things slowly. Jack, who was head over heels, was almost desperate to move things forward. He was working at his house because a friend of Cindy's, Armando, was there to hang the pictures he had purchased. Cindy had been honest, telling him that not only was Armando a lifelong friend and former fellow artist but they had once been lovers. She also shared that she had broken up with him over an infidelity and she no longer had any romantic feelings toward him, so Jack should, at no time, become jealous. Jack had promised to try.

Armando had given up painting, finding a niche hanging pictures. He was considered one of the best. He hung them for galleries, rich people, anyone who had the money to pay or could provide good company and beer or both. Therefore, the price of his services varied. He concluded, rightly, that Jack was both a good drinking partner and willing to pay his highly priced, ever-changing fee structure. Jack was reluctant at first but Cindy insisted. Armando had stayed overnight to get a feel for the natural light in the rooms. They had consumed 24 beers before they moved onto Jack's scotch. Armando had an assistant, Tito, who was his match in the drinking department. At first, they all, Cindy included, argued over the chosen hanging locations. In the end, Jack had deferred to the experts, hiding in the study while they completed their work. Even Jack's housekeeper, Ursula, normally the boss of the house, where outside tradespeople were concerned, retreated upstairs until they were finished.

In his study, Jack attempted to study the file. An actress they represented had signed an agreement to appear in a film. This had happened over a year earlier, back when she had different representation. She was only 18 at the time. Her parents were inexperienced people, too trusting and they had used a family friend, a lawyer who normally dealt in property and tax. Her parents and the lawyer had read the contract but been more focused on the sections pertaining to payment than anything else. They had missed several clauses, relating to nudity, inserted by the director. In the interim, another film, that she had appeared in, was released. This film was very successful and she received favourable reviews that glowed about her burgeoning talent, praising her performance. With her star on the rise and large offers beginning to come in, they wanted to re-negotiate her contract and have the nude scenes removed. Jack had read the script. It was concerning and could derail her career, although filming had commenced.

At 18, she didn't need her parents' permission to sign the contract. She was an adult and it had been entered into freely. They really didn't have a leg to stand on. She was being well paid. The only question was, if there was a deal to be made here. He rubbed his temples. Publicity for the film had already begun and it was hotly anticipated.

There was no question of litigation, they had no basis. Could he convince them to re-write the scenes? Why would they? He needed something to offer. There were only a couple of things he could think of, one was money. She was set to receive 2.5 percentage points on the film. She could forego these or they could offer to sign a contract for one or two future films.

Jack wondered how important the nude scenes were to them; at their last meeting they were adamant. He wondered if that would change. Projections for the film were good. Maybe they would change their minds, then the chance to see her topless might bring in even more revenue. There were two topless scenes and one scene where her buttocks were on display. This scene was scheduled to shoot in the next week.

Her parents were adamant that she would not appear naked in the scenes. Jack feared a lawsuit for expenses if the film was cancelled. Insurance companies, the studio, everyone would be lining up for a piece of her. He couldn't allow that to happen. If push came to shove, he would side with the studio and his counsel would be to appear in the scenes. He wouldn't like it but she could not afford a multimillion-dollar lawsuit. Even if it affected her career, at least she would still have one. He would arrange an 11th hour meeting to try and make a deal. How much would they need to give to get what they wanted? That was the question.

He was interrupted by a knock at the door. It was Armando.

'We are ready for you,' he said through the closed door, in a thick accent that made him sound drunk, which he probably was.

When Jack opened the door to his study, there was nobody there, nobody in the living room when he went in there either. He looked up and there were his paintings. Cindy was right, Armando was a master. He had enhanced what she had created. Jack sat down, forgetting the case and everything else. He stared up at them. They were even more beautiful than he had remembered. He barely moved for the rest of the day.

18

JOHNNY WAS LESS than happy with how things were turning out. He was being ignored by his family, who were yet to visit him at the private clinic he had been moved to. They hadn't even sent Randle to check up on him. His only visitors were Rory and Chloe, his girlfriend. Rory had some news to share, news he was certain would be unwelcome. He decided to wait until they were alone.

'How are the boys holding up?' Johnny asked.

'As well as can be expected. From what I can tell, they are still in shock. They are looking forward to the vacation.'

'Vacation?' Johnny looked straight at him but Rory avoided his eye. It was an icy cold look, filled with disgust and jealousy.

'Your father's sending everyone down to Mexico for a couple of weeks. If you ask me, it's just what we need.'

Johnny fell back against the pillows.

'He can't even bring himself to visit me.'

'I'm sure he is keeping tabs on you.' Rory leaned forward. 'Listen to me, Johnny. We were lucky this time. You were almost killed. These games of yours, they have to stop.'

'Games of mine? You were all equally involved.'

'I'll never participate in one again, neither will any of the other boys. We've had enough.'

'All the games?'

'All of them.'

'Then how will we ever learn?'

'Learn what?'

'Learn about human nature, be able to understand the psyche of man.'

'This is sick, Johnny. A man died. Haven't you seen the reports in the papers, we were nearly caught. What would happen to us?'

Johnny cut him off. 'We didn't, get, caught. Had the old bastard followed the rules, he may well be still alive.' He scowled after saying this. Rory tried to remain friendly but firm.

'I'm your friend, I love you Johnny, but I will never play another one of these games again.'

'What about the bedroom games.'

Rory stared at him.

'Them too.'

Memories of the bedroom games flooded back, bringing with them feelings of self-loathing and disgust, ashamed of himself, of the glimpse into his secret psyche. He struggled to remain composed.

'I want no part in any of it. Why are you so obsessed with them? I hate to be the one to point this out but the time has come to grow up.'

'You're being naïve. Everyone plays games. Life is the biggest game of them all.'

'Your games are different; they are manufactured.'

'And what is all of this?' Johnny said, gesticulating at the world around him.

There was a noise just outside the door. Chloe entered, followed by the governor and Randle.

'Look who I found lurking in the corridors,' said Chloe.

'Hello, Son.' The governor approached the bed, patting Johnny on the arm. Johnny was cold in his response.

'Hello Father, Randle.'

'Rory, good to see you, my boy.' Rory smiled, as the governor shook his hand, taking hold of his arm with great affection.

Johnny took the afront well. Chloe noticed this difference in greetings. Randle did not say hello but shook Rory's hand, once the governor was through.

'Chloe, I wonder if you might leave us, for a few moments. We have something important to discuss with the boys,' said the governor.

Chloe looked around, Johnny avoided her gaze.

'Yes of course, Mr Hollingsworth.'

'Close the door behind you please.'

As soon as she closed the door, Randle began.

'Gentlemen we have a problem.' They looked at him. Rory became instantly ashen and Johnny wore a blank expression.

'I took a look around the site of your little accident, Johnny,' he continued, 'In the course of doing so, I had trouble reconciling the story the boys told us, so I contacted a friend of mine at the police. He did some digging. Now I'm sure that you had your reasons Rory, however, we need to know about this mystery man. Who shot Johnny and what motivated him to do so?'

Rory felt as if he was going to be sick. He looked at Johnny, only to be met by a blank stare. There was nothing else for it. Swallowing hard and with no other choice, he found the courage to speak.

'Because, Sir, we accidentally set the old man on fire.'

'Thank you, Rory. God damn it, Johnny. What's wrong with you?' the governor yelled. None of his anger was directed at Rory. He paced up and down the room 'Explain to us, Johnny, exactly how did you accidentally set this man on fire?'

Randle and Rory watched on as Johnny bore the brunt of his father's anger. This time, Rory couldn't cover for him, he would have to speak for himself.

'It's a game. We burn their possessions, only this time there was an accident.'

'Their?' His father was quick to pick up on the pronoun.

'Homeless degenerates.'

'Degenerates? This man was a war hero.'

'As I said, it was an accident. I'm very sorry.'

'I'm sure the judge will take that into consideration.'

'Alright, James, he's suffered enough.'

Suffered enough? Rory thought, *Was he serious? They all deserved jail for this, him included.*

'This other man, the one who shot you, where did he come from?' continued James.

'I don't know, all of a sudden he was just there,' replied Johnny.

'And he just shot you?'

Rory found his voice. 'He told us to stop, to leave the old guy alone.'

'What were you doing to him Johnny?'

'We were cleansing the streets; it was a humanitarian mission.'

The governor was disgusted.

'This is a new low. You were all beating up a helpless old man when, when this guy tells you to stop. You think, "Fuck him", only this guy, this nobody, he's got bigger balls than all of you.'

'He fired a warning shot first,' Rory said, now disgusted in himself.

'And still, Johnny, you didn't leave the old guy alone. Why? Because you thought you were the bigger man? Then he shoots you, well I hope you're happy and I hope that it hurt, because let me tell you, you deserved it.'

'After he shot Johnny, the old guy caught fire, I think. It was an accident,' said Rory.

'No Rory, no accident. If you hadn't been there, it would never have happened and you would never have been there if my son, my own flesh and blood had not taken you there?'

'Why does it matter? He shot the son of the governor. It should be him that is getting the third degree, not us.' That was Johnny.

'Son, this is what leadership is. You talk of yourself as a leader. Being a leader is all about choices and you have made some terrible choices. Hell, I could shoot you myself for what you have done.'

Randle took up the conversation.

'Johnny, are you aware that we cannot find this man? That we have not the slightest clue of who he is or where he is from? Any day now, he could walk into a police station, then, I hate to say it, your life as we had planned it and that of your father's, all the plans that have taken years to bring to fruition, would be over.'

The boys exchanged glances.

'You said the cops were involved,' said Johnny, still angry about what had happened to him, compounded now with why nothing was being done to bring his attacker to justice. 'So go find him, I want him jailed for what he did.'

Randle and the governor both laughed.

'I'm sure he'll get a long sentence for trying to stop a group of rich kids from killing a war veteran,' said Randle.

'That's enough, Randle,' interrupted the governor, 'You heard Johnny, it was an accident, a tragic accident. Don't worry son, we will do all in our power to protect you, you know that, but this has to be the end of it. You have a bright, wonderful future in front of you. It's time you took responsibility for your actions and grew up!'

'What's going to happen to me?'

'You will remain here until you are ready to be discharged, then I've organised for you to stay at your grandparents, to convalesce, until you are ready to return to the dorm. Now you get some rest. Rory, you come with us.'

They left Johnny to stew over all that had been said. As they stepped out into the fresh air, the governor turned to Rory.

'Rory, I wanted to thank you again for all that you did for Johnny. Oh, I know you had your reasons for bending the truth. Consider yourself forgiven.'

Rory was still suffering the effects of the earlier conversation, he could only manage a very weak, 'Thank you.'

'Now onto happier things. My niece is very taken by you; she'll make a wonderful wife for someone one day, don't you think?'

Rory looked at him. Was he being serious? After all that had just been said, it was tactless in the extreme, but he knew better than to say so.

'Yes sir, most definitely.'

'Very good. I think that I could safely say that you would be warmly welcomed into the family. Give it some thought and, if you need help with an engagement ring, you give Randle here a call.'

'Thank you, Sir.'

'Very well, I look forward to the happy announcement.'

Rory stood watching as Randle and the governor walked away, in disbelief.

Did the Governor just propose to him?

Did he just accept?

Johnny was right about one thing, human behaviour was fascinating!

19

Armando stayed on for several days. Jack had learned to enjoy the company of his uninvited guest. Armando was moody, irritable, drank too much but he knew his stuff. The paintings looked amazing and Cindy was happy. His presence brought with it many things to be thankful for. One morning, Armando announced he was leaving. A job back east, one worth a lot of money, beckoned. Their final conversation, before he left, would change the course of Jack's life. They were breakfasting out on the terrace opposite the pool. Armando hungover, was slugging whiskey straight out of a bottle.

'English people, they love to eat sausages for breakfast. You Yankees, some of you do also, no?'

Jack nodded.

'We must give them thanks.'

'Maybe your, what do you call her, she could make us some? They help with hangovers?'

Jack's patience was plentiful. Ursula, on the other hand, had reached the end of hers.

'You can ask her if you want,' suggested Jack.

Armando stared at the bottle in his hand then took another slug.

'Women, they are my, how would you say, Achilles heel!' he said.

'One minute, they can't get enough of me, the next, they are trying to scratch my eyes out. I don't think I'll risk it.' This made Jack laugh. 'Jack, you know that that guest house over there opposite the pool?'

Using the hand holding the whiskey, he gesticulated in the general direction of where the guest house stood.

'Yes, I've never used it. It's more of a pool house than a guest house, not even sure anyone could live in it, legally, you know.'

'Shame. It would make a great studio for Cindy. I could help convert it, then she might stay here a while longer, rather than head back home to Mexico!'

Jack was shocked. Cindy hadn't said anything to him about heading home.

'Still, if it can't be used.'

Jack was not consciously aware of the words he spoke next; he just opened this mouth, letting them out.

'I could, check with the city. Do you think she would stay?'

Armando shrugged.

'Why not? She likes it up here; you're a nice guy. a good patron, you like her, yeah?'

'I do.'

'If she had somewhere nice to work, it could help convince her.'

Armando winked, taking a fresh slug.

'How long would it take?'

Armando looked around.

'Couple of days, three maybe.'

'Okay, yes, let's do it.'

'Can't do it, I have a plane to catch.'

'I'll pay extra.'

'Sorry Jack, this is a good client. I can't turn them down, I already agreed.'

'Please, delay them for three days, that's all I ask.'

Armando rolled it over in his mind.

'If they agree to wait three days, if you can convince your housekeeper to make us some sausages, then I'll do it.

Jack jumped out of his chair.

'Ursula, we urgently need some sausages, here.'

Good to his word, three days later, Armando was finished. They showed Cindy, who was ecstatic. It was perfect, she exclaimed. Armando had moved windows, knocked down walls, painted, changed the furniture, filled it with a small fortune in art supplies and had even installed a hammock for afternoon siestas. It was a huge step forward. Cindy would still live with Elanor but she would work here at Jack's.

On a sunny Tuesday, Cindy and Jack drove out to see Tommy. A nurse showed them through to the rear garden, where they found him sitting in a chair alone beneath a tree. They sat on a nearby bench. Jack hadn't been expecting Tommy to be very talkative, but he was cordial, saying hello then making small talk. The improvement was remarkable; he was far more lucid, the few times he drifted away, they waited patiently for him to return. Tommy picked up the conversation without missing a beat. Jack had not shared much information with Cindy, beyond letting her know that Tommy was his friend and he was not well. Now, here in front of Tommy, he wanted to tell her everything. He found the compulsion to do so, overwhelming.

He held back though. Now was not the time for all that. They exchanged glances, her smile was, as ever, radiant. Cindy instinctively seemed to understand what was happening, squeezing Jack's hand when things became silent or awkward, in a gesture of support, sharing, in her expressions, genuine understanding and concern. After 20 minutes or so, Doctor Feldman arrived, smoking a pipe. He exuded his usual calm demeanour. This was nothing out of the ordinary, not in the world in which he lived.

Joining them on the bench, pipe still firmly in his mouth, Jack made the introductions. Doctor Feldman moved closer to Tommy, whispering something to him. Tommy's eyes brightened. Smiling, he turned to look at Jack.

'I just want to say thank you for everything.'

Jack wasn't expecting this. He felt both touched and embarrassed at the same time.

Tommy was then silent, drifting off and Jack motioned to the doctor.

'When he is like this, is he aware of us?' he asked.

'Oh yes, very much so,' the doctor replied. 'He knows that we are here, hears our conversation. He is aware, yet unfocused, too many competing thoughts occupying his mind.'

This made Jack feel more uncomfortable than before. Tommy remained silent and Jack sensed that he was done with them for the day. When the conversation with the doctor petered out, Jack motioned to Cindy that it was time to leave. He said goodbye to Tommy, then Cindy approached him to say goodbye. To Jack's surprise, Tommy whispered to her for a good few minutes. Jack pretended to not be interested.

When Cindy and Tommy were finished, Doctor Feldman walked with them back to the main building. Out of Tommy's hearing, the doctor explained, in more detail, how things were going. Jack would not later recall any part of this conversation. He was too preoccupied with what had passed between Tommy and Cindy. To Jack's surprise and disappointment, at no time did the doctor ask Cindy to share what she had been talking about with him. When they were safely back in the car, he could wait no longer.

'Well?'

'Well, what?' Cindy looked quizzically at Jack.

'Are you going to tell me?'

'Tell you what?'

'What Tommy said to you, before we left.'

She thought for a moment, 'Oh, that,' then she nodded. 'He described something that happened to him during the war. It was very vivid, disturbing.'

They drove on in silence.

'Can you share with me?' asked Jack.

'No, no, not in words, it would be far too shocking to talk about,' replied Cindy.

She remained quiet for the remainder of the drive back to the house. As soon as they pulled up in the driveway, she excused herself, heading straight out to her studio, locking the door.

She worked throughout the entire afternoon, evening, then into the night. Jack visited, the door remained locked. Each time, he was politely told to go away. He returned one final time around midnight, was once again rebuffed, gave up, then went up to bed.

The dawn sun woke him. This time, when he visited the studio, he found the door unlocked. As he entered the room, he saw what had kept her up all night. On an easel, in the middle of the room, was a large canvas, approximately six feet by three feet. In dark tones, greens on a background of burnt orange, was depicted a horrible battle scene. He stood transfixed by its grotesque beauty. Recognising the setting, a chill ran up his spine.

It was a camp where they had lived, a camp located in the middle of enemy territory. It graphically depicted a man who had been shot through the head, being held by another man, he recognised as Tommy. An enemy sniper stood passively in the background and they seemed to be admiring their work. The detail was incredible. It was no photograph but he recognised the camp, the green tents faded from the constant rains in monsoon season and the belting sun bleaching them. The muddy tracks that served as paths between the tents, how could Cindy, who had never seen this camp, reproduce it with such incredible accuracy? She was, he thought, truly gifted.

She was asleep in the hammock. As if sensing Jack, she stirred. He looked across as she woke. Dressed in only her underwear and a paint spattered man's shirt, she sat up, climbed out, then crossed the room to where Jack was standing. There were no words spoken. It wasn't necessary. She draped her hands around his neck, kissed him then led him back to the hammock.

20

ROUGHLY A WEEK after their morning in the hammock, Cindy announced, that she had decided to do a series of paintings she was planning to simply call, "WAR!". She showed Jack a painting that was based on an image she had seen in an old book, of a Japanese soldier charging with a bayonet, his mouth wide open. Cindy had focused on the mouth, using yellow, orange and gold hues, to make it stand out against a black background, representing the dark volcanic soil of Iwo Jima. It was another striking image. He loved it, yet it had left him uncomfortable; the dark haunting undertones nagged at his psyche. There were horrors, in this painting, he was not ready to confront. She told him of her plans for a poster, based on the picture, that could be printed in bulk. Beneath the image she would paint, "WAR!" in blood red underneath. He shivered at the thought.

'My plan is to speak to old soldiers, from all over the world and then interpret what they tell me visually,' she said. He smiled, hiding his true feelings. 'It will take some time and a lot of effort but it will be worth it.'

Jack did not share the same excitement or enthusiasm as Cindy, his feelings of discomfort would not go away, though he said nothing. The thought that he would soon be surrounded by dozens of these images, was not something he cared to think about. With difficulty, he pushed the thoughts from his mind, covering his emotions, being joyous for her.

When he analysed his feelings, he also found he was envious of her. Envious of how she was able to conceive an idea like this, from one brief moment of inspiration, then to be able to create it, going after it fearlessly, with no concern as to whether it would be worthwhile or not. She trusted her instincts. People would come, they would be interested in the subject, they would pay to view the exhibition. Some, those that were able, would buy her work. There was no doubt, no second guessing and if it wasn't successful then, so what, she would recover, then keep on going, moving onto the next project.

Jack was the happiest he had ever been. Cindy had moved in with him, awakening a passion within him that he had never thought possible. At any time of the day or night, he found himself pursuing Cindy with a lust he had thought only existed in books, a lust that was reserved for myth and fantasy. Jack loved being in her company. They spent hours together, sitting sharing a bottle of wine or walking along the beach.

Cindy, though, was far more disciplined than he was when it came to work. Nothing stood in her way. The studio door was barred while she was working. Cindy knew nothing else then, as she was completely consumed. He, on the other hand, was plagued by the inability to focus, with growing feelings of the pointlessness of what he was doing.

He wondered sometimes, how little he still knew about her. She was independent, managing her own affairs, paying for as many of their dates as he did. He found this sometimes difficult but then, he had no idea of her finances nor, he had reasoned, should he. She had threatened him with the gift of a watch but, of late, had said she was saving that for their trip to Europe.

He had agreed to taking the trip the day after Cindy moved in. Now she was seeking a date. She had threatened him that she would just go ahead and book the tickets without him and then done so. Make it work, she had told him, when she announced the date of their departure,

He had broken the news to his office and they accepted his decision with less concern than he thought they would, which did nothing for his fragility. Tim, the first person he had hired when the firm was growing too big for him to handle alone, was stepping into the role of Senior Managing Partner. Everyone seemed happy about Jack's trip, congratulating him on taking some time for himself. He appreciated this, yet it unnerved him. Could the firm continue without him?

Jack had three cars including the sports car. A big Ford station wagon that was getting on in years, that Ursula drove, declaring it was fine, every time he broached the subject of replacing it. He also owned a 1967 Ford Mustang he had fallen in love with on return from his final tour of Vietnam. Dark blue with white leather interior, customised sports wheels and engine.

Cindy shared driving the station wagon with Ursula; she didn't seem to care. As far as he knew, she did not own a car of her own. He was vaguely aware of a studio and storage facility somewhere near her family home in Mexico and an apartment in New York. As for possessions, she had little. Money and the items that came with it, just didn't seem to interest her. The car was an example in the differences between them. For Cindy, it was a method of transportation whereas, for Jack, it was far more.

He laughed at himself for having these thoughts. Here was this beautiful woman, a soul he could fall in love with, marry then spend the rest of his life with, instead, his mind was conspiring to ruin it for him. *You are not worthless,* he told himself, *your work is important. Consider this, you represent artists, actors, singers, etc. They all have agents and accountants, people like you, to advise them. Why should she be any different? Thank your lucky stars that you haven't found someone who is dependent on you for everything, needs you to balance their cheque book, hand them an allowance each week. Someone who wants a new Mercedes. Be happy for what you have. Take every wonderful day, one at a time, go to Europe, enjoy every moment, live, see where this takes you.*

The day of the departure soon arrived. Tommy would not be released from the clinic until some undetermined time after they returned. He had Louise, so there was no stress associated with leaving him behind.

As Jack boarded the flight, he committed to forgetting everything else except spending time with Cindy. They landed in London, then spent the first few days getting acclimatised. True to his word, Jack stayed away from his London office. Cindy was anxious to get to France, so they boarded the boat train and headed across the English Channel but only after visiting the Imperial War Museum as part of Cindy's research for her project.

The museum visit left him cold, once again hiding his emotions, as Cindy wandered, fascinated, from one exhibit to the next. On their first night in Paris they stayed in a fancy hotel, not far from the Champs Elysees.

On their first night, while they were lying in bed naked, Jack, sitting with his back against the bedhead, Cindy, her head resting on his stomach, gazing out of the open balcony doors at the Parisian night, she interrupted the serenity of the moment, speaking in a soft tone.

'Why do men go to war?'

Jack considered the question carefully. It seemed like the perfect time for a cigarette. He had smoked from junior high school, right through his stint in the army but had quit after a chance meeting with a man who had smoked two packets a day for 30 years and was in the final stages of dying from emphysema. Before he could answer, she asked another question.

'Would you have joined the army, if there hadn't been a war on?'

This time there was sorrow and fear in her voice, like she was scared of the answer.

'I've never thought about that,' he replied, answering honestly. After a momentary pause he continued, 'There was certainly no need for me to do so when I did. I was a volunteer, my family weren't rich but we weren't poor. I could have finished law school, done my masters, avoided it completely.'

'So why did you?'

'Well, perhaps if I explain the events that led me there, maybe you can gain a better understanding,' he said. 'High school was almost finished when we had a visit from a group of army recruiters. I was in the junior ROTC, a military program for young people, who might like to become officers in the army one day. My father had encouraged, but not forced, me to take part. I found that I enjoyed it. Because I was in the ROTC, they spent additional time speaking to me individually. This recruiter guy kept saying that that there was a shortage of good officers in Vietnam, that they were needed more than ever. His words struck a chord with me; they stayed in my memory at the back of my mind.

'That was in 1964, a year after President Kennedy was assassinated, patriotism was high. This recruiter told me he could get me into an officer training program, encouraged me to stay in the ROTC in college, then if it was what I wanted, with the training I had and was going to receive, I could be in a good position to join an accelerated program which, if successfully completed, would see me gain a commission as a second lieutenant. They needed me in Vietnam, he insisted. Men with my qualifications were difficult to find, then after I had served just four years in the army, I would be eligible for benefits, a pension, paid education etc. Well, I thought why not, how can it hurt.'

'Weren't you scared for your life?'

'ROTC in college was like playing a sport or joining a club, except during vacations when we actually spent time training at military bases. I didn't think about it. I had made no commitment beyond staying in the ROTC while studying. At that time, I wanted to finish prelaw and my accounting courses, then find a good law school.'

'So, you still wanted to become a lawyer?'

'Yes, that was my main goal. The army didn't even come second.'

'When did that change?'

'Sixty-six, I was coming to the end of my studies and had been clerking at a local law office close to the college. After graduation, I avoided the ROTC and spent the summer working there, assisting on a murder case. At the end, I decided I needed some adventure in my life, before settling down. Stupid, I know. The irony is, the army had been in contact and wanted to assist with finishing my education with a guaranteed job in the legal division.'

'When did you first realise you may be in danger?'

Cindy was desperately trying to understand this side of him.

'My first mission was in June 1967. We flew in from our base by helicopter. I was leading a small platoon of men. There was a more experienced officer in charge, leading another; he was a captain and had been in the country for seven months. There was another platoon led by another newbie. We were checking enemy activity near two villages. As we were entering the first village, a firefight erupted. I was knocked unconscious, receiving a small wound when a grenade exploded not far from where I was standing. Two of the men under my command were killed instantly, another badly wounded. Their bodies absorbed the explosion, taking the bulk of the blast. I remained unconscious for hours, only came to in the helicopter.'

'How did you feel about your men?'

'Heartbroken. I had only been assigned to lead them on this mission 24 hours before, yet there was a bond. I was entrusted with their lives. I failed them.'

Cindy turned this over in her mind. Jack could feel her wrestling with emotions in the darkness, trying to understand who he was back then. He knew she would never be able to; that person and the one she was laying on were completely different.

'After that, I was in constant fear of my life. I pushed it to the back of my mind in an effort to get on with it. Bravado, it was all a lie, the fakest of the fake. When I made it back home, I vowed I wouldn't go over again, yet it ate at me, something drove me to prove myself worthy.'

This made Cindy shed tears. She hid them from him in the dark.

'A commission to captain, some bread, I didn't need much convincing. Just three months after I went home, I was back for more. Another promotion, along with the promise of an easier assignment, saw me go over a third time. Then something happened on that tour and that was that. The end. I was back studying, the army a distant memory.

'What happened?'

He never answered her. Instead, he reached for her naked body in the dark.

21

CINDY WAS SO happy as she led Jack around Paris, showing him the world she had first discovered when she was a student. Everything about the city fuelled her imagination, filling her soul with inspiration. It also fuelled her romantic desires, bringing her closer to him. They visited galleries, including the Louvre, where Cindy showed him the famous paintings he remembered seeing in textbooks and encyclopedias. They visited districts where artists lived and worked, ate fine food, saw cabaret shows, made love in doorways, under bridges, on park benches, visited the tourist spots. Jack found her energy infectious; Cindy was fuelled by Jack's curiosity, his eagerness to learn and the raw energy that generated between them.

They rented a small car to travel through the countryside. Cindy was seeking inspiration from two sources: from the natural beauty of their surroundings and from the many battlefields of the two world wars, which stood in stark contrast, still bearing many scars. Jack enjoyed the battlefields less than the museum at the beginning of their journey, still he tried to make the best of it. Those stretches of land where men had died were eery, leaving him cold. There were too many dark memories buried beneath the surface, he could not help but wonder how many bones and unmarked graves lay beneath their feet. For Jack, familiar with such things, the smell of death, was everywhere. It lingered. The open countryside, on the other hand, was beautiful. It jumped out at him like pictures from a book; he loved their time there.

In the villages they passed through, they met many veterans of both wars. They chatted and drank with these men and women, Cindy gathering information as she conducted interviews, sifting through their memories, then noting the most detailed information for the successful candidates, the ones she would immortalise. She photographed them, not that they would be painted as they appeared now, but the person they were 30, 40, 50 years earlier.

Some happily shared photographs of their younger selves, many in uniform. She was kind to each and every one of them, taking their details and promising to write, saying she would send copies if she featured them.

While in the alpine region near the border with Switzerland, Jack heard talk of a local legend. The story interested him greatly. He was told that just beyond a small heavily wooded forest, outside of the village they were visiting, they would come across a perfect valley. A place where you would expect to see a village, the perfect place for one. Only, for reasons nobody knew, nothing was ever built there. For years, generations had simply ignored the place, dismissing the possibility of building anything there. Unable to help himself, Jack asked why. He was told it was believed by many, that in this place there was a village already built and lived in, only no-one could see it. It was named "Ames Perdues", the village of lost souls, that it was built and inhabited by the victims of war, souls that, as the name described, were lost.

'They live there happily,' one old man proclaimed, 'only we cannot see it.'

Another said that on certain days, especially when the fog sat low, if you were standing in the right spot, you could catch a glimpse of it.

Cindy had realised, the descriptions from the old soldiers made Jack uneasy. She stopped reading them to him. His years as a soldier held a fascination for her, try as she might, she couldn't reconcile the man she was with, the man she was falling in love with and the soldier of his past. She still searched for answers, only being more careful in her investigations.

He treated her as an equal and that was one of the things she loved about him. Not once had he ever spoken to her about money or about how she made a living. He had altered his house for her; she loved him for it. It was an acceptance by him for who she was. She knew he felt that his work was not as important as hers; it was something that she couldn't understand. In her mind, his work was equal, it should, therefore, be just as fulfilling. It was something she was determined to work on.

Armando had warned her that she would fall in love when she least expected it. He had been right. She loved Armando, he was one of her oldest friends, the complete opposite of Jack. Disorganised, haphazard, but he was brilliant at what he did. He hung and lit paintings in some of the best houses and galleries in the world. Though, a brilliant artist still hid beneath this new façade he had constructed. When he became disillusioned with the world, she felt, in many ways, partly responsible for this. It was dangerous ground, she had loved cared for him, shown him affection. Cindy had not forced him to sleep with other women. And she had paid, no she thought they both had, only he was and would remain unforgiven. It cost him far more than her; she could still paint, now he could only hang!

22

WHEN THEY REACHED Switzerland, Cindy bought Jack a watch. He had resisted; she had insisted. It was engraved and once he put it on, he never took it off. In Venice, he reciprocated when, by chance, they found an antique diamond necklace, with matching bracelet, in a small jewellery store. Cindy wore the bracelet every day, keeping the necklace for special occasions. When she did wear it, it sparkled, enhancing her natural beauty. Jack noticed she touched it constantly with her left hand. When he saw this, his heart raced. In Rome, he had found some diamond gold earrings, along with a gold anklet. That night, alone in their hotel room, she wore nothing else.

They travelled through Greece, into Turkey, spending three wonderful days wandering the bazaars and sites in Istanbul and exploring the beaches along the turquoise coast. Cindy filled sketch books with drawings along the way. She had filled volumes of journals with the information gathered from the old soldiers. Although sad that their trip was coming to an end, she was equally excited to find her way home to her studio. It had become home at some point during their journey, no longer thinking of it as Jack's house.

The world caught up with them when they returned to London,

finding two boxes filled with letters and messages waiting for them. They spent a precious day dealing with them, deciding in the end to cut short their vacation and travel home via New York, where they both had some business to attend to.

Jack was impressed with how well Cindy knew the city. She regaled him with tales of her adventures, from when she called it home, showing him around the places where she had once lived. A loft in Soho a, penthouse apartment in Manhattan with a partial glass roof, that she still owned and was uncertain now what to do with. Jack felt she should keep it. He could happily live there, he thought. Why not maintain an east coast base? He had suggested. She smiled at this but was uncommitted. Her family had a history with the city, she explained, but didn't elaborate further, pulling the veil back down.

Jack had remembered fondly visiting New York with his family when was a boy. He had never forgotten walking around the city, staring up at the skyscrapers, amazed at the people rushing about in the busy metropolis.

On their third and final day in New York, Cindy had told Jack she had some business to attend to, that she would be busy all day but would meet him back at the hotel for dinner.

'What business?' he asked, his curiosity piqued.

'A meeting with my lawyer,' she laughed. He wasn't sure if she was being serious or not. 'Then my family's estate lawyer, then lunch with my business manager, then in the afternoon my agent.'

It was a lot for poor Jack, who looked bewildered, to take in.

'Don't look so glum, you can spend the day shopping, go to a movie or something, then we will meet for dinner to celebrate the end of our journey.'

He realised that Cindy had shifted out of vacation mode, her demeanour was changing. She moved and spoke with purpose, her mind engaged, bursting with ideas. They were booked on a 10 am flight the following day. The realisation it was all coming to an end, hit him hard.

Jack was lost without her. After eating lunch in a coffee shop, he went to the movies then wandered around the city, doing some shopping before heading back to the hotel to wait for her to return. Cindy's day had been far busier; she had hired a car and driver for the day to make traveling a little easier. Her lawyer had a stack of documents to explain, then have her sign. One of her ideas for the upcoming project was a picture book, with back story of the origins of each painting. Her agent had found a publisher and the contract was ready. This, along with several other contracts etc, took up the first part of the morning.

Her next appointment was with the family's estate lawyer. Cindy's family had amassed a large property and business portfolio across four countries. Some assets she owned herself, some with siblings, some with the wider family, each protected by trusts to manage the finances. They had used the same firm to manage their interests for over 100 years. She visited the same offices in New York that had been visited by her great, great, grandparents. There were more documents to sign and decisions to be made, before she raced off to lunch with her business manager.

Her business manager, Carmela, a tough Italian woman, who had grown up in Hell's Kitchen, then forged a career on Wall Street, managed everything from her personal income, property and investments. Carmela had nothing but good news for Cindy. Revenue from sales was good, her investments were all doing well and Carmela had put aside a large amount to fund the new project. Her final meeting with her agent took all afternoon, as they planned the logistic and promotional details for this latest project. Scary and exhilarating at the same time, Cindy enjoyed the experience, planning the finer details of was her most ambitious project to date. They became so engrossed in their work, they lost track of time. Cindy raced back to the hotel and into the arms of Jack, who looked a little down.

Dressing for dinner, Cindy looked stunning in a silver evening gown, highlighted by the necklace Jack had given her. She wore high heels to mark the special occasion and perfume they had bought in

Paris. He wore a black suit with a blue shirt and tie. They dined in the elegant hotel dining room at a private table behind screens. Soft classical music played in the background as they were served by their own personal waiter. After dessert, they went for a horse and carriage ride through Central Park. All evening, Cindy had said nothing of her day, giving her full attention to Jack. Back in their room, they sat together on the lounge with a bottle of champagne. It was the perfect end to a wonderful time spent together on holiday.

23

ANNIE MILLER WAS the second lawyer Jack employed. Recommended by Tim, his first hire, the new Senior Managing Partner, had been at law school with Annie, who was originally from Canada and they had become close friends.

Annie's family had their roots in Jamaica, where they had lived for generations. Life had not been easy for the family. She was tough, hardworking, with an inbred desire to succeed. Annie had won a scholarship to an exclusive school in Toronto, where she had finished at the top of her class, winning a place at university. She had come south to study Law on another scholarship and great things were expected from her. She had set her eyes on a career in international law and was working in Washington DC at the Canadian Embassy when Tom called her.

The timing couldn't have been better. Annie's girlfriend had recently moved to California. Annie, herself, had been assigned to a terrible boss who she was happy to say goodbye to. She had come west with a happy heart. Two years later, she had packed up once again, along with her girlfriend, Yvette, and their two-year-old daughter, Rochelle, to establish the new office in London. It was an offer too good to pass up. They had returned to Los Angeles to see her Yvette's family. As she hadn't had the chance to catch up with Jack in London, she was looking forward to seeing him here.

'I joined you three years ago and we have experienced an incredible amount of growth in that time,' said Annie when she finally caught up with Jack. 'I thank you again for your faith in me by making me a partner last year and putting me in charge of the London offices. Something I wouldn't have achieved anywhere else in such a short time at my age. Perhaps never, given the nature things.'

Jack stopped her. Annie had a way of selling herself short.

'You've earned it,' he said.

'That being so, for a firm that is only seven years old, we are doing incredibly well. I believe we can do even better. Everything is in place, we know who we are, we know where we are going, our core principles are sound. That's why our clients join us; it's what keeps them here.'

'That's true.'

'They are progressive people, far more accepting than many others, open to new ideas.'

'Where are you going with all of this?'

Annie continued, 'We've expanded our offices and I think it's time to expand the services that we offer.'

Jack sat back in his chair. He was interested. Annie had obviously put a lot of thought into this.

'Such as?' Jack said keen to hear what she had in mind.

'An accounting and financial advice division, for starters,' said Annie, excited that Jack was keen. 'I also think... I also think we should consider a rebranding, with a name that encompasses better who we are and what we do. We should expand our clientele to include sports people.'

Jack felt a stirring for the first time in months. What Annie was proposing, was exciting to him.

'Okay, where do we begin?'

Annie smiled, 'Let's start with the name.'

'We should bring Tim in on this.'

As soon as Tim arrived, they started brainstorming ideas. Within a short time, they had the new name "Global Sports & Entertainment Services Inc."

Jack marvelled at how far they had come, from a small shopfront in Santa Monica to this. They would need more people and that would mean an injection of capital. Jack had spent his reserves on the new offices in London and New York but he had some shares he could sell. The other two would need to find some also.

All of a sudden, the excitement for his work life had returned.

24

TOMMY WAS RELEASED from the clinic in the second week of June. Greeting him at the front door was Jack, pleased to see his friend back to his old self. He looked nothing like the person he had seen in the garden of the clinic the day he had described his image to Cindy. He now resembled the man he had known, the picture in his memory. He walked into the house, accompanied by the doctor who had driven him personally. Jack retrieved his belongings from the car then joined them along with Louise, Cindy and Ursula, around the kitchen table for coffee. At no time did Dr Feldman discuss treatment, expectations or anything else. It was as if he was dropping someone off for an extended stay.

Jack was interested to hear more about what had happened to Tommy on the night he had hidden the gun. It sat just a few feet away in his safe: the literal smoking gun. He had considered disposing of it, however, he had made an agreement with his friend, one that he was bound to keep. There were more than a few loose ends to be tied up but now wasn't the time. Marcus arrived in time for dinner on the patio. Jack manned the barbeque under the careful eye of Ursula. After dinner, they took a swim in the heated pool, before gathering in the games room for some pool. As they laughed, it was if they didn't have a care in the world. Tommy, for all his outward appearances, was apprehensive, though he did feel the warmth surrounded by people who cared about him. He felt at home.

<h1 style="text-align:center">25</h1>

JOHNNY, RORY AND the other seniors, graduated from university. Johnny's father, momentarily lost in the euphoria of his son's graduation, agreed to fund one last vacation for the entire gang. The chosen destination was Cabo in Mexico. Two weeks of sun, sand and partying lay ahead of them before they began the next phase of their lives. Some had jobs to go to, others were headed for graduate school, others would settle into a life provided for by their trust funds. Still others had plans to conquer the world. Johnny had yet to decide but, in his case, the wheels were already in motion.

James Hollingsworth had other things on his mind. His second term as governor was coming to an end. The next chapter of his political career was about to begin. He had decided to keep an eye on Johnny by having him assist with campaigning. Rory, who was about to begin his career with the family bank, after they returned from Cabo, would also be given a minor role to keep Johnny company. The road to the presidency was open. It would soon be 1980, a new decade, with a democrat in power in, what was considered, a weak government.

With public discontent at an all-time high, oil prices through the roof, the rising cost of living, there might never be a better time to bid for the ultimate prize. All he needed was the republican nomination which his father-in-law had promised would be his. *Johnny wasn't all that bad*, he argued with himself, *he was just prone to over exuberance and running wild occasionally*. He managed to convince himself that all was okay. Then he would catch something, a look in the boy's eye, something that told him that things were not normal.

Yet he was convinced he could find a way to get him to settle down, like his friend Rory. Rory had become engaged to their niece over Christmas; he was envious and proud of Rory. Johnny had promised both his father and his grandfather, had sworn on the bible, that nothing like last year's incident would ever happen again, that he was completely reformed and, who knew, politics might be something he could aspire towards. Perhaps well... he stopped that line of thought as he remembered the look again. It was evil, pure evil. What had they done? What had they brought into the world?

No, it would be all right. Johnny would marry Chloe. She was a nice girl and he would marry her. They would have some children, everyone had the power to change, he thought. Yes, but change is only possible for those that want it!

Johnny's grandparents had bought him a new sports car, a Ferrari, as a graduation present. His parents had gifted him some money on top of the vacation with his friends. Secretly, Johnny wanted to play the game again. He lay in bed at night, dreaming about it but he found no supporters amongst any of his friends. Rory was right, he had managed to convince them to stop. In Cabo, they split into two opposing factions. On one side were the extreme party goers, led by Johnny, who spent all night in the bars, strip clubs and brothels, drinking heavily and taking drugs. Then, there were the more sedate party goers led by Rory, who enjoyed a beer or two, flirted and danced with the girls in the hotel bars or around the pool, went deep sea fishing or sightseeing.

Yet the game was off, even for Johnny's most ardent followers. Nobody would even consider any of his proposals. As the vacation progressed, Rory's group grew in numbers as more and more of Johnny's followers found it difficult to maintain the regime of round the clock indulgence. By the end of two weeks, Johnny was reduced to just three followers.

When they arrived back home, Johnny was bored. Rory was busy with his career, working 12-hour days and his parents were spending more time at the governor's mansion, in between campaigning. Alone on their vast Beverly Hills estate, he grew listless, his mind turning to his bad habits. Surely it couldn't hurt to play the game one more time, but with who? None of his friends were interested. Then a thought occurred to him, what about some of the younger guys from the frat house? He could invite them out, then talk them into playing *Nobody would ever find out*, he convinced himself. A few hours later he was back in that dark world he had grown to love, exploring, as he termed it, humanity.

26

OMMY HAD SETTLED in well at Jack's. Not long after his arrival, he answered a knock at the door. There he found a young man wearing an old-style cane hat. He thrust out his hand and asked if he was excited about the upcoming election. Tommy smiled at the sight of the young man who was bursting with energy. Rather than waiting for Tommy to answer, he went on extolling the virtues of the incumbent governor, how he would make a fine president, didn't he think? Could they count on Tommy's support to see him safely into the Whitehouse? Tommy, who had not voted in some years, promised to give it his full consideration. The young man was joined by another young man, roughly the same age. He looked somehow familiar to him. They both shook his hand. The second young man seemed less enthusiastic than the first.

Tommy thanked them for stopping by. They handed him some literature telling him to contact the campaign office if he had any further questions. He promised that he would. It was only later Tommy realised that they had mistaken him as the owner of the huge house. He laughed at being mistaken for a prominent citizen.

The "WAR" project was progressing full steam ahead. Cindy had recruited five additional artists to help her produce what had grown into a huge body of work. They were planning their first exhibition in LA. Along with her first two paintings, "One Man" and the project image, "Bonsai" of the Japanese soldier she had used on the poster, she had added: "Horror", based on a British veteran's memory of encountering a German flame thrower squad in the trenches of France and "Terror" from the memory of a Japanese soldier, who was waiting to die on Iwo Jima without food or ammunition, as the marines closed in.

All the images were provocative, horrible and stunningly beautiful at the same time. She had been very impressed with a painting by a young French artist, Phillipe, who she had met while traveling, adding him to the group. His painting, "Peace at Last" depicted men walking home through the graveyards of their comrades and it was especially touching.

Cindy wasn't the only one overwhelmed with work. Jack's business was expanding rapidly. In just a few short months, their client list had almost tripled with many taking up the offer of the services provided by the financial division. Adding sportspeople had been a stroke of genius. They had needed to hire account managers who were assigned to clients to help manage their needs, transforming them from service and advice managers, to providers of representation in many cases. The reputation they had created saw so many requests for representation, more than they could comfortably handle at this stage. Jack had been wary of making enemies of existing talent management agencies, however, in the end, he saw it as a natural progression of their business. He made a decision early on that they would not poach clients, rather they would always wait to be approached.

A never-ending stream of baseball, football, basketball and tennis players came looking for advice and representation. On top of this, half the rock bands in Europe had become clients of the London office almost overnight. Jack had even gone over to assist with his expertise in this area. He was always amazed at how some of these musicians had been crooked managers who had stolen entire fortunes from those they represented.

They were thriving. Tommy was helping with the organisation of the first exhibition of the first series of paintings which were being photographed for the book. Everything was as good as it could be. They were all busy, but they were happy.

27

THE URGE WITHIN Johnny to play more games was strong, overpowering. The promises he made to everyone, along with the declarations to himself, fell aside as his desire took over. He had found willing helpers, players in some of the younger men from his old fraternity. The plan was more elaborate than for the last one, that had ended in him being shot. He had been more cautious, taken his time preparing. His choice of players had been careful too. He had found two couples: one young, the other old, living in the same flop house.

For a $100 tip and the fee for the room upfront, he had rented rooms from the desk clerk, next to each of them. For $100 more, he had learned their stories. Each couple was about to be evicted; something that he rectified immediately. He learned that the old couple was down on their luck, that the man had a gambling problem and the woman liked to take prescription drugs. He was told that the younger couple fought all the time, that they caused the desk clerk no end of trouble with a high number of complaints from the other residents. He was a reformed drug addict, not long out of jail, who constantly fell back into addiction to get money to fund his habit. His poor wife whored herself out for him. She liked to drink. It was not uncommon for him to find her passed out in front of the building.

Johnny's family owned an old film studio lot on the outskirts of Hollywood. It had stood empty for more than a quarter of a century. Johnny befriended the caretaker, who introduced him to the security guards. He convinced them to give him the keys and, on certain nights, to make themselves scarce so he could hold, what he told them were, parties there. They agreed to stay on the opposite side of the lot but wouldn't leave. However, they assured him he had free reign to do what he wanted, on his side.

Inside one of the studios, using an old movie set, he had constructed a game zone. It was a simple room with a table and four chairs. There were four doors, which opened into four identical smaller rooms he had also constructed. In each, he placed some basic furniture: a bed, a small table and a chair. Suspended from the roof, in the rafters, was a metal gantry, that must have been used for film making, where he could observe everything, directing any necessary changes as the game progressed.

The game was called Temptation. He had played it many times with his friends. Johnny had taken a game board and then glued white carboard over the game squares, making his own. The rules were simple. Four players rolled the dice and moved their chosen pieces around the board. When they landed on a square, they had to perform the action stated within. These were basic: kiss the person to your left, right or opposite, go back three squares, say the alphabet backwards. If you failed any of the tasks, you had to take a shot of whiskey. On the board were four squares marked "Temptation". This was where Johnny was going to have fun.

Mindful of the players addictions, he had put together a series of temptations he felt would show, not only their ability to resist, but also, their loyalty to one another as a couple. Players who fell to temptation, had to return to the start. Those who resisted, moved forward three spaces. The winner was the one who made it first into the winners' circle in the middle of the board. Each of the players had been drugged before being transported to the venue. They were laid out on their own, in one of the rooms on the bed. Johnny had laid out clothes for each to change into, along with some water, when they should wake up.

All was at the ready.

It was time to play!

28

28

JOHNNY COULD FEEL the excitement in the air as he strode back and forth along the gantry. He had longed for this day, the culmination of all his work. He felt a deep satisfaction. Along with his helpers from the frat house, he had recruited a nurse, a heroin-addicted woman who was high functioning; she had helped drug the players, four prostitutes, two men and two women. They would help deliver the temptations; the boys would do the rest.

Slowly, the players awoke, sitting groggily on their beds. Highly disoriented, they found the water but it took some time for them to become aware. Confusion moved to fear, then anger. It took some time for them to calm down, then Johnny began the show.

Picking up a microphone, he spoke with the confidence of his father addressing a group of eager voters. His voice boomed in the large empty space above them.

'Welcome all, welcome. Before we begin, please change into the clothes that have been laid out for you, then step through the door into the game room.'

A cacophony of angry voices filled the air; the boys dropped a number of fresh $100 bills from the gantry that floated down into each of the rooms. The players watched, mesmerised, as they floated down like large flakes of snow.

'Gather them up,' came Johnny's voice, 'they are your reward for any inconvenience. All I ask is that you hear me out, change, then step through the door into the game's room to hear my proposal.'

Silently, they picked up the notes, changed clothes and stepped into the games room.

'Now isn't that better?'

His question hung in the air unanswered. There were no tearful reunions, the players already devoid of affection, stared awkwardly at each other, across the room.

'In front of you on the table, is a game. The rules are simple. It is easy to play; you just need to follow your instincts. If you would like to stay for a while and play, you will be richly rewarded. If, instead, you would like to leave, then the doors will be opened and you will be free to go, your pockets full. You should understand though, if you do stay, then you must agree to play to the end.' Johnny paused for effect. 'Now what say you?'

The older of the men spoke. His name was Paul.

'What is the purpose of this game?'

'I am a professor of the mind; this is an experiment in human behaviour,' Johnny said, with a believable confidence.

'And what will we receive by way of compensation?' Paul continued, his voice growing in confidence.

He lifted his eyes, staring up into the lights. He could not make out Johnny, yet feeling his presence, knew he was there.

'Each of you has been gifted $1,000. You will each receive another $500, regardless of the result, however, the winner of our little game, will receive $3,000 in crisp $100 bills.'

Paul looked at his wife, for the first time in a long time, with any form of affection. She was worth $1,500 at a minimum. Suddenly, she meant the world to him.

'Forgive me, Paul and Pamela, our distinguished mature couple, meet Tony and Josie, the younger members of our party.'

They nodded at one another, Tony spoke for them, 'We'll do it, you can count us in.'

'Paul?'

'Why not?'

'Good then let us begin. Please take a seat at the table.'

Each of them was wearing a button up shirt of a different colour. The female and male shirts differed but were of a business type. On their legs, they all wore track pants with running shoes on their feet. They each took the seat closest to the door they emerged from. This made Johnny smile. There had been much debate, ending in large wagers as to whether or not this would happen.

'Now, this game is simple,' said Johnny, high up in his vantage point, 'you simply spin the dice and then move your piece around the board from go to stop. When you land on a square, you perform the task or take a shot of whiskey from the decanter on the table. Should you land on a square called "Temptation", you will be offered that. If you resist, you advance three spaces, if you succumb, you indulge your pleasures but return to the beginning. The winner is the first player to enter the winners circle in the centre of the board.'

They looked to one another.

'Are we ready?'

There was silence.

'Then let's begin. Everyone has a coin in front of them. Flip it in the air, catch it and hold your hand over it.'

They flipped the coins.

'Tails,' he yelled. 'Raise your hand if you have tails. Good, Paul.' The only one with his hand raised. 'You're first.'

They continued in this manner until it was settled that Tony went second, Josie, third and Pamela last. Paul picked up the one dice and rolled a six. Tentatively, he moved six spaces.

'Kiss the person opposite,' he said, looking across at his wife.

Coolly, he reached for the whiskey bottle, poured a shot and drank it in one gulp. Tony was next and he rolled a one.

'Hey, what is it with this game? I thought it was some science experiment. I feel like I'm 12 years old in my friend's basement. Kiss the person on your left.'

His accent surprised them; it sounded more like someone from the Bronx than California. He looked to his left. It was Pamela again. His eyes went to the bottle, then he caught the sadness on the older woman's face. He leaned across.

'Do you mind?'

'No.'

Here goes, he thought, *might as well make it memorable.* She closed her eyes and he leaned in, kissing her on the lips, his hand moving to the back of her head. It was the best kiss Pamela had received in years; wet, with an element of passion. When they broke, she was blushing. Josie felt a pang of jealousy, wondering when he had last kissed her like that.

Up above, Johnny noted what had happened. The stranger showed more compassion than the husband of a lifetime. The passion displayed in the kiss, had changed things. He couldn't tell how, up on the gantry, yet he could feel it. *A sign*, he thought, *to his superior intellect.*

It was Josie's turn now. She threw a five. Both her and Pamela's turns continued in the same vein as the first two. They were just kids' truth or dare. It was Josie who scored a three with her second turn of the dice that hit the first temptation square.

'Temptation,' she said, smiling.

She was actually enjoying the game. It was a welcome break to the grind of her everyday existence. Johnny smiled. He motioned to one of the boys; they had prepared temptations tailored to each of their players.

'Return to your room, your temptation will be waiting there.'

Johnny had decided that at least some temptations would be better tested in private. He felt the players would struggle more with their demons in private. Josie stood to leave the room, Tony looked across at her.

'Be strong,' he said, with a weak smile.

It was a half-hearted attempt at support. She was the strong one far stronger than him and he knew it.

In her room, Josie found nothing. She glanced at her surroundings but it was as empty as before. She looked under the bed, under the table, nothing. Then a noise from above caught her attention. Something was being lowered. At first, she couldn't make it out. It fell into her arms: a white dress, a wedding dress. A note was pinned to it that said, simply, "Change".

She looked around, then quickly removed her clothes. There was white lingerie and she put it on, then squeezed into the tight dress. A pair of white shoes was lowered. There was no mirror, so she had no way of knowing how she looked. Just as she began to feel embarrassed, there was a knock on the door.

Josie was stunned, frozen in place. There before her was an image she had dreamed about. It was Tony, or was it? It looked like him, no, resembled him. *It's not him*, she told herself. The man was young, well, younger maybe, yet only by a few years. He was smartly dressed in a tuxedo. She stared, unable to move. How long had she fantasised about this moment?

Without a word, she fell head long into this fantasy, allowing him to lead her out of the room. An hour later, as she changed back into her game clothes, she giggled to herself. What had just happened? Those few precious moments were something she had longed for, the touch of the man she loved, on her wedding day, the stolen moment together while their guests waited. The fantasy that had sustained her through a thousand illicit encounters that had ruined her self-worth, to get money for her husband's irresistible urges.

Husband, yes, they were actually married. That had been some judge or social worker's bright idea, she couldn't remember which. Perhaps it was time for all of that to change. Maybe, somewhere out there, was the man of her dreams, waiting for her to come along. She placed her hand on the doorknob, then paused. *It was time to get out, win this*, she thought, *get Tony high, take off, run and keep on running until all this is long behind you. Start again, somewhere far away.* In an instant, her mind was made up, determined. She turned the knob, entering the room, with renewed confidence.

Above, on the gantry, Johnny smiled.

29

ETECTIVE LAWRENCE'S DAY was moving from bad to worse. Two, as yet, unidentified bodies had been found in exactly the same spot where the homeless veteran had been found. Not only that, there was now a new star witness, a homeless woman named Elyse, who had arrived on the scene, claiming the first incident was no accident. That, in itself, would not be so bad, except she hadn't spoken to them. She had reported it directly to a TV crew who happened to be on the scene reporting live for the morning news. He was told, her impassioned statement, that included a plea for protection for elderly, homeless people like her friend, "The General", a World War Two veteran, burned to death by a bunch of hooligans and if it wasn't for the man with a pistol, he would have been dead, was being broadcast across the nation. This had the desired effect with calls from everyone, from everyday citizens, to politicians, including the mayor, for immediate action.

This had thrown Lawrence's world into chaos. He had requested the file on the earlier incident, that had been classified as an accident. He picked up the report from his desk. Fresh reports were included that confirmed that kerosene was present on the victim's clothing and skin. Among the homeless man's possessions was listed a kerosene heater. This seemed to confirm the accident theory.

In this latest case, the bodies were burned beyond recognition. It was no small fire caused by a heater that had injured these people. This had all the markings of a calculated attack. Hell, it looked like they were assassinated then placed here and set on fire. What did that mean? He pondered for the first time, realising he had been too busy to give it any thought. Everything or nothing?

With the absence of any plausible evidence to the contrary and ruling out self-combustion, someone wanted these bodies found, but why? Set them on fire to destroy any evidence, but why do it publicly? Why not bury them somewhere or slide them over a cliff into the ocean? The cruelty of the act, the deliberate nature of it, hit him hard. It was a horrible way to go and he found himself struggling to isolate from the emotion/ He balled his hand into a fist, punching it into his other hand with such force that it hurt, leaving an ache that remained for the rest of the day.

Closing his eyes, he tried to calm down, imagining a nice riverbank shaded by tall trees. It worked but his mind drifted back to Elyse. The witness. What did she have to tell them? Was she more than a crazy old bag lady? Had she seen something or was it pure fantasy? He picked up the file again. She had known the first victim, that was confirmed. The word "burned" jumped out at him, it stuck in his mind. She had said it, of course. She would have known he was burned but she had said, 'burned by a group of hooligans.'

She would only say that if she had seen it. Was it a clue? Right now, it was their only clue. It linked the accident to this new case. A link, a tenuous one, yet still a link. Why would she use the word hooligan? That was more of a British term, young people maybe. The police report had reached the conclusion that it was an accident, that there was no suspicion of foul play.

The report also detailed a witness who had provided assistance to the victim, one who was at the scene when the emergency crew arrived. The officers had informally interviewed the man, who confirmed the accident theory. He had accompanied the victim to hospital, however, he had left before officers had conducted an official interview. The mystery man's name was recorded as Thomas. There was little more to go on in the report: some references to first aid given by Thomas, reference to a passerby he had flagged down to help. No details, just a name, Simpson. He assumed this was the person who called it in.

He found the lack of information frustrating. Both of the officers had been present at this latest crime scene also. He mulled this over. They thought it had been an accident. There were no suspicious circumstances. He went in search of Reynolds and Palmer, finding them in the squad room, preparing to go back out on patrol.

'Gentlemen wonder if I could be so bold as to indulge in a moment or two of your time?'

They smiled.

'Let's take a seat,' said Reynolds, motioning towards the chairs that were lined up in rows for the briefings.

'I've been assigned to investigate this morning's case. I've also been going over the case of the veteran, the accident, the one the new witness, Elyse, spoke about on national television. The file, if I might say, seems a little light.'

Reynolds glanced at his partner before answering.

'Good luck with her. She's battier than, well, I don't know what.' Palmer interjected.

'Well, it's light because there weren't much to tell. All of the evidence pointed towards an accident. There were only two witnesses who came forward at the time. One was the man who called us, the other disappeared before we had a chance to properly speak to him,' said Reynolds.

Detective Lawrence opened the file.

'I get the impression from this that she saw it happen. Is this Elyse lady British by any chance?'

Palmer replied, 'I couldn't rightly say. She could be anything. They call her the queen of the screen. Apparently, she was once quite a beauty, used to be a bit player back in the thirties but never quite made it, or so the legend goes. Hell, she probably doesn't even remember herself.' Detective Lawrence frowned and wondered if this was a waste of time, 'We interviewed her. It's all there in black and white. She claims that the old man, the General, was set upon by a group of young men and then this stranger, the man we have identified from her description as the same we encountered at the scene, Thomas, stepped forward from the darkness and shot one of them. Then one of the others set the old man on fire and they sped away in their cars. You can ask her; we left her upstairs for you.'

'Thank you kindly, I will, tell me about this mystery man Thomas, now known as the man with the pistol?'

Palmer continued, 'He was there when we arrived. He knew his stuff; he was triaging the victim, had administered morphine, was doing what he could for the victim who was severely burned.'

'This wasn't his first rodeo. This guy knew his stuff. Not his first burn victim either. When the ambulance team arrived, he gave a very professional summary before he handed him over.' Reynolds added.

'Ex-military, do you think?'

'Probably, either that or he was a paramedic. Very calm under pressure. If I had to guess, I would say military, someone who had dealt with those types of situations.'

'Nam?'

'I would say so. Here's a guy, confronted with this horrific scene, just gets in and deals with it. Doesn't even raise a sweat. I would say he has seen worse, much worse.'

Reynolds' assessment was accepted by Palmer. who nodded in agreement.

'Did you ask him how he came to be there?'

Palmer responded, 'We didn't get into details but he mentioned that he was nearby. With the amount of gear he had on him, it was obvious he was sleeping out, for whatever reason.'

'And there was no sign of a weapon?'

'None. The guy had a fairly hefty knapsack, though. I wouldn't rule it out.'

'Were there any signs of a gunshot victim blood trails, anything?'

'Not that I saw.'

'Me either,' Reynolds added. 'Though, there was blood around the victim, we weren't looking for blood trails.'

'You know, this guy gave me the impression that at one time he had been one of us. Definitely ex-military but I think somewhere along the line he carried a badge,' Reynolds said with authority.

'Interesting, so what happened to him?'

Reynolds continued, 'We only spoke with him briefly. He told us, from what he could tell, it was an accident. He pointed out the kerosene stove. We planned to speak to him further at the hospital. He was concerned about the old guy, rode along with him in the ambulance, then we were called away. When we came back, the old man had passed away, our new friend was gone.

'What did you think about that?'

'Nothing sinister at the time. He had helped the old guy, done all he could, even if there was trouble, geez it's a tough one. You know what these guys are like, they don't want to be involved, he was staying under the radar for a reason. I hold nothing against him, maybe he should have hung around, as now we have this new incident, claims of a weapon. It puts things in a different light.'

They sat in silence for a moment, considering what Reynolds had just said.

Detective Lawrence resumed the discussion.

'After what Elyse told us, we will need to contact all municipal, private hospitals and clinics in the area. See if anybody remembers treating anyone for a gunshot wound on the night in question. Doesn't mean that it didn't happen, just means they were either treated elsewhere or outside of the mainstream system. In all, it seems like it was a pretty quiet night. The only other report involving a firearm was three hours earlier during the robbery of a liquor store on the other side of town. In that case, the firearm was not discharged. I'll go upstairs and speak to Elyse, see if I can learn something more. I'll keep you boys posted.'

Lawrence noticed that Palmer was in deep thought.

'What's on your mind Palmer?'

'Something Elyse said, she described the attackers as hooligans on the TV but when she spoke to us, she used the term boys. Clean cut boys, was what she said. What about colleges and universities? They have doctors, right? Student doctors anyway.'

Detective Lawrence considered it.

'That's a good point. There is at least one student hospital I know of. You know, at that fancy university, where all the rich kids go?'

'Barker University?'

'That's the one. You might be onto something here, Palmer. I'll get you boys to speak to the sketch artist, maybe we can put something together on our mystery man. It's a longshot but you never know. In the meantime, if you think of anything, give me a call.'

They were making progress but he had a long day ahead. He decided to get some air before meeting Elyse. He reflected on the information they had so far gathered. The shooting was interesting. The shooter, who was likely Thomas, the good Samaritan, had decided it was best to remain anonymous and may well have always planned to slip away, otherwise, he would have told the officers when they arrived on the scene.

The shooting victim had been committing a crime that had turned into murder. It was in his best interests that all details, regarding the incident, never be discovered. It made for a unique scenario. By remaining silent, both the shooter and the victim remained safe, free from persecution. How could he flush them out into the open? That was the million-dollar question. If they were rich college kids with everything to lose... a chill came over him. Wealthy people, with so much to lose, could become very dangerous, especially if they were well connected and powerful.

The thought made him up his guard.

30

JOSIE STEPPED BACK into the game room, a look of serenity on her face. She sat back down and, without a word, picked up her piece and returned it to the beginning. Her husband, Tony, scowled in her direction. Pamela picked up the dice. It was her turn. She landed on the square that said stand up and dance. It put them back into the world of adolescents and she picked up the whiskey bottle and took a slug straight out of it.

The game laboured on. After three hours, Johnny was growing tired of it. One by one, they fell to temptation, addictions claiming them. Alcohol and drugs. They had expected this in a way; it was sadly predictable. Paul was the only one to show any signs of discipline. He had refused them all, had shown no interest in the most elaborate and seductive scenarios. In the privacy of his room, he had turned down every proposition. Even when, at times, it seemed he would snap, he had come out clean, his will as strong as ever. Men women, groups, combinations, none could tempt him. They had tried alcohol, drugs, even resorting to having others drink or take them in front of him. Nothing, yet he had ruined his life due to temptation, had fallen into the gutter, yet now in this place, had somehow found the strength to resist. It was baffling. *Why was it?* Johnny wondered, even as he was tired of the game, even when he wished it to end. This showed his own need for self-gratification, the rush adrenalin, for he too was impatient. So, they trudged on, relentless.

After what seemed to them like an eternity, Paul found himself in sight of the winner's circle. It was time for what they all hoped would be the final temptation. He was three squares from the finish and had been stuck there for two turns. He rolled the dice and got a two. He was now one square away. There was a collective sigh from Johnny along with all up on the gantry.

'One, two, Challenge card,' he said with reduced enthusiasm. Johnny perked up, looking down with renewed interest as Paul selected a card.

'Change identity, roll again, swap places with the player to your right, they take your position on the board along with your turn.'

Reluctantly, Paul stood up and swapped seats with Josie. She picked up the dice and blew on it before rolling. They all watched, their eyes transfixed. It was a one and landed on the final temptation. Johnny's heart leapt. He picked up the microphone.

'Final temptation. That's it folks, 10-minute break while we get ready.'

Johnny called the boys together.

'What do we think?'

There was silence, as they considered. One of the boys, Stevie, spoke up.

'She'll walk, offer her a fresh start, she'll break the door down to get away.'

Johnny considered it.

'Does everyone agree?'

There were shrugs amongst the smiles, as what Stevie had said, sunk in.

'Okay, here's what we do. I'll sell it to her then, if she walks, Stevie, you bring the car round and load her in. You're taking her to the airport, Daryl.' He pointed to one of the boys. 'You go with them then, before you get through the gate, drug her. Drive around until she passes out then, come back. I'll have the nurse drug the other three, then we'll put them back in their rooms. Man, she is going to be pissed when she wakes up next to him in the morning.'

This brought laughter from all of them. Cameron, another of the boys, spoke up, 'I'm not convinced she'll leave him. I mean she whores herself for him, I'll take some of that action.'

The boys placed their bets, then got into position. Johnny picked up the mic.

'Josie, here is your final temptation, you have 60 seconds to decide.'

A package was lowered down onto the game table.

'Inside that package is $20,000 and a contract. The contract dictates that you must stand up right now and walk out the door, leaving Tony behind. We will convey you to the airport. One of the conditions of the contract is that you do not return to California or contact Tony for five years. You have sixty seconds.'

Johnny knew these terms were unenforceable, however, he gambled that they would not question it. Besides, he didn't care. It was a test. Would she leave this man she had loved enough to have ruined her own life? Josie sat staring at Tony. She loved him, she loved him, however, it was over. She stood up, picked up the package, then disappeared through the door. The other players stood as one.

'This is an outrage,' said Paul, 'How can she win? I was the only one to resist temptation. I should be the winner.'

Tony was next. 'Open the door. I demand that you open the door.' He grabbed it, throwing his weight against it but it didn't budge.

Josie picked up the bottle of whiskey, draining it. Upstairs, Johnny had had enough. This game had been a failure. It had provided some light entertainment, only not anywhere near the thrill that he was hoping for. The absence of death, that was it. He should have had things like Russian roulette similar. Time to pack it up.

'That concludes our game,' came Johnny's voice, 'players, please return to your rooms, change, then await the doctor's clearance before your transport home. Thanks for playing.'

Johnny climbed down off the gantry. He noticed the nurse was looking a little worse for wear.

'Toby,' he called to one of the boys.

'Yes boss?'

'Maybe you should give the injections.'

'I can inject them, I've injected a million, like them,' the nurse said, slurring her words.

Johnny smiled. The nurse was a junkie with an expensive heroin habit. Even though he knew better, he decided to be nice, just so they could get out of there.

'Okay, you do the old ones. Toby, you do Tony, I want to get out of here tonight.'

Twenty minutes later, they were heading in the direction of the flop house. Johnny helped carry Tony in through the back door. Everyone else in the house was asleep. They laid him down on the bed, then went back out for Josie. He arranged them so they were hugging one another. This brought some muffled laughter.

As they emerged from the house, it was to the sight of everyone else standing around the trunk of the car. From the expressions on their faces, Johnny instantly knew there was trouble.

Later, he would admit that he panicked!

E LYSE WAS SITTING bolt upright, in a seat at the interview table, waiting patiently, when Detective Lawrence entered the interview room. A female officer stood silently near the door. He nodded to her and she stayed as he took a seat. He still carried with him the file of the supposed accident victim, a classification that may be about to change.

'Elyse, my name is Detective Lawrence. May I call you Elyse?' he said, having already done so without permission. She nodded. 'I'm the detective assigned to investigate the discovery of two bodies this morning and the accidental death of...'

She cut him off.

'The General's death was no accident.' She stared at him. It was a look of contempt, mixed with some anger. 'We are the forgotten people, Mister... apologies... Detective Lawrence. We have been without a voice for too long. Well, that time is over, the General was murdered, as were these two people.'

He seized the moment.

'These two people this morning, you witnessed them being murdered?'

He hoped her answer would be yes, wanted, wished it. It would certainly make his life easier.

'No, I arrived in the aftermath. However, I was there when the General was murdered by those hooligans, have no doubts on that score. I witnessed the entire thing.'

'Yet, we are only hearing about it today.'

The rebuke brought tears. He offered a box of tissues.

'Yes, detective, sometimes courage is slow to arrive!'

'Tell me, you've got my attention.'

'I seen the whole thing. I was right across the street. I saw them burn the General alive, then a man appeared out of nowhere, shot one of the boys and they ran away.'

'Elyse, that man was killed in an accident, burned by his own campfire, it's all here in black and white.' He tapped the file sitting on the table in front of him.

'No, he was not. No sir, indeed, he was not. I'll tell you I was asleep minding my own business when a big black or, maybe blue, car pulled up. They raced out from it and a moment later the whole place went up in flames.'

'Had you been drinking, Elyse?'

'No sir, sober as a judge. I'm the chief witness, it's time we had justice, so you take your fancy notebook and pen out and write this down.'

'Did you happen to see the licence plate of the vehicle?' he asked out of hope.

'No, but I got a good look at them. Young, clean cut and I would recognise that car and those boys if I saw them again.'

He took out his pen and wrote on the outside of the file. What to do? He had nothing else.

'Okay Elyse, tell you what I'm going to do. If you're serious about this, I'll find you a place to stay, somewhere you will be safe. You work with us and maybe we can do something but I warn you, Elyse, I won't stand for any crazy behaviour. I want you to spend the rest of the day gathering your thoughts, then I will come see you in the morning. I want you to think about everything, leave nothing out. Do we have a deal?'

'Yes.'

It was all he needed; it was all he had. He had no sooner returned to his desk when the duty sergeant came to see him.

'Detective Lawrence, there's a lady downstairs I think you should meet.'

'Oh yeah, why's that? I've had my quota of crazy broads for today.'

'She saw the story on the TV and she thinks the dead bodies may be her uncle and aunt. She was meant to meet them at some flop house, the Chicken Coop. Know it?'

'Chicken Coop? Dive downtown?'

'Aren't they all? Well, they have disappeared. Coincidence?'

'I'm not that lucky.'

'I'll tell her you're on your way.'

'Thanks.' Lawrence rubbed his temples.

32

THANKS TO A story in the LA times, Cindy's upcoming exhibition "War" was generating an extraordinary amount of interest. So much so it had stirred up discussion about veterans' affairs. Ever keen to jump on the bandwagon and be immersed in the campaign trail, the governor's office had been in contact to see if a special gala preview could be arranged. As a sweetener, the governor's own personal foundation would donate $100,000 to the Veterans Association. With this offer, Cindy could hardly say no. She was already feeling the pressure, having moved the opening date from November to July and now, on top of that, this was being forced upon her.

It had been decided to hold the preview in the ballroom of the governor's mansion. Armando had been brought in to work his magic, along with help from Tommy, Marcus, Elanor and even Jack, as busy as he was. They somehow managed to get everything ready and organised. Doctor Feldman had shown a great, previously unknown, skill in handling the press. He articulated himself so well, Cindy happily stood aside, allowing him to take the role of spokesperson.

The guest list was a who's who of Californian Power Brokers and celebrities. A gala dinner was to be held before the exhibition and Jack found a nervous Cindy pacing the ballroom in her evening gown beforehand.

'They look amazing.' Jack's voice echoed in the vast open space; he spun around, gesturing to the walls with his open hands. 'And you, my lady, look stunning as always.'

Cindy blushed. Jack looked handsome in his tuxedo. They had been asked to stand with the governor and his wife at the entrance, to greet the guests. A great honour they had been told; a task Cindy was loathing. He tore across the ballroom to where she was standing, sweeping her into his arms. He kissed her deeply, dipping her backward in a rush of heated passion. Cindy's knees buckled, her breath caught but she just managed to hold on.

'Stop it, you'll smudge my makeup, you crazy man,' she said when he allowed her up for some air.

Try as he might, he could hardly believe how far they had come in such a short time. He had to keep pinching himself, to stop from thinking he was dreaming. Cindy was wearing some of the jewellery he had bought her on their vacation and some more that he had bought, under her constant protests of spending too much money, since. The antique diamond necklace shone around her slender neck, while a new addition, a gold, diamond-encrusted bracelet did the same on her left wrist.

'You know you have forgotten to put on a piece of jewellery.'

'Really? Which one? I can't wear them all at the same time, you know.'

'This is a very important one and you should never take it off.'

Cindy looked confused. She looked into his eyes as Jack went down onto one knee, reached into his jacket pocket, pulled out a ring box and opened it. She started to cry as Jack placed the ring upon her finger. He had been carrying it since his solo shopping trip in New York months before, waiting for the right moment, which he decided, upon entering the empty ballroom, was now.

33

JOHNNY AND RORY, along with Chloe and Claire, were riding in a limousine to the governor's mansion. Unlike the boys, who felt stifled in their tuxedos, the girls relished the opportunity to dress up on such a pleasant evening. Rory was becoming more comfortable at these events; Johnny would sooner just find a bar and get drunk.

Claire had been watching Rory carefully as he worked on her uncle's campaign. She was impressed by what she had seen. She had begun to daydream about a life as a first lady and why not? Her grandfather was making it happen for her uncle, why not for Rory, who knew, in 20 or 30 years? After all, they were the future, weren't they?

The radio blasted rock n roll. It felt phony to Rory, while he was wearing a tux. The campaigning was going well, expectations were high, talk about the Whitehouse was becoming louder as more and more people started to see it. The possibility was real.

Claire watched Johnny carefully, also. She had grown up with him, knew that he had a complex personality, though she would be always forever grateful for him introducing her to her future husband. She now wished their association would end or, at least, be reduced. There were things in his past she knew about, things that unsettled her. Yes, he could be incredibly generous, yet there was always a sinister motive to his generosity, always something he wanted in return.

For a brief moment, uncomfortable memories flooded her mind. She had not been able to decipher what Johnny wanted from Rory. There was a price for all he had done for him, this she knew. She wondered if Rory had already paid some of that bill. That thought was nasty. Rory was hers now; she would protect him, no matter what.

Johnny was bored with everything. The spice had disappeared from his life; he was searching for something new. He missed the thrill of the games, missed the devoted group of followers from his school days. He was tired of watching his father play the big shot. Everyone knew his grandfather was the real source of power. It was bad enough that his father had become governor, now people were speaking about him as a future president. The thought made him sick. Had he never met Johnny's mother, he would be nothing more than an inn keeper!

Johnny's grandfather, Michael Lethbridge, always said that he was born lucky, whenever anyone asked him. He had always been secretive about his origins, rising out of nowhere to become one of the wealthiest and most powerful men in the world. Few knew that he had been born in a small, extremely poor, village in Wales, for he held no trace of that accent, nor could he speak his native tongue any longer, something that embarrassed him. If little was known about him, almost nothing was accurately known about his business or the composition of his net worth. If people investigated carefully, they would find little more than a few thousand shares in a company called Infomax LLC, a company with no listed assets and a personal bank account in the family-owned bank, with less than half a million dollars in it. The lavish homes where he lived, the fancy cars, the yachts and planes, nothing was in his name. In truth, he only owned these things to please his family. He was not someone who coveted possessions. They did, however, seem to mean a lot to his wife, children and grandchildren. One of his few pleasures in life was seeing them happy. He liked to tell people that every day was a gift, one that should be treasured.

When someone would say that not every day was a good one, he would simply reply, any day you don't have to go down a coal mine in order to live, was a good one. Unlike his own father, uncles and three dead brothers, as the youngest, he was allowed to go to school. There in the one teacher school, he met a man who taught him everything that he knew. The man was a walking encyclopedia who read 10 books a week and had that gift rarely found in his profession, a talent to actually pass on knowledge and teach, along with an ability to inspire those who he taught.

Michael would stay behind after the daily lessons ended, hanging on his teacher's every word. He learned about politics, deception and treachery from the War of the Roses and other tales of ancient dynasties and empires. The rise and fall of the Roman Empire also taught him much. He learned about trade from stories about the silk road, the Knights Templar and the Rothschilds.

'History repeats,' Carter, his teacher, would tell him. 'Study the world around you and choose your moment.'

Timing, he insisted, was everything. He taught him if you are truly in business, to be in business, utilise the labour of others and save your own labour for the important things.

With little fresh produce available in their small community, Michael started a small business selling fresh fruit and vegetables, door to door. He never once sold the goods himself, instead employing friends from school to do the work for him. When the local company run store insisted he close his operation down, he offered to sell it to them. When they threatened violence, he paid someone to set fire to their small delivery truck. When the man who ran to the store complained to the mine boss, Michael threatened to expose him for several indiscretions with other men's wives.

A deal was brokered and Michael went into the money lending business. After his brothers were killed, he declared his education complete. He convinced his mother that they should try their luck in a new country.

Landing in Chicago, Michael opened a small money lending and pawn shop. Then when his moment came, he built an empire.

34

T HE LIMO PULLED into the governor's mansion, interrupting Johnny's thoughts. He looked across at Chloe, who looked stunning in a satin, green evening dress. He had been thinking a lot about marriage lately. Since Rory's proposal, his parents had made discreet inquiries, but he was reluctant, wasn't certain about his feelings. Sure, Chloe was fun but did he want to spend the rest of his life with her? Did he want to spend it with any one individual?

He offered Choe his arm and escorted her to the door, where his parents welcomed them and introduced them to Cindy and Jack. In his perception, they were far more enthusiastic when introducing Rory and Claire, which put him in a bad mood. Champagne and hors d'oeuvres were served in the crowded entry foyer before dinner was announced.

Johnny found himself struggling to stop yawning during the speeches. Unable to contain himself any longer, he excused himself and went in search of a drink. Stepping out onto the terrace, he found he wasn't alone. There standing, looking off into the distance over the balustrade, smoking a cigarette, drink in hand, was Tommy.

'Nice evening, do you have a spare one of those?'

Tommy turned startled.

'Sure thing.'

Tommy reached into his jacket and brought out a packet of Marlboros. He offered one to Johnny, then reached into his pants and brought out a silver zippo lighter.

'Know where I can get one of those,' Johnny said, pointing to the drink.

Tommy motioned towards the other side of the terrace and a waiter stepped out of the shadows. Johnny took a glass off a silver tray, drained it then took another, thanking the waiter, who retreated back into his former position.

'Thanks, I needed that. Way to stuffy in there for me.'

Tommy smiled at the young man.

'Where are my manners? Johnny.' Johnny held out his hand, Tommy hesitated for a moment then shook it.

'Tommy, friend of the artist.'

'Ah, you're the reason for all this, congratulations.'

'Thanks.'

'I'm looking forward to the exhibition, I've heard great things.'

Tommy smiled. 'It's a subject close to my heart.'

'Are you a veteran?'

'Yes, Vietnam.'

'I see, very commendable. I believe, as does my father, that our veterans deserve far more recognition and assistance than they receive.'

Tommy showed a humble expression.

'Thank you, it means a lot. As veterans, we carry a lot of baggage. For some, it is a never-ending struggle. Life often becomes too tough: alcoholism, dependency on drugs, for some it leads to ruination and homelessness!'

Tommy stared deeply into Johnny's eyes as he said this. He expected to see a flicker, something. There was nothing, not even a hint.

'Hopefully, exhibitions like this, in some small way, help to raise awareness. Excuse me, I had better head back in.' Johnny dropped his cigarette, squashing it with his foot.

After he had left, Tommy drained his glass and called for another.

His hands shaking, he lit another cigarette. Tommy made it back inside just in time to see everyone stand up to go and view the exhibition. He sidled up to Jack.

'You see those two young guys walking out with the governor.'

Jack looked across the room to where the governor and his wife were led by Cindy to view the exhibition. They were followed by two young men and their dates.

'Yeah?'

'They are the ones I told you about; the ones who came to the house campaigning.'

'Okay.'

'I couldn't place him before but I just ran into him out on the terrace.'

'Which one?'

'The tall one on the left.'

'We were introduced to him earlier; he's the Governor's son.'

'I know, yes he is.'

'So, what of it?'

'He's the guy I shot!'

35

JOHN STANLEY'S DAUGHTER, Julia, had received a letter informing her that the investigation into her father's death was being re-opened. She didn't know what to make of the letter. That sad chapter of her life had been finally closed. They had buried him. It was over.

In a cardboard box, in their messy garage, were her father's possessions, the few that had not been destroyed by the fire that was. She hadn't opened it. There were other boxes in the garage also, ones she had collected over the years, ones nobody else wanted, ones she could not be parted from. When enough time had passed after his last disappearance, their mother had gathered them altogether, then gone through the house, "boxing up", as she called it, their father's life. All his things were so stored away, then over time they had ended in the care of Julia. All except his firearm collection. Their mother was unsure what to do when it came to his precious guns.

She had called Hal, a friend of her husband's. for advice. Hal was surprised at the size of the collection; John had nearly 30 rifles and shot guns in his cabinet. Amongst them, he had found five old lever action Winchester rifles, that looked like they might be worth something and two shot guns. One "Holland and Holland" he recognised from pictures in magazines. He suggested they take some photographs and send them to a few speciality firearms dealers. The remaining guns, which he felt had a lower value, he suggested they take to the local gun store and see what they could get for them.

They took them to the store and were surprised to come away with almost $1,500. That was nothing when compared with the offers from the gun dealers for the others. All told they received $22,000, a fortune back then. Enough to pay off the mortgage; enough to start over.

It was time, she had decided, to sort through her father's boxes, to go through them all, to face whatever demons were lurking in there. To feel, to reconcile. She started with the one the police had sent. Most of the items were damaged by the fire but some remained untouched. In a small tin, she found a $20 bill carefully folded up. She started to look in everything for money and uncovered more. There were several, small school exercise books, some had been burned and showed water damage. She pried the pages of one apart. Inside, every single one had been filled, in neat handwriting with a ball point pen. She started to read it. It was a diary and gave her an insight into her father's life. She could hear his voice clearly as she read. It was as if he was reaching out to her from beyond the grave.

Everything he had done, had seen, was carefully documented. Every day played out in her mind like a movie or documentary film. It was like being there, from where he slept, to what he ate, the people he encountered, the things he did to fill the day. He also recorded his thoughts and feelings. He criticised himself and performed some brutal, she felt, analysis of his actions. He was strict with himself but sometimes fell off the wagon and went on benders that lasted for days. He was clever and street smart. He had learned it was safer to find a public place to sleep in, hiding away could open you up to assault or worse. She felt a chill when she read this. *No Daddy, there were no safe places.*

He liked to go camping when he could and had spent years living in the national parks and forests. As he got older, it was hard living off the land. It was easier to camp out in the cities.

She found a few entries that referred to her and her brother and the pain he felt at being separated from them. *Pain?* she thought, becoming angry, *not so painful that you ever came back though!*

Later, when she calmed down, she wondered why. Desperate to understand, she read on. Her mother wasn't mentioned at all. There were only six books and she wondered if it had been a lifelong habit or just something he started when he went out into the world. She began searching through the other boxes. In the third one, Julia found what she was looking for. Stacked together and tied with string in eight piles, was the documented account of his life up until he had left them from ages seven to 48.

There were 51 books in total. She took the books into the house, found a pair of scissors, cut the string off, then stacked them on a coffee table in separate piles by decade. After that she went into the kitchen and brewed a pot of coffee. Returning to the living room, she settled in for a long session of reading.

The first few revealed a happy childhood spent playing games, swimming in the river, his first ever trip to the cinema aged 10, the Christmas gift of a BB gun, his first crush on a girl.

When he was 14, things turned darker. A favourite uncle, who took his own life after the stock market crash, had a profound impact. His aunt and cousin had come to live with them, although his father, who worked for the government, kept his job, the devastation wrought by the depression didn't escape them. He had written descriptions of seeing hundreds of people walking down the roads outside of town, destitute, searching for work that didn't exist.

At 15, he had gone on his first date and had his first kiss. When he was 16, his parents had bought him a second-hand car, a Model T Ford, that he used to go hunting, fishing and for drives into the country with his friends for picnics.

He wrote of his desire to become an engineer. Life at 17 was full of struggles with attempts to improve his mathematics for entry into college. He wrote about his failure to do so and the angst it caused him. At 18, he had graduated from high school but didn't go to college.

He wrote about his father finding him a government job. They had enrolled him in night school. The first references to Julia's mother and of hunting trips with Hal. The purchase of an old house outside of town and fixing it up, giving him an interest in carpentry but still working as a clerk for the government.

By the time he was 25, John had owned his own house and bought a new car but had nobody to share it with. He was heart-broken when Julia's mother left town.

At 26, he was dating a girl from another town, the daughter of a minister. There was reference to a letter from her mother who was in the navy now, based in Washington DC in the communications division. He was still dating the minister's daughter, had proposed to her but she wanted to wait. He joined the army reserve, did an NCO course and was promoted to sergeant.

Age 27, Julia's mother visited his home and they double dated, with Uncle Hal accompanying her mother. The sadness that accompanied this outing. The Japanese attacked Pearl Harbour and he was called up into the army. No fear, no trepidation, almost a macabre happiness.

Julia looked up. It was getting dark. She hadn't noticed. There had been an emotional farewell with his girlfriend, advanced training, then more training and he was asked would he take an officer's exam due to a chronic shortage, then left for England on a troop ship as a second lieutenant.

On landing he received a "Dear John" letter from his girl. Met an English girl and went on a few dates, liked her family and was happy.

Aged 28, there was the frustration of waiting around, then more training, practicing for beach landings, more training and by December 1943 he was a First Lieutenant. He described the bombings in England and the bleak, dreary outlook. How the people were suffering. He described their eyes and how they looked hollow and empty.

In January, 1944, he was on a troop ship headed for Italy. His mother had been writing to him; Uncle Hal had evidently met somebody else. His English girlfriend had wanted to become engaged but he had said "no" as he did not know what would happen in the war.

He was scared but the landing was unopposed and they were moving inland. His combat experiences were frightening, several times she had to put the books down, there was genuine feeling and emotion as he confronted death.

The futility of war was something he had to come to terms with, now as he lost the first man under his command. There was deep sorrow and remorse in his words.

Riding in a jeep behind their commanding officer, when a mine exploded, killing all those on board the leading vehicle. The horrible description of having their body parts rain down on them. Would they ever be clean again? he asked.

Heavy fighting, many casualties, one entry read that his corporal was badly wounded, loss of arm likely, unable to sleep, nightmares.

Catching a German prisoner and how one of his men shot the man in cold blood, while the others laughed. Horrified as every time he closed his eyes, he saw the young man.

It went on and on like that and she felt closer to her father than she had in her entire lifetime. Wounded, he was evacuated to England where he was joined by his heavily depleted platoon then promoted to captain.

The landings in Normandy were heavily opposed and in direct contrast to Italy. Moving inland, the fighting was ferocious. She noticed his change in attitude as he calmly, without emotion, killed a teenage German soldier. How he had gone on a killing spree when one of his men was taken down at his shoulder, in an ambush, covering him in blood. Those deaths were obviously a turning point for him. From that point on, he never spoke about mercy for the enemy again.

Half his men were dead, reinforcements arrived daily, some were buried that same day. He barely learned some of their names.

The months rolled by, he had written, as they slowly edged their way towards Germany. They were resupplied again and sent in as support troops for 'Operation Market Garden', a mission designed to capture bridges across the Rhine. Once again, they were in the thick of it.

They had fought on in the Netherlands. There was an entry, called Black Wednesday, where they were awoken to the sound of artillery fire. After half an hour of repeated fire, the Germans attacked en masse. It was chaos and completely unexpected. They tried to regroup and form a defensive position. The unit next to them collapsed under the weight of enemy attack and were annihilated.

His father had written him a rare letter. He had only just finished reading it, before turning in the previous night. He prayed to live long enough to write a reply. The fighting was the most intense he had been involved in against fresh fanatical SS troops. Their position formed the shape of a square and was shrinking quickly. They called desperately for reinforcements as they were being overrun. Eventually, they retreated, along with the remnants of the other units into a nearby forest. The fighting was almost, in some cases was, hand to hand. Just when they thought it was all over, the cavalry, as he described it, arrived. He collapsed against a tree and thanked God once again for sparing him.

The Rhine was just in front of them but he would never cross it. Wounded again and with only five of his men still alive, they were shipped back to England. His war was over but it wasn't time to go home yet. They spent the final months recuperating in the English countryside, bored and weary. He was lonely. His English girlfriend had married another; he wrote to her mother but received no response.

Hitler was dead, and the war was over.

As he was in one of the first troops to arrive in England, they were given a priority return home. He, along with the five remaining survivors of his unit, flew home on a B17 Bomber. In New York, they boarded a train and when he arrived home, there were celebrations welcoming him.

Julia could tell by the entries in his diary that he was a changed man. She could tell he probably needed some psychiatric care. He fell into a dark depression and his diary reflected this. He didn't return to work straight away, even though there was a job waiting for him. He travelled to DC to their mother; this trip did nothing to lift his spirits.

He was 30 years old but said that he felt 50. He decided to move to a big city and sold his house. The next entry shocked her. Her mother was pregnant and he offered marriage, even though he was not the father. She accepted.

He had planned to study engineering, now all that changed. He bought a lot in the middle of town then took a mortgage to build them a large house. He had never enjoyed his job, even if it was with the federal government. Now he was stuck. He became a supervisor but was universally unhappy. After two years, their mother fell pregnant again. Shocked, she read that he was not certain he was the father.

In 1949 his father fell ill and died. He now had to look after his mother. His frustration grew as he wrote how he had missed the boat of life.

When Julia's family returned home, she stayed on the lounge, while they had dinner in the kitchen. She ate without stopping and, at some point after midnight, she dozed off. When she woke, rather than head to bed, she opened a bottle of wine and continued reading. The house was quiet, except for her page turning and sipping from the glass of wine.

In 1950, he recorded her own birth and the start of her father's 35th year. The Korean war had begun. Desperate, he attempted re-enlistment but was too old. Her mother was asked to return to Washington DC with a new government agency, the CIA, offering a role. She wanted to go and, in the end, she went.

In 1951, John's mother became ill and passed away. He had wanted to pay off their mortgage with the money from the sale of his parents' house. Julia's mother didn't agree. She wanted to sell everything and would only agree to move to Washington DC. It seemed to her, reading between the lines, their marriage, that had been showing cracks, was all but falling apart.

Another bombshell was dropped in 1953 when her brother was five. Her father wrote how much her brother reminded him of Hal. Up until this time, reading the diaries, she had never considered it but could now see clearly the resemblance. She went into the bathroom, looking deeply into the mirror and began to cry. Her father was becoming more paranoid as future entries revealed.

The unhappy years flowed on by. In 1955, he had turned 40, hated his job, doubted the paternity of his children and was stuck with a woman who didn't love him. What Julia couldn't understand, was how he allowed Hal to stay involved in their lives. She began re-examining her own memories.

Then next entry was interesting though, as it was a story she both lived through and had heard repeated many times. It was Friday and, as usual, he visited the bank. While waiting in line to be served, the bank was robbed. Behind him was a woman with her daughter. The girl was scared and began to cry. One of the robbers screamed at her mother to shut her up. The mother, not thinking, opened her handbag and reached inside; the robber panicked, thinking she was reaching for a gun and raised his own. John didn't even think, throwing himself in front of the mother and her little girl. One bullet struck him in the arm, a second, his leg and the third, his stomach.

Distracted, the robber was tackled by another customer. His two accomplices panicked and ran from the bank.

Her father was strangely upbeat about the whole thing. She wondered if his euphoria was another symptom of his continued mental illness. He was in hospital for three weeks and the entire town rallied around them to celebrate their hero. A thousand dollars was raised in a public collection to cover medical expenses. He was decorated by the mayor and the governor sent him a citation and a letter.

A period of happiness followed but another bombshell was only months away. Her parents' fighting increased. In the heat of the moment, she told him that none of the children were his. He responded that he would divorce her and that she would get nothing. She didn't care as she was going to live with Hal, who was far more of a man than him. That he wrote this out verbatim in his diary, told her how much it had hurt.

He walked out of their lives for the first time that night. Hal had obviously refused to take them in, because they never left the house, though he visited often.

His entries became dark. There were constant rants; he would leave and return then, over the next few years, they tried to reconcile but the damage was done, the wounds too deep. She cried when she read the second last entry in book 51 that detailed his withdrawal of half the money in their bank account and planning a move to California. His last entry was one word.

'Sorry.'

The sun was rising as she finished the last book. She would love to have the missing editions that she was sure existed somewhere. Exhausted, she finally turned off the light and headed to bed.

36

THEY WERE IN Tommy's hotel room, trying to decide what to do next. Jack knew the right thing to do was to call the police and report everything. He would catch hell over the pistol but that was a tomorrow problem. Maybe he could claim attorney-client privilege or maybe Tommy could claim he threw it into the ocean. Hard to explain if his home was searched; better to just come clean.

Tommy had shot the governor's son. The lack of reporting the incident on their side was interesting. Did it mean they knew the boy had killed someone? Highly likely, therefore they had made the decision to hush the entire thing up. It dawned on Jack that if Tommy had recognised the boy, then maybe...

'Did he recognise you?' he asked Tommy.

'No, but I may have made a mistake.' Tommy recounted their conversation, and the governor's son's abrupt exit.

'Doesn't mean that he knows you were the shooter. Could be a coincidence.'

'He knew I knew something. I can feel it.'

Jack ran it over in his mind.

'What are the dangers here?' he said, pausing to ponder them. 'They have a lot at stake, a damn lot. If the father was involved in the cover up

149

and, we have to assume that he was, then if this all came out, it would be very damaging, career ending.'

Jack paused to take a few breaths before continuing.

'They hushed it up for two reasons: the first, to protect the son from a murder charge, the second, to maintain the governor's image. Now that they have made their decision, there's no going back. He's a powerful man and he's shown us that such people are capable of anything.'

Jack and Tommy both were silent. Tommy felt scared. It was a feeling that would haunt him in the days to come. It was not unlike being back in combat, never knowing from one moment to the next if it was to be your last.

'What do we do?' Tommy asked, reaching into his pocket for a cigarette.

'I don't know. It really depends on what they know. If they suspect nothing, then...' Jack paused. No, that was not right. He hated himself for almost saying it.

'I take that back; it depends on what we are going to do.'

'Justice.'

'Yes, justice. Do you want it?'

'Why are you asking me?'

'This is your show, old pal. It's your call all the way. If you say so, we find a way to end it here and now. If you want justice, then...' Jack tailed off, hardly believing what he was about to say. Then, like tearing off a band aid, he spoke the words he was so scared of. They came racing from his mouth at great speed.

'Then we find a way to see that it's delivered.'

There was silence. Tommy felt overwhelmed. He looked at Jack who wanted an answer. It was all too much.

'What if...?' He looked at Jack. There was no delaying things; he raised his lowered eyes. 'All the way.'

37

THEIR NAMES WERE Pamela and Paul. They had once been affluent, successful people by all the measures of society. However, through a series of events, it had all fallen apart. Abandoned by their own children, they had been living in dive hotels and flop houses on a downward spiral. A favourite niece had come to rescue them. She had offered the small apartment above her garage and promised to take care of them. She had spoken to the owner of the flop house, in order to organise payment for them to stay until she arrived and was surprised to learn that they were all paid up.

Detective Lawrence had heard it all, reading, then re-reading, his notes until they were memorised. So, why had they turned up dead, burned beyond recognition, on a bench in the same location where John Stanley's blanket, partially burned, was found a few feet away. The supposition was, they had been sleeping beneath it and it had blown off during the fire. Unlike John Stanley, there was no kerosene stove. In fact, there were no other possessions found at the scene. Everything they owned was back at their paid room in the flophouse, where they had been staying. *Why,* he continued to ask himself, *would they have been there? There was no reason for them to be.*

Identifying the bodies had taken time. If the victim's niece hadn't come into the station on a hunch, they may have laid in the city morgue for years. Dental records had been required to confirm what they suspected, then by the time he had visited the flop house, it had been too late. Though there had been some things that were suspicious, they were suspicious because they were unusual.

He had interviewed the owner of the flophouse, who also was running the place at the time because he couldn't find anyone else desperate enough to take the job. They spoke at the small desk just inside the front door of the old three-storey wooden building.

Pamela and Paul's room had been paid for; this was important, yet it got him nowhere.

'Who paid for the room?' he had asked. He got no answer but after an age, the owner responded.

'The same guy who paid for the other room,' he eventually said. 'Look Mister, a guy comes in and wants to pay for two people's rooms. I don't argue. Do you know how hard it is to get these people to pay?'

'Don't you keep records?'

'Of course.' He opened a large book that sat on the counter.

'Looks like two rooms, one for a Mr and Mrs Peach and a Mr and Mrs Antonelli, were paid for in cash for two weeks, both dated the same time. Here, see?'

'Who paid for them?'

'We don't record that information,' replied the owner. 'Look, I wasn't the one who was working. That was my manager, he quit later the same day. Said he was going to Phoenix to visit his sister. Before you ask, I haven't seen him since.'

'And his details?'

The owner shrugged.

'Top notch organisation you're running here.'

'This is a flophouse. People come, people go, the residents, the workers. Hell, I'd go myself if I could find someone to buy the place.'

This was pointless, the detective thought. He was just about to leave when he noticed two entries just below.

'What are these?'

'I asked about those when my manager quit. Same guy. He booked rooms opposite the ones he paid for, never stayed in them though, as far as I can tell. Young guy, rich looking.'

'His name?'

'I can't make it out. Is that a J?'

He turned the book around so Detective Lawrence could see it. He frowned; the entry was barely legible.

'Could be. Tell me you didn't find that at all interesting, that someone wants to pay for two people's rooms, then rents the rooms opposite and you never see them.'

The owner shrugged again. 'It is what it is.'

Detective Lawrence had left a card, as pointless as he thought it was. He remembered the feelings of helplessness he had felt as he walked out of the flophouse. He felt that way now. The niece maintained contact, calling him every week. He could feel that, although she wasn't losing interest, she was approaching the point where she wanted to put it behind her. He felt a sudden burst of energy.

Sitting up straighter in his chair, he picked up a pad and pencil and began scribbling.

This case was a dead end but what if it was connected to the John Stanley case? That was the only way it could be solved, if he believed what Elyse had told them. If there was a mystery shooter out there, if Stanley was murdered and he could find the killers, then maybe it was the only chance. It was such a wild theory, though. It was preposterous, yet at the same time, it made sense. Something bigger was at play, something he could not yet see. With renewed enthusiasm and determination, he began again.

38

For Jack, life was good and getting better every day. That was until he learned that it was the governor's son that Tommy had shot. Now it was full of headaches. Tommy, who was himself, now flourishing, had made, in his own eyes, a fateful error, that had the potential to endanger them all. Yet justice had to be done. Despite the fact they had both met women who had the potential to be the loves of their life. Despite the fact that Tommy had begun to overcome the many issues that had been haunting him, denying him happiness for so many years. That Jack was slowly finding purpose in his life. Everything they had was now in danger.

But your actions, they both had agreed, defined who you were. They owed it to the victim, they owed it to themselves and, most importantly, they owed it to humanity, because if they walked away from it and did nothing, then they did not deserve the things that they had been given. If he could do this, then everything else in life would be easy.

They had finished a six pack and Tommy had gone to bed. Jack had returned to his room to find Cindy asleep across the bed in nothing but her underwear, her dress draped over a nearby sofa. Deciding not to wake her, he went back into the other room, then moved on to scotch. It was late, there would be no sleep but at some point, he nodded off.

Events of the following morning would put everything on hold.

The phone started ringing at 6am. They slept through it. At 6:30am, the operator, tired of trying the room, yet convinced by the caller of the importance of the call, sent a bellboy to investigate. The bellboy, unable to raise anyone in the room, went to find the night manager. The night manager, who really wanted to go home, passed it over to the concierge who, after his own unsuccessful attempt at knocking, used his room key.

Cindy heard the concierge knocking at their bedroom door. After the initial surprise and a few good shakes, a semi-conscious Jack was handed a phone.

Thirty seconds later, shocked into lucidity he was switching on the television and searching for the news channels.

His timing was perfect. The newsreader's expression was grave.

'There are serious reports today that a leading Hollywood actor and producer have been caught with others in a drug-smuggling operation led by detectives. John Hansen has more.'

'Thanks Ken, I'm standing outside this palatial Beverly Hills home, where authorities responded in the early hours of this morning, after reports of a disturbance. Police say they discovered three minors amid, what officials described as, a "wild and out-of-control party."

'Inside one of the bedrooms, a fourth teenager was found unconscious. Paramedics attempted lifesaving measures but the young woman was later pronounced dead at City Hospital. Her identity is being withheld pending notification of next of kin.

'During a search of the property, detectives uncovered what one law enforcement source called "a significant stash" of illicit substances, including pills and powdered narcotics, believed to be tied to a larger smuggling operation.

'At the time of this report, investigators are said to be executing a search warrant at a second property in Studio City connected to one of the male suspects.'

'My God,' Jack said, instantly recognising the house of that belonging to one of their biggest clients. He switched the TV off.

Maria was still waiting on the line; he picked the receiver back up.

'Get on the phone to Jim Teal, he's the only one in our firm with the experience to handle this. Tell him to drop everything and get over there immediately, send anyone he needs to help. Our message on behalf of our clients is no comment, name, rank, serial number only, got it?'

'Got it.'

'We will leave here within the hour. Gather the team and set up a war room.'

'Okay, see you soon.'

Hanging up, he turned to Tommy, who looked the worse for wear.

'Go back to your room, shower, pack. I'll wake up Cindy and do the same. Let's aim to meet for breakfast downstairs in thirty minutes.'

Tommy headed back out the door without a word.

<h1 style="text-align:center">39</h1>

THE OFFICE WAS buzzing when he arrived in the middle of the afternoon. They had dropped Cindy at home and Jack had brought Tommy for moral support. Dressed in jeans and a t-shirt, Jack stepped into the war room. All eyes turned to him and Tommy.

'So, tell me, how much of it is true?'

'Lots,' Maria blurted out. Jim Teal raised a hand.

'Some of it.' Jim was more serious, less panicked than everyone else. He continued, 'They'll be out this afternoon. They aren't being charged, not yet anyway. I'm confident the kid will walk.'

'And Conner?' Jack asked, beginning to pace up and down the room. Conner was the one described as the older man by the news reporter. He was a hot shot producer. Jim Teal shrugged.

'The girl died of an overdose in one of the guest rooms. She was 17. They can't prove he invited her there; her name isn't even known to our boy. She was just rounded up and brought along for fun. There were maybe 20 people there, four of the girls are under 18. I paid a visit to the coroner's office after a tip from one of our friends. She has track marks, heroin,' Jim said, his voice emotionless. Jack rolled it over in his mind.

'Go on, Jim,' Jack said, as calmly as if he were discussing the weather.

'If our tip is correct, then she died from a mixture of heroin and cocaine, which is the drug that they found in a large quantity.'

'How much?' Jack showed his interest.

'Just under a kilogram.'

Jack pondered this. When he raised his eyebrows, Jim continued.

'Once again, there's no proof it was his. Yes, it was found in his house but it was in the open, on the kitchen table of all places.'

'Who called the cops?'

'One of the girls. It sounds like a bit of a setup, all except the tragic death, that is. Press arrived there at the same time as the cops.'

'Could have been tipped off by one of them!'

'Maybe, I'm looking into it. If you ask me, it has all the makings of a newspaper set up. Only one of the girls partied a little too hard. Stories like these sell a lot of newspapers.'

Jack could see the logic.

'What about the kid's house?' he asked fearing the worst.

'The kid was Mario Deluca, a 22-year-old former teen star who was outgrowing his audience. They were trying to transition him into more adult roles. So far, it wasn't working. A scandal of this magnitude, if it didn't land him in jail, could definitely spell the end of his career,' said Jim. 'His place, was clean when they searched it.'

'It's very careless. I mean, how do you allow a teenage girl to come into your house then pass away like that?' Jack asked. Jim couldn't believe the question, so he put it down to Jack being tired.

'Happens. He didn't invite her there. I doubt he knew how young she was.'

Jack felt unsettled. Jim was right, of course. Well, in the context of a lawyer protecting his client, he was. Morally though, it was tough. What was a grown adult doing hosting drug parties with teenagers? He made a note to have a serious think about who they represented.

'Okay well, good work everyone. I guess we will need some help,' said Jack pacing again, 'We need a top PR person to help us with the press. Let's be proactive, get them both into rehab. We don't discuss the death of the girl though. If pushed, say that we are working with the authorities over the tragic death. Don't speculate about her being a user or anything like that, this girl has a family. Let other people spread those rumours. If the drugs do come up and I'm certain that they will, just say that no drugs were purchased or supplied by our clients. Jim, push that angle with the police also, speak to a judge, prosecutor, someone. Maybe they can both avoid a charge.'

'Already on it.' Jim stated. He had been working the phones all day.

'It's both a PR war, and a legal one. We need to win this in the realm of public opinion.'

Maria interrupted Jack.

'If we send them to rehab won't that admit a drug problem?'

'Good point do they have drug problems?' Jack looked around the room and was met by blank stares. 'Okay, find out. Maria, get onto Marty Wilson at Global. He is the best PR person I can think of. Get him and his team on this. I want something out on the 6pm news, regardless of the cost.'

'On it.'

'Jim, let's meet for breakfast. My phone line is open if anything changes. Once again, good work everyone.'

Tommy drove them home. He was impressed with how Jack led his team and a little envious. *Cool under pressure, he had always been like that,* Tommy thought. Tommy had seen Jack show the same coolness under heavy fire in the jungle. They didn't speak on the trip home. Tommy respected the silence; Jack was deep in thought and he knew that it was not the fate of his clients that was troubling him.

There were far more difficult problems to deal with.

40

Tommy woke in a sweat. He had shot the governor's son. Why had he done that? Because he was the leader. It was the old communist leader thing he had learned in the army. Communist trained troops rely heavily on their leaders; take out the leader and they fold. Well, that was the theory and it definitely worked against the regular troops who relied on weight of numbers to overrun the enemy.

He didn't know what to do. If it all came out, Jack Cindy, Louise, they would all be in trouble. He could not, would not, allow that to happen. He was panicking. *Calm down*, he told himself. *Be rational. How can I? There is no way out of this.*

He would run, pack up right now and go: Mexico Canada. He experienced a moment of joy, thinking of himself free, out on the open road but it was fleeting, undeserved and he chastised himself. *NO! No more turning away. Time to face things. There is a solution to this, there is a solution to everything, think.*

Doctor Feldman had taught him some breathing techniques. He employed them there in bed, in the dark. Turning his mind to happier thoughts, he started to calm down. He thought about the work he had been doing with Cindy, how much he enjoyed it, how much he enjoyed growing closer to her as their relationship grew. He thought about Jack, how their bond had returned, stronger than ever. Finally, he turned to Louise, realising, not for the first time, that he was falling in love with her. He thought about her smile, the velvet softness of her skin, the gentleness of her embraces, her luscious lips when they kissed. She was one of the calmest people he had ever met and she could sit patiently for hours saying nothing.

His life had become stable. There was happiness and hope, plans for the future were forming. He needed this problem like a hole in the head.

Jack was right, they owed it to the old man that had been killed. There was no questioning that, but how and against what odds?

He had fought hard to keep the old man alive but, in those precious seconds it had taken to shoot the boy and then extinguish the flames, irreparable damage had been done. He had known this as he fought, had seen it, yet something had spurred him on, because you just never know. *Never underestimate the human spirit*, he reminded himself. He had held men in his arms, men who were dead, only for them to rise from the ground with a cough, brought back to life with his hands.

Still there was a detachment in this case, not when it was happening, it came after. It stemmed from his expectations. He had expected to be arrested at the scene but the boys had run; detained at the hospital, but the police had left him alone, giving him the opportunity to walk away. They had not even properly identified him. It was, sadly, as if they didn't care. They had quickly moved on then so had he, so had the other side. The governor's kid, from what he could tell, showed not a shred of guilt or remorse. Nobody cared for that homeless old man, not even him.

Feelings of guilt and shame flowed through his body. A veteran like him, a brother in arms, left to die in such a horrible way and for what? Then he had helped cover things up, hidden the gun, not reported properly to police, implicated others. He could have… he stopped. He should have done a lot of things. Then he was seized by a thought.

More importantly, what would he do now? The past was written but the future lay before them. Somehow, with the help of those around him, he needed to make things right. By doing that, perhaps yes, a warm feeling came over him. By doing that, he would atone for his sins.

He would see if he could find out more about the man who had died, that was the first step. It was a comforting thought and it allowed him to fall back to sleep.

When Tommy woke again, it was with great purpose. He quickly showered and dressed, then borrowing Jack's Mustang, hit the streets. He parked not far from where he had spent his last night on the street, bought a coffee then started wandering around. He tried to approach a few homeless people without success, then he came up with an idea.

He bought some cigarettes. Sitting on a brick wall near the beach, he spied two men, a shopping cart close at hand.

He walked up, smoking and said, 'Good morning.' in an exaggerated friendly manner.

As he thought they would, both men kept glancing at the cigarette. He offered them one each; the ice was broken. Three packs of cigarettes later, he had had several conversations and learned a great deal. One man told him the victim's nickname was "The General". The General, it turned out, would often talk about his military service with the people he got to know. He was an officer in World War Two. His ex-wife had swindled him out of his savings and his pension, another told him.

'He was the nicest fellow; would give you his last dollar.' Then the man had become serious leaning close to him. 'Can you keep a secret?'

'Yes, of course.'

'Don't believe what you read in the papers. It was no accident. He was murdered, only you didn't hear it from me. I heard that from someone who saw it happen.'

Tommy went cold. There were witnesses. The man leaned close again.

'A friend of mine, fine lady, used to be an actress, saw the whole thing from across the street. He was murdered by a group of young men who drove fancy cars. She was sitting there the whole time. The cops came, the ambulance and fire brigade also, but there wasn't anything they could do and the General died.'

The man leaned back again, his cigarette was almost finished. Tommy offered another, desperate to hear more. Then, something occurred to him, perhaps this wasn't the only time something like this had happened.

'Can I ask you another question?' Tommy asked, offering the man the rest of the packet.

'Certainly, ask away.'

'Has anything like this happening before?'

The man leaned in close again.

'Another friend of mine, everyone calls him Othello, sleeps down near the pier. I saw him one time, the whole side of his face was just one large bruise. I asked him what happened. He told me that a group of college kids had beaten him up. I asked him how he knew they were college boys and he said one of them was wearing a college football jacket, that he recognised the school as some fancy rich kid's college. They beat him real good. He passed out at some point. When he woke up, all of his things had been burned, you didn't hear it from me though, I got troubles enough of my own!'

Tommy thanked the man, standing to leave. The man looked him straight in the eye.

'Could you spare a few dollars?'

'I tell you what, if you agree to meet me here tomorrow with your friend, the actress, I'll give you $50.'

The man smiled.

'Can't help you there, son. She's gone MIA, haven't seen her in days. I'll ask around though, if you want me to, maybe someone knows something.'

It was better than nothing, Tommy took a 50-dollar bill out of his pocket, handing it to the man who held it up, inspecting it.

'Same time tomorrow?'

'Agreed.'

Tommy walked back to the car and drove home.

The following day he returned but the man didn't show. An hour passed. He was surprised, certain that the man would keep his word. He went for a walk to stretch his legs, keeping an eye on the meeting place the entire time. He sat back down again. It was then that he noticed a teenage boy looking at him. The boy nervously approached.

'Are you a friend of Cornelius?'

He had seen the boy approach, yet was startled when he spoke. The boy looked around nervously awaiting his reply.

'You look like him. Cornelius told me to give you this.'

The boy handed him a piece of paper then quickly backed away, his eyes darting in every direction.

Written on the paper in neat handwriting, was a simple message:

'Apologies, same time and place tomorrow.'

'Thank you, let Cornelius know I'll be here.'

The boy nodded and was gone.

The following day, Tommy was running late. He had overslept and never got back in front. He was almost half an hour late for the meeting with Cornelius. He was hurrying along the street when he spotted something that stopped him dead. Beyond where he could see Cornelius waiting, he spotted someone he immediately suspected was a detective. He was standing casually against a wall, had probably been standing back but had grown sloppy when Tommy hadn't shown. He was wearing dark sunglasses, a baseball cap and smoking a cigarette. Tommy could spot a detective a mile away and he knew, almost definitely, that this man was. It was in his mannerisms the way he stood, the way he casually looked around. Tommy turned around then, without any sudden movements or panic, began retracing his steps. Holding out for as long as he could, he gave in, looking over his shoulder. There was nobody there.

'Damn you, Cornelius,' he said under his breath, carefully making his way back to his car, then quickly driving away.

<h1 style="text-align:center">41</h1>

JOHNNY HAD NOT visited anyone from the frat house since the last and, what he had decided would be, the final games night. Well no, not technically true, for the pull was still strong, only it was the final one that would involve his alumni. That, he had decided, was too dangerous and, besides, it was time to move on from his college days. He had lived in a mixture of fear and shock in the days that followed until he reasoned that there would once again be no repercussions for what had happened. Then he had employed the lessons learned from his father and Randle, to hush things up on his own.

The boys had been paid off with a vacation and cash. The caretaker and security guard at the studio lot his family owned, knew nothing of what had happened, nor did the prostitutes, nor the nurse, whose drug induced incompetence had been the cause of their problems. Therefore, he was saved any worry there.

The other couple posed a problem as they could link him through the flophouse to the game, though they had not seemed to make the connection. Still, it concerned him enough and, along with the press coverage, he was sure it would only be a matter of time until they connected everything together, so he had needed to take action. Though what, he wasn't sure. In any case, they had disappeared from the flophouse. It was a loose end that haunted him. He was not so upset by the unfortunate demise of the older couple, more disappointed in the events that followed.

On discovering the bodies, he had panicked. In the fog of his memory, he had formulated the plan to dump the bodies in the same place of the previous "accident", though he could not, for the life of him, remember why he had thought that was a good idea. After they had left, he returned to the scene with a gas can and started the fire. This brough back memories of the night he was shot. It was that moment when the reality of it all had hit him, followed by more panic. This had caused him to seek out Rory, who was unhappy about being woken in the middle of the night. Johnny had told him everything and his response had not been kind.

'Why, do you love these stupid, irresponsible games so much?' he had asked, his voice filled with contempt

'Because they allow me to escape reality,' Johnny had responded.

'Escape reality!? You have everything a person could ever want, why would you want to escape from that?'

He had studied Rory carefully at this point. He felt distant, cold. He had thought his friend understood him; it appeared he was wrong.

'Possessions are nothing more than anchors that weigh you down, all of it can never make up for what's lacking.'

'Lacking, I'm sorry Johnny, I can't see anything lacking.'

'Then I suppose you will never understand.'

'I suppose not.'

And with that, Johnny had left. They were still friends only things were different now. They still socialised, even planned vacations together, after all, Rory would soon be family, but there was a change, a distance between them.

What Johnny had not known was Rory had been upset by his friend's late night visit, upset enough to pick up the phone to call Randle. He was about to dial when he decided not to. Then concern crept in and he raised it once more, only to put it down again. *This was a mess*, he had thought, *a mess that somebody needed to clean up.* If he didn't want to call Randle, he thought, who did that leave?

Silently, Rory, went out into the night.

42

JACK HAD FACED the media, appearing in front of the cameras with his clients. Cindy got a kick out of watching Jack on TV. She had cut clippings from all the papers sticking them into a scrap book as a keepsake. When she learned the details of the case, the experience was tainted.

'The poor girl,' she said with tears in her eyes. Jack tried to mimic Jim Teal's cool assessment of the situation. 'Do all of your clients behave like this, drug induced orgies with minors?'

This was difficult to answer, he honestly didn't know.

'Not as far as I'm aware.'

'Do you condone it?'

'Of course not, only it's not as clear as…'

She cut him off.

'So how can you defend them?'

He looked carefully into her eyes. She was serious so he took his time to answer.

'Because he is our client. It's our job. It's not for us to judge or decide what is right or wrong in their behaviour. It is to look after our client's interests by providing the best possible defence.'

'So, you agree with their actions?'

'I don't agree or disagree. My personal feelings and morals don't come into it. Our clients find themselves in trouble, it's our job to find a way out of it. In this case, there is substantial evidence exonerating our clients.'

'What if it was your or our daughter?'

'That's not fair. It isn't, it's a girl who, for whatever reason, lost her way or was just careless. She was taking heroin, then mixed it with a little too much cocaine and alcohol. There are hundreds of girls and boys out here doing the same thing every day.'

Cindy looked horrified at his response. Jack felt terrible. He felt the need to continue the argument, even though it was obvious that this was unwinnable and he would do better to simply fall on his sword.

'Everyone is entitled to a rigorous and proper defence. We would not be doing our job if we did not do everything in our power to provide it.'

'Murderers?'

'Yes.'

'Child molesters?'

'Everyone!'

'Why?'

'Because that is the nature of the game we play. The prosecutor will go all out to gain a conviction, even if they suspect or, know for a fact, the person is innocent. Therefore, we must go all out to defend our clients regardless of what we know or think. Remember one thing, clients are people and people are innocent until proven guilty.'

Cindy looked angry.

'Look Cindy, you have a lawyer in New York, correct?' he asked.

'Yes, you know I do,' she replied.

'And why do you pay your lawyer?'

Cindy shrugged. Immediately, she saw where this was heading and disliked it, though the answer was clear.

'You pay them to protect your interests, correct?' Jack stated, answering for her.

'Correct,' Cindy said begrudgingly.

'Now we are in love, correct?'

Cindy smiled, 'Correct.'

'And we have agreed to enter into holy matrimony, yes?'

'Yes.'

'I expect at some point, you and your lawyer will have a discussion about this change in your circumstances, that this discussion will involve your money, your assets etc. It will include the "what if?" questions?'

'What if questions?' she asked, confused.

'What if you're wrong about this man? What if he turns out to be a wife beating asshole? What if he goes broke? What if he wants you to loan him money? What if he dies? What if you die? What if he gets sick or you get sick or you both get sick? What happens if you have children? What happens if he decides to wander off with a young blonde? What if a bear eats him?'

It worked, the mood changed. Cindy laughed and Jack continued.

'At some point, if you haven't already, you will have this discussion, regardless of how madly, deeply, head over the heels in love, you are,' he paused for effect, 'Because, that's what you pay them for, to protect your interests! And protect you, they will. They won't concern themselves with the morals, won't give a damn about your assessment of me, won't give a damn about me, because their sole purpose is to protect you. And believe me, that is exactly what they will do.'

Cindy thought about this, thought about it a lot over the next few days. She understood but she wasn't by any means comfortable. There was a difference in her mind, between protecting someone's assets and defending a man who allowed underaged young women to die from drug overdoses in their house. She decided, in the end, though, to drop the subject and move on.

The delayed visit to meet Cindy's parents had finally arrived. Cindy's parents were staying at their house in New Mexico, a palatial Spanish mansion on a golf course, as Cindy described it.

Cindy's father came from a long line of cattle ranchers; they could trace their roots back 100 years before the Spanish American war. They held large land holdings on both sides of the border and, at one time, owned massive tracts of land in Texas, Mexico, California and what was now New Mexico. In the late 1940s, her grandfather had sold the Texas land to oil speculators and they were gone.

Over the years, they had continued to sell and the last of the cattle ranches passed from their hands in the mid-1960s. Wise investments in property, stocks, bonds and a million other financial vehicles, had built their wealth considerably. Cindy's father was a mystery to Jack, who had no insight into the extent of the family's wealth. Cindy said little, something about involvement in a farm machinery business and some philanthropy.

Their lifestyle was quite modest. Cindy warned him, it was conflicting as they lived in a palatial mansion modestly. He could not help but wonder.

Cindy's mother had been a ballerina when she was younger. At 15, she had gone to Europe to study, including a stay in Moscow. She was also from a wealthy background as her grandparents had been large land holders and owned an enormous department store in Mexico City and some incredibly valuable land in the Hollywood Hills. Her dancing career had ended with a knee injury, when a male dancer, who was meant to catch her, slipped. Her dreams in shreds, she returned home then fell into a deep depression. Her grandmother forced her from her bed one evening, to attend a gala ball.

At the ball she met Cindy's father. When introduced, she famously asked him what he was doing there.

His reply was simple and honest. 'I'm looking for a wife.'

'Why?' she asked him, smiling.

'Because it feels like the right thing to do!'

Six months later, they were married.

Cindy had always been stubborn. Her parents loved that about her. Born with incredible talent, even before she could properly read or write, she could draw. Even before the years of study, her talent was obvious. A gift from God. Despite their wealth and assistance, she had forged her own path and they were immensely proud of her.

Jack and Cindy were met by her parents at the door and welcomed into a large sitting room, while servants unloaded the car, taking their bags up to separate guest rooms. Lunch was served outside in a courtyard. It was peaceful as the only sound was coming from an ornate fountain, as the water bubbled and sprayed.

Vines were growing up the walls and, overhead, a canvas pergola shaded them from the sun. It was a comfortable, peaceful place to while away the afternoon, eating and sampling wine from their abundant cellar. They stayed out there most of the latter part of the day. When they staggered up to their rooms, for a nap before dinner, they were drunk.

After dinner, they relaxed in a large, living room complete with a huge fireplace that was not lit. Jack studied the many pictures of Cindy and her siblings and other relatives that were scattered about the room. He answered the standard questions about his life. Cindy was embarrassed. Jack didn't seem to mind. Her parents seemed unimpressed with Jack.

When the conversation stalled, Cindy's mother ushered her from the room. Jack remained mortified as the silence devoured them. Cindy's father stared at him, smiling. It took Jack quite a long time to understand what was happening. Then, finally, the penny dropped.

'Sir we would be honoured to receive your blessing,' he stammered, feeling faint.

Cindy's father realised that this was the best he could hope for, in the "asking permission to marry my daughter" department so, with a smile, he gave his blessing. Cindy and her mother, who had been patiently waiting in the hall, came bursting back into the room. Her father called for champagne.

Cindy wanted to go dancing. Jack, on the verge of a nervous breakdown, wanted to sleep. They finished the bottle then Jack excused himself with a promise of dancing the following night. While

Jack staggered up the stairs, Cindy stayed to speak to her parents. She desperately wanted sex but she didn't want them to know that. She still felt extremely self-conscious about sex when it came to discussing such a topic with her parents, preserving the illusion of innocence, even if it had long since gone.

Hanging on the wall at the end of the hallway near his room, Jack spotted a painting. He was drawn towards it. At first, he wasn't sure what he was looking at. It was a mix of reds, blacks and oranges. A as he drew closer, he could make out the shape of a naked woman, as seen from behind, standing in a doorway, her curves accented by the bright reds and oranges. It struck him as dark and mysterious. The woman's black hair flowing freely, the skin of her back looked exquisite. He reached out to touch it, withdrawing his hand at the last moment. It was Cindy. He was stunned. *Who had painted it?* he wondered. Was it a self-portrait? It didn't look like one of hers, so he searched for a clue.

Mounted on the wall, beneath the picture, was a brass plaque that was inscribed:

'What Awaits'

Cindy 18 A

A for Armando, he thought. It was beautiful. Then it dawned on him, Armando had loved her, loved her deeply. He stood staring at the painting for the longest time. He truly was the luckiest man in the world.

<h1 style="text-align:center">43</h1>

JACK WOKE EARLY. When he came downstairs, his future father-in-law was already at the breakfast table.

'Good morning, Jack. Come, join me. I'm thinking about going out for a quick nine holes after breakfast, while everyone is asleep. Would you like to join me?'

Jack swallowed hard.

'Sure, sounds great.'

Jack had been playing golf with Doctor Marcus, friends and clients for years. He could hold his own on the golf course. Still, he was nervous as he stepped up onto the first tee. After driving the ball, what he considered, an acceptable distance, he watched Cindy's father, Eduardo, out drive him by several yards.

On the drive back to the house, Eduardo turned, asking him directly, 'So do you like living in California?'

'Well,' Jack replied, a lump forming in his throat, nervous about answering such a question at such short notice, 'I have a nice home and my business is there. I enjoy the climate.'

Eduardo nodded.

'My family once had large holdings out there. We still own land in the Hollywood Hills. Cindy, her sister and cousins all have some,' said Eduardo.

'Really? I didn't know that. Cindy has never mentioned it,' Jack said surprised at the revelation.

Eduardo continued, 'My daughter has always moved around a lot. How does she feel about remaining in one place?'

Jack answered cautiously, 'We haven't really discussed it, there's nothing to say we will settle permanently in California.'

'But your life is there, things like this are important. Not that it matters to me, I just never imagined that she would settle down in one place. Not like that. Not so soon.'

'Well sir, I guess I should add that topic to the top of the list.'

The old man laughed and Jack breathed a sigh of relief.

'How do you feel about it?'

'My business is changing; I'm hoping that soon I can live anywhere.'

The old man smiled.

'While ever you are both willing to listen to one another, approaching everything with an open mind, you will always be happy.'

On Saturday night the whole family, including Armando, who had arrived unannounced with her sister Sophia, and one of Cindy's friends, Claudia, went out for dinner. The restaurant was loud and interesting. They ate too much, drank way too much, without exception. The dancing went on until well after midnight, when her father ushered them into waiting cars for the drive back to the house, where they drank champagne, toasting the newly engaged couple.

Jack loved the way Cindy's family celebrated. He loved their zest for life. As they celebrated, their love and affection for one another was intoxicating, as everything was pushed aside to enjoy the moment. When the last hug had been given, when all the others had gone to bed, Cindy took Jack's hand then, on unsteady legs, led him through the labyrinth of corridors to a small door just near the kitchen.

Cindy turned, kissing him, pushing her tongue into his mouth. Jack, a little stunned, then followed her through the door, which she locked behind them, down a narrow staircase and into a cellar beneath the kitchen. A dull light revealed a table surrounded by chairs, which she pointed to. When they reached it, she kicked off her shoes and kissed him again, while undoing his trousers. As they fell around his ankles, she sat him down on the chair.

Jack caught a quick glimpse of her naked body as she lifted her dress, sat in his lap, then in a frenzy of passion, made love to him with total abandon. Jack placed his hands on her thighs, concealed beneath her dress. Her skin was like touching a thousand electrodes as she moved against him, kissing him between breaths and clawing at his body. He pushed himself off the chair to meet her. Their intensity increasing until, with a deep moan, Cindy went stiff, desperately holding onto the pure ecstasy of her climax, before letting out a final long moan, then collapsing against him.

The following morning or what was left of it, found Jack wandering around the house. He made his way to the games room, which was complete with a full-size bar, billiard table and jukebox. This room opened onto the patio where the pool was located. The terrace surrounding the gigantic pool was littered with sun lounges and umbrellas. It reminded Jack of a hotel rather than a house. On one of the lounges, he found Armando in a relaxed repose, drink close by, cigarette burning in an ashtray. He was all smiles.

'Good morning, Jack,' Armando said, in a long drawl that suggested it wasn't his first drink of the day. He motioned to the sun lounge next to him, Jack sat down.

'How's the water?'

'I was hoping that it might help sober me up. 'Tell me,' Armando said, taking off his glasses, 'why, when you have a beautiful woman upstairs, what you are doing down here?'

'The princess is sleeping, plus I'm not exactly allowed in the same room as her, unchaperoned. I was wandering around, looking at the art.'

Armando's ears pricked up at that.

'I think that's more her,' he said, 'she was always a little embarrassed about these things in the presence of her parents. Believe me, they aren't as old fashioned as she thinks.'

'They put us in separate rooms.'

'Yes, but I don't believe her father would demand satisfaction if you entered hers,' he chuckled. 'Did you see my painting, the one hanging in the hall?'

'Yes, it's stunning.'

That made Armando smile.

'She modelled for that. Her beauty was profound, even then. It's more so now, don't you think?'

That caught Jack by surprise. It was strange, speaking so openly to a man who had known Cindy as intimately as Armando obviously had.

'Yes,' Jack said sheepishly. Armando handed him a beer.

'Come on, don't be embarrassed. She has a past; you have a past. She's a beautiful woman, an amazing person. I have known her all my life and, although that flame has gone out, I still have a memory.'

Jack immediately wondered how extinguished the flame was. He pushed the thought from his mind.

'Why did you stop painting?' Jack changed the subject.

'That's not easy to answer. I come from a line of artists, my father, my grandfather, both were well known throughout South America and Europe. My grandfather is a sculptor, my father a painter, like me. My mother is a poet.

'My grandfather originally came from El Salvador; he is most celebrated there. His works are revered and are displayed in the national gallery and many public landmarks. He is an institution and has received many public honours and awards: land, a house in the capital, San Salvador, a government pension for life, grants for his art. My grandfather was commissioned by the Mexican government for a statue. Our family moved there while maintaining our home in El Salvador. Other commissions followed. He built a huge house there, prospering.'

Armando took a swig of his beer before continuing.

'By the time I came along, our family was well established in Mexico and were known in Europe and New York. My father's career was also going well, so when I showed some talent, there were great hopes for me. That's when I met Cindy, a young artist, who was also a kindergarten teacher. She had the idea of holding art classes for kids. It was very progressive. We learned about shapes, how they related to space, learned about colour shades, very abstract. Our aunts used to sit at a café downstairs and drink coffee.' Armando went quiet, then continued, 'Cindy and I went to the same school. It was also progressive. I don't know when I first felt the weight of my father and grandfather, perhaps it was always there. It grew worse, the older and more successful I became. The more praise that came, and the more people used the word prodigy, the heavier it felt. I would be doing fine, then go to an unveiling or visit their studios. Their work was so superior to mine, I would be physically ill. Meanwhile, my relationship with Cindy grew. It became overwhelming and this became an even heavier burden. Then one day, I discovered alcohol. Quite by accident I discovered that by drinking etc. I could sabotage my career, my life and the heavy burden disappeared. I did this to the point where it took on epidemic proportions. It worked, all except where it concerned Cindy.' He took a deep breath. 'Cindy loved me unconditionally. I gained weight, she didn't care. I was mean to her, she didn't care. When I flirted with other girls, she laughed. The years passed. Now everyone forgave me. I was a genius they decided; I was someone for whom concessions had to be made. The heavy burden returned. Our relationship became physical.'

This hurt. Jack struggled to contain his reaction, which was a mixture of pain and anger. Armando didn't care, forging on.

'It was pure, innocent, beautiful, yet it carried an even heavier burden of the brilliant, young, artist couple.'

Jack looked straight ahead. He was talking about a teenage romance but he could feel his jealousy building.

'Cindy kept talking about our future, taking off for Paris, there were all of these places she wanted to visit and explore. I was jealous of her. She didn't have a father and grandfather looking over her shoulder, didn't have the expectation of the artistic community. I had to end it.

Not long after I painted that picture, during her 19th birthday party, I made a decision that changed the course of our lives forever. We broke up, the dream had ended. Heartbroken, I told my family that I could never paint again. It killed me but I was free!'

Armando stood, then started to walk towards the pool. Jack stared after him, stunned into silence.

'You know, Jack?' Armando called out, without turning around.

'What?'

'I like you, we all like you.'

He dove into the pool.

Spying Cindy in an upstairs window, Jack returned to the house. He caught his girl just after she had come down the stairs. He pulled her into a nearby room, backed her up against the door and lifted her dress. Cindy wrapped her arms around his neck as he lowered her down. She kissed his neck, placing little bites up and down it, as they took back up where they had left off the night before.

Cindy was breathing heavily.

'How is it that you still have this much energy?'

His head was filled with images of her naked body in the painting upstairs and he was ready to go again. Noises from outside the room, put paid to that. Cindy repositioned the strap on her dress, that had become dislodged in the throes of passion, uncovering her naked breast and brushed down the front of her dress. Jack couldn't resist a final kiss and was disappointed when he was pushed away, his tongue still in her mouth.

After the longest lunch of his entire life, one that stretched from noon until 5 o'clock, her father looked at them.

'My apologies to you both if earlier I showed any misgivings. Jack, welcome to our family.'

44

ERB COLLINS HAD been just 13 years old when a shotgun exploded in his hand, taking with it, two of his fingers and permanently damaging the sight in his right eye. It was a bad injury and it took time to recover. Eventually, he learned to live with it. When he was 15, through a friend of a friend, he found a job as a message boy for a large newspaper in London.

He wanted to become a journalist one day and, when Henry Powell, a seasoned veteran, needed an assistant to accompany him to France in 1917 to cover the war, Herb jumped at the chance. Watching everything with his one good eye and listening intently to all that was said, he quickly learned what it took to fulfill his dream. With Henry's encouragement and advice, he began writing a few pieces and was thrilled when they were accepted for publication. At the end of the war, he accompanied Henry to Versailles and witnessed the entire Armistice negotiations, firsthand.

By 1920, he achieved his ambition and was promoted to full reporter status. By the time World War Two began, he was editor-in-chief. Although successful in peace time, war reporting was his specialty. He had reported on every major and some minor conflicts since, including Malaya, Korea and Vietnam. In the 1950s he had given up the cold streets of London for the sunshine of LA. He was meant to be retired but it was in his blood and he still went to work every day, writing his stories and offering advice that was gratefully accepted by everyone, from the youngest cub reporter to the president of the corporation and everyone in-between. He kept his finger on the pulse and his ability to sniff out a story was legendary.

His many years of war coverage had given him a soft spot for veterans, so it took little convincing to gain his support, when he received the report of the homeless veteran, killed in a brutal unprovoked attack on the streets of his adopted city.

Appalled, he sought the help of a fellow Vietnam correspondent, Peter Martin, to do the leg work. He told Peter, in no uncertain terms, that they needed to uncover the perpetrators and bring them to justice. Use the power of the paper, he said, to put pressure on the police and the politicians until they achieved results. Peter found this unnecessary. Detective Lawrence was his first port of call. He found in the detective, someone who was willing to share everything he knew.

He introduced him to Elyse, who shared her story. Next were the attending officers, who filled him in on the details of the mysterious stranger, a hero, in their eyes. He had been told about the shooting of one of the perps, however, this detail was being withheld for now. He spoke to John Stanley's daughter by phone, making plans to meet with her. Herb was committed to running the story as a Saturday feature.

Momentum in the case was growing!

45

JOHNNY, ACCOMPANIED BY an entourage, including Rory, their partners and another of his cousins Alexis, took a short vacation to the family's estate in Martha's Vineyard. When they weren't resting by the pool or playing tennis, they ventured out on the motor yacht, cruising up and down, with no preset destination, whiling away the hours.

Johnny was in a good frame of mind and remained well behaved throughout the entire trip. Alexis, well aware of her cousin's proclivity for excess, was more surprised than anyone at his newly discovered mellow demeanour. The truth was, he was planning an escape. Working on the election had shown him how different he was to the other members in his family. A chasm so wide that he saw it as being unbridgeable.

He would retire to Europe, he decided, buy an even larger yacht than the one they were currently using. He wanted a classy one, an old design like they had in the 1930s with all the modern features. He would crew it full time and base it in Monaco, where he would buy a villa. His other large purchase would be an island. He was, as yet, uncertain where. His preferred locations were either, somewhere off the coast of Sweden or, somewhere in the Mediterranean, perhaps close to Greece.

He would rarely, if ever, return to the US, become a resident of Monaco where he would base his family, freeing him to live alone on his island. He would claim the stress was all too much and that he was dedicating himself to strictly philanthropic pursuits, while raising the next generation, which he would use as leverage, whenever he wanted anything. He would ask Rory to head up his interests, forcing him to remain connected with him. He would also insist the family buy Rory and Claire a villa in Monaco also.

Chloe, after they married, would be allowed to spend her days living a luxurious life in Monaco. She could do what she wanted, with whoever she liked, with no restrictions placed on her spending. After an agreeable period of time, she would bear, then raise their children, largely unaided by him. The only stipulation would be, that when he wanted her, she needed to make herself available.

He would stay on his island or boat. She would not be invited to the island, where he would live in self-imposed exile for the majority of the time. As the years went by and the family realised he could be trusted, he would look to gain more unrestricted access to his money but would allow some form of governance because, heaven forbid, he should ever have to one day do something. This was the utopia he was seeking. A dream, yes but in his world, dreams like this were not unobtainable.

Alexis had figured out early on, how to avoid all responsibilities, which is why he had invited her along for this vacation. Sick as it was, he had always had a thing for her. Not that he could now, in good conscience, act upon it. Alexis was an interesting character, a real genius, in his opinion.

In adolescence, she had portrayed autistic characteristics and traits with activities like still playing with dolls at age 16. Sweet and loving towards her grandparents, who wrongly assumed her to be mildly retarded, she was prone to removing her clothes at important gatherings and running around naked, making inappropriate gestures to the esteemed guests. Her grandparents were quick to react. As soon as she came of age, they set up an enormous trust fund for the poor girl who, they were convinced would never be able to lead a normal life. It was also hoped, by keeping her happily spending and enjoying the high life, that she might in turn spend her time removed from the public eye.

To this end, she had developed a proclivity for extravagant spending and decadence. Alexis honoured their unspoken agreement by only attending one or two of the family- only functions, held during any one year, just enough so they didn't forget she was alive. At all other times, she remained in happy exile. A card, attached to a large bouquet of flowers, would arrive, offering her most profound apologies for being unable to attend. These were carefully composed by professional writers and poets, designed to provoke emotion and promote affection, maintaining the myth of the poor afflicted child. Always delighted to receive them, her grandparents would, without fail, instruct the accountants to increase her allowance and pay any invoice or bill without question. Johnny was desperate to follow in her footsteps.

Carefully choosing his moment to speak to her, it came one morning early, while the others slept.

'Alexis, surprised to see you awake so early,' he said, warmly but with a lack of sincerity.

It was a lie, of course. He had asked one of the crew members to track her movements and had woken especially.

'Johnny, how's my favourite cousin on this beautiful morning?'

'As good as can be expected. Tell me, as we are alone for once, how is everything going with you?'

She was seated at a table at the rear of the yacht where they usually took breakfast. Johnny took a seat, uninvited.

'Well, as I'm sure you can appreciate, life is never easy when you suffer as I do,' she smiled ironically.

'Oh, cut the bullshit, Lexi. I can see right through it.'

'Bullshit, why dear cousin whatever do you mean?'

'The nudity, the dolls the tea parties with the dolls. I bet if they tested you properly, your IQ would be off the scale.'

She laughed. 'What about you, going the psychopath route. You're a hundred times worse than me!'

'Touche.' Johnny grinned. They both knew, in Johnny's case, it was no act. 'So cousin, how do you do it?'

'Like you I started young, (action beat here) 'though, I may add, it's a bit different being a bit looney, to what you do. A bit looney they can deal with. They like problems that are solved by money and, in this case, it was money they would have spent anyway.

'Imagine how much I would cost them if I wanted to run the bank, the fucking oil company or one of the others. This way, they don't have to find me something to do, as well as everything else.'

'Good point, so how much do you get?'

'Well, I have never been shopping without buying everything I want, never worried for a second about how much things cost. I have three homes full of servants but, here is the tricky part, you have to live where they don't live.

'You see dearest cousin, you may have already worked this out for yourself, they don't want us anywhere near them, anywhere you might drop in unannounced. Therefore, I live on the east coast on Long Island. They all live on the west coast. I'd love a place in Malibu, but I stay away. Instead, I have a house on the beach on Grand Cayman. New York is a big city, but I don't have an apartment in Manhattan, where they have places. Mine is in Soho.

'I decline every invitation where I know I won't be welcome. Send birthday and Christmas gifts to everyone. I never attend. I extend my own invitations, only when one of the lawyers suggests it and generally stay out of the way.

'I give false names for any event I attend, anything that might remotely get in the papers, give anonymously to charity and sign anything anytime they want it.

'For this, I receive generous gifts I like to call bonuses on top of my trust fund. The more well behaved I am, the larger these are. Poppa and Nanna have bought me all three of my houses, separately to my

TF. They gladly pay for my personal staff.' She smiled. 'You though, dearest, I hear, are in between being given a role in the family business or being packed off to a facility with rubber rooms.'

'I've had a taste of life in the family business, I...' He stopped, not wanting to say it. Alexis finished it for him.

'Want out?'

'Yes, how can I do it?'

'Alone or with Chloe?' She eyed him seriously.

'I'm very fond of Chloe.'

'Okay, knock her up, keep helping your father but, at some point, start becoming overwhelmed, suggest seeing someone for some counselling or better, wait until it's suggested for you. Do something embarrassing that won't cause harm. I've set a precedent but perhaps appearing naked at the inauguration ball might be a good start.

'You need to really work hard at this, then have a breakdown. You are simply unable to cope. Suggest a peaceful life away from the pressure; they will want rid of you anyway by then, so suggest Europe. Move there, stay away from everything, from everyone. I'm a wealthy philanthropist avoiding the limelight, something like that.

'Then, if they become reluctant, threaten that you are well and want to return to public life. Threaten to run for office. That should buy you a nice villa or two in Switzerland!'

'I prefer Monaco.'

'Monaco, it is. Only, realise there is no going back. Others will get the power, the money. We all get the same amounts anyway, bonuses excepted, I've checked. For us grandkiddies, the cash share and asset amounts are almost identical. Remember, the others will receive bonuses for what they do. You and I will receive them for what we don't!'

And with that Alexis excused herself, leaving Johnny to ponder his future.

46

A S HAD BECOME his routine, Tommy woke up early. He had decided to get in better shape so every day he would go for a one-mile run, while the rest of the household slept. He left Louise asleep in his bed. He felt awkward about her overnight stays. He had never discussed them with Jack, nor sought permission of any kind. They had just started to happen.

He found himself to be shy, vulnerable in the bedroom, making love only when the lights were off. They reached for each other in the darkness, finding solace in one another's arms. In Louise he found an experienced passionate lover, a soul willing to give herself completely, as if living for those stolen moments of intimacy. Tommy had been unable to so far. Not as completely. He tried to hide this, finding great vigour in the darkness. *Perhaps*, he had wondered, *it was a mental thing*. That, in his mind, he had not given himself.

There were many reasons for this self-diagnosed. But physical efforts aside, he knew, deep down, that she knew. He also knew from bitter experience, that questions like this, if left unanswered, became chasms. Chasms that became ever wider. Chasms that in time would begin to consume. These questions rolled over and over in his mind as he ran along the streets of the place that was beginning to feel like home.

As Tommy ran up to the front door, he picked up the paper from where it lay on the front lawn. In the kitchen, he poured himself a glass of orange juice then sat down at the table to read. Relaxing after his run, he turned a page and saw an article that sent his heart rate straight back to the level it had been when he was exercising. It was s short piece on the election and the relationship between Johnny and his father, the governor. *If only his father knew,* Tommy thought, then remembering what Jack had said, became angrier as the full realisation hit him. How could this be okay? A mixture of feelings: anger, disgust, even hatred, washed over him.

The article, that portrayed their relationship as being bult on genuine affection, respect and loyalty was, in the light of what he knew, absurd. Boiling with anger, he struggled to finish reading it, especially when he read that, in his father's opinion, Johnny was an ideal candidate for a future leadership role within the community. A possessor of great morals and the pride of his illustrious parents. Unable to calm down, he sat for the longest time, paper open, simply staring into space. He was still sitting like that when Jack found him. Without a word, he slid the paper across the table.

When Jack looked up, after he had finished reading, he was met with Tommy's steely gaze.

'We have to stop this; we cannot wait any longer,' said Tommy.

Jack was surprised by his friend's conviction; his look was scary. There was real anger there, he could see it in his eyes.

'It's not that easy, Tommy. There are other factors at play here. These people could be dangerous, very dangerous.'

'Are you worried about your involvement? The gun?'

Jack looked back at his friend, smiled. Was he that transparent? Guilt permeated through his veins for a moment. He did not share Tommy's determination.

'Yes, of course but that's only a small part of it.'

Tommy responded, his voice filled with anger.

'Forget about your involvement. Nobody needs to know. We just leave out the part about you bringing the gun back here.'

Jack looked with great affection towards his friend.

'I am involved. I can't simply forget that this ever happened. Can you accept that you aren't alone in this world, that there are people who care about you? For whatever reason, right or wrong, we are in this together, until the very end.' Jack could see that Tommy was still angry. 'People like this stick together, they have powerful friends.'

'You don't know that for certain. There is something called justice. I can go to the authorities and explain.'

Now it was Jack's turn to become angry.

'I know enough to know that you don't get to where they are, without powerful people behind you. I've seen enough to understand that the laws of society don't always apply in the same way, that justice is flawed.'

The image of the young woman who had died at his client's party flashed into his mind. Jack closed his eyes, shaking his head to force it away, before continuing.

'Nothing just happens. A good, noble person doesn't wake up one day and say, "Hey, I'll run for president", then is elected for being pure of heart with an unshakeable foundation of core values. It's the manipulators, the corrupt masters of the art of deception that are elected, but only after they win the support of those who really control things: the people who live in the shadows. Do you, for one moment, believe that if we drive down to the police station right now, that before the day is done, that boy and his friends will be in prison?'

Tommy's expression slowly softened. Jack was right, yet he wasn't quite ready to concede.

'What about the facts?' he said. 'They can't deny. That it never happened. There are witnesses, I can corroborate their story. The boy was wounded, how can they explain away that?'

'In a million different ways,' Jack replied. 'As it stands right now, it's your word and that of some homeless people, against his, Tommy. You say you shot him, he will deny this. They will contend that, although you may well have shot somebody, you did not shoot him. There may be a witness; they will tear this person to shreds and, if all else fails, they will claim mental illness. They will call in a never-ending number of experts, who will place their hand on the bible and offer their opinions.'

'How can you know that?'

'Because that's what I would do.'

Tommy's resolve weakened. He attempted to add one final plea to his case.

'Will justice not prevail?'

Jack did not wish to answer this question directly, found he couldn't, then offered a glimmer of hope.

'Not in the way that you think.'

Tommy could settle for that. He didn't want to as it scratched at his core. He wanted to believe the world he had fought for, existed. No, he definitely did not want to, however, he could.

47

THE ACCIDENTAL DEATH case weighed heavily on Jack's mind. Perhaps not for the first time, yet definitely the first serious time, he began to question the morals of the people they represented. Yes, many of their clients had been treated unfairly in the past, exploited, had money plain stolen from them, by people they trusted but then, did that justify behaviour like this? He was sitting in the closed courtroom, next to Jim Teal, who was eternally unflappable and their clients who were both extremely nervous. Jim leaned close to Jack.

'Relax big guy, I told you I went over this with the DA and the judge. This is just a formality.'

Jack offered a weak smile. He hoped they were doing the right thing. The judge spoke.

'I understand that the coroner has ruled that the tragic death of the young woman, Deanna Standing, to be accidental, a tragedy after consuming a toxic mixture of heroin and cocaine. Neither of which were supplied by the defendants, is that correct?'

'Yes, Your Honour,' Jim replied sombrely.

'That the young woman in question, did not arrive at the invitation of either of the defendants, even though the party was organised and hosted by them jointly.'

A thought flashed through Jack's mind, a moment of understanding and clarity.

'That is correct, Your Honour.'

'That neither man, when tested for traces of illegal narcotics, returned a positive result?'

'That is correct, Your Honour.'

That had cost Jim some favours and a little cash. It had been handled privately. Jack was not aware and it could not be linked back to him.

'And I understand that the defendants, even though they are not guilty of any wrongdoing, having now come into close contact with the tragic outcome of illegal narcotics, have agreed to produce a network television special on the dangers of drugs and have already begun production by convincing some of the biggest stars to appear.'

'Yes, Your Honour.'

'Mr Pierce is the state satisfied with this?'

It was now the public prosecutors time to speak.

'Yes, Your Honour, the state wishes to thank the defendants for their assistance in the fight on drugs.'

'Very well then, I declare the case closed.'

As they exited the courtroom, Jack turned to Jim.

'Good work. Tell me, our clients in there, are they a couple?' Jim just smiled and looked at Jack. 'And the drugs?'

Jim shrugged.

'That's how you knew that they had no knowledge of the girls, wasn't it?'

Jim checked to make certain that they were out of ear shot.

'Jack, sometimes I wonder about you. If you don't want to get your hands dirty anymore then perhaps just leave this stuff to me. Look, I'm not saying I like what happened. Hell, give the word and I'll stop representing these people tomorrow but we have a job to do in defence of our clients and I'm damned if I'm going to risk losing my licence for malpractice. We have acted 100% above the law, not just in this case but in every case.' Jim placed his hand on Jack's shoulder, to both calm and connect with him. 'Look, I get it, you're reevaluating your life, I understand. Who hasn't at some point but the world keeps turning and a lot of people are relying on us now, for pay cheques, mortgage payments and to feed their kids. Both of those men are married. The drugs in their circles, it's more of a question of who isn't using but what do I know? When the police arrived, neither was in the vicinity of them. From what I gather, this was a sting, along with the girls and a newspaper looking for scandal. Maybe, if they had just filmed what was going on in the master bedroom, nobody would have died. The toxicology report cleared them of any wrongdoing. We have people who work with us who lead that lifestyle. Justice was done.'

Jack took it in, though he wasn't listening. Maybe Jim was right, maybe this world just wasn't for him anymore, maybe he should leave it to the others. He shook Jim's hand and they parted.

Was justice done? Jack wondered, as he walked back to his car. *Was it?!*

48

PETER MARTIN FILED his story.

Tommy was the first to see it. He brought it to Jack, who read it carefully. Tommy was all for contacting the newspaper immediately but Jack counselled against it, insisting that they continue to wait. Reluctantly, Tommy agreed, on the proviso that they began moving their plans forward. Jack agreed, still uncertain of what their plans actually were. The "how" simply alluded him.

He wondered if some ego was creeping into Tommy's sudden eagerness, who was described in the article as, "The mystery hero, who rode in the ambulance with John Stanley to the hospital", was it going to his head? Jack further wondered if his cautious approach was stemming from fear. A fear of loss. There was so much at stake now, so much to lose.

Cindy had found a gallery in Washington DC that would be the next stop on, what was developing into, a world tour once the LA exhibit closed. *Perhaps,* Jack thought, *Tommy could be distracted with that, while he decided on their course of action.* He chuckled to himself. The grand plan that would ultimately see the governor's son and, perhaps, the governor in prison and, by that way, grant posthumous justice to John Stanley. Yet, he doubted it. There was a slim chance, yes, yet it was fast fading, the passing of time diminishing the possibility, with every tick of the clock.

Washington. Right into the heart of enemy territory. Anything they did must be delayed until then. Any hint of a scandal like this, connected to them, would stop Cindy's beloved project dead.

It was another unwanted complication.

Two days later, Jack called Tommy into the study. He had a file marked "Tommy's Incident" in front of him. He opened it and picked up the top document. He was in lawyer mode, so his voice took on a serious, business tone.

'We need help, Tommy,' he started, 'professional help. Jim Teal has given me the name of a private detective, extremely qualified, but he doesn't come cheap. He's available and waiting to be briefed. That's our first step, gathering information.

'We need to be practical. I'm going to ask Cindy to bring our vacation forward and we will leave this weekend. It will be up to you and Armando to close the exhibition, pack it up and move it. You will also have to liaise with the investigator while I'm away.

'In three weeks, the week before the exhibition opens in Washington DC, you will return here to the house. I'll drop Cindy off in Washington, then she can finish preparations with Armando. You, me and the private investigator will meet here and see what he has come up with. From there, we will plan our next move. I can't represent us in this, if it comes to a legal stoush, so I will ask Jim Teal to take over. I'll brief him on everything. We will have attorney-client privilege and he can help you liaise with the PI, also. Jim's a clever guy and he's very street smart. Learn to trust him as you would me.'

Tommy, frustrated, wanted more. Yet, what could he do? This was all beyond him. He could not afford private detectives, didn't have the contacts that Jack had. So, he remained silent, simply agreeing with a nod.

They emerged from the study with sombre expressions. Jack went to deliver the news to Cindy. He stopped, turning to his friend. He had been expecting more from the meeting, more interaction, to be challenged at least, to hear more of Tommy's insights. Not wanting to end things like this, he spoke with a very definite and serious tone.

'Tommy, this is a dangerous world we are walking into, just as, if not, more dangerous than the jungles we played in back in 'Nam, when we were kids.'

Tommy offered nothing but a weak smile.

David Savage had lived an interesting life to say the very least. Born in 1934 in Poland, his father, an officer in the Polish Army, had been killed by the Russians in 1940. His mother, who worked at a radio station in Warsaw, lived through the German Occupation and the loss of her husband during the Soviet annexation. She also lost a second husband: a half German, half Polish police officer, who was killed when the Russians returned to liberate them. The family was middle class and it had seemed as though the future was bleak for young David.

When the war was over, his mother wrote to a distant uncle who lived in Chicago. She received a reply in just a few weeks and her uncle, who was in the car repair business and doing well, offered to sponsor, bringing them to the US, to form a new life with him. Her uncle had never married and was lonely, with no other family. She accepted his offer and they packed up what little they had and left. She abandoned their house because she knew it was pointless to even try and find someone to buy it.

David could still remember the journey, traveling by train. It was a difficult experience at the end of the war, surrounded by devastation and endless delays. They spent a magical day wandering the streets of Paris, then caught a train to Calais, where they boarded a boat across the channel and a final train to London. The uncle had booked them into a very nice hotel and wired some money. They felt rich. Wartime London was as desolate as everywhere they had passed through; there was little to spend their newfound wealth on. A few pieces of clothing, some second-hand luggage, with the help of a friendly concierge, was all they could manage. At least it was an end to the suitcases tied with string, the parcels wrapped in brown paper.

They travelled in comparative style to Southampton, where they boarded their ship, first class to New York. Feeling uncomfortable, they spent most of their time in their stateroom. New York proved to be their Shangri-La. Unlike Europe the shopping was plentiful, with the stores packed full of goods. They walked around, almost in a dream, for three days before traveling to Chicago and riding in his uncle's Cadillac to their new home.

The house was large. It came with servants, gardeners and maids. It sat on a leafy, tree-lined street where their every whim, was catered for. The garage contained three cars. Along with the chauffer-driven Cadillac, was a sporty convertible, then there was a more homely sedan that was used mainly by the staff and to drive him to school. Their English was poor and a tutor was employed to improve it.

It wasn't long before he was doing well at school and his mother found a job at a radio station that broadcast in Polish. She also wrote articles for a Polish newspaper and this, along with the wealth provided by his uncle, gave them a wonderful life.

David's bedroom was huge, filled with toys and books. At times, he could hardly believe it, thinking that he must be lost in an impossible dream.

Uncle Peter, as they called him, was really his mother's first cousin. He had come to live with her father's family after his own parents passed away, when he was young. He had immigrated when only 18. His love of motor cars led him to the auto industry in Detroit. Through saving and a small legacy from his parents, he eventually was able to open his own repair shop.

A natural businessman, he eventually owned several, plus a car dealership. He prospered, moving into manufacturing parts. During the war, he had won government contracts. His wealth had grown substantially. Shy when it came to women, he had never married. With no family, he had been thrilled to receive the letter from his niece. He had no hesitation in welcoming her and her son into his life.

With plenty to share and nobody to share it with, they had filled a void in his life, bringing happiness and purpose outside of business.

They chose a private academy for David's education; he did well there. In 1952 he went to university and in 1956, after graduation, joined the Chicago Police Department. A lover of detective novels from when they had arrived in their new country, it had been a long-held dream to become a detective. He worked hard and by 1960 was awarded his gold shield.

For three years he was happy but then he started to slowly become dissatisfied. He left the force and worked with his uncle but they both knew his heart was not really in it. His uncle decided to sell his business interests and retire to California, taking David and his mother with him.

They bought a big house in Pacific Palisades. More for a purpose in life than any financial need, David became a licensed, private detective. His mother had never married again and he wondered, more than once, about that, if either his uncle or his mother had liaisons with anyone. He had never seen any evidence of it. They shared, it seemed, a preference for a life of celibacy, devoted to a chaste relationship with each other. He did often wonder what would happen to his mother, who was 15 years younger than his uncle, when he died. He just assumed, she had decided that two husbands were enough. Although he had no real idea of his uncle's actual worth, trusts, already established, provided incomes for himself and his mother, even though she had her own savings though her work. They would both inherit, however much it was, on his passing.

A friend of his from the force had also decided to try his luck out west. He contacted David and they rented a small office and started to work. It was slow at first but, with hard work and a reputation for discretion, the business had grown. Work now flowed regularly and they could pick and choose jobs.

Jim Teal was more friend these days than a client. Bonding over several cases, they had progressed from drinking buddies into a full-blown friendship. Jim came to see David in person at his office. After the usual pleasantries, they got down to business. As Jim trusted David, he held nothing back, telling him almost everything he knew, only holding back Jack's involvement with the gun and his warnings of the potential dangers.

David felt that a trip to the university might yield results. Jim agreed and it was decided that he would begin there. They scheduled to meet in a week's time. Leaving the office together, they headed to a local bar.

49

UE TO THE altered timetable, their relaxed vacation started in a chaotic rush. Flying out late on a Thursday, their carefully laid plans were now laid aside. The long cross-country flight allowed little rest, a three-hour stopover in Miami passed with painful slow monotony, before they boarded the relatively short flight to Grand Cayman in the Bahamas. Spending just one night there, the following day, they climbed aboard a yacht that would be their sanctuary for the next five days.

Cindy was relaxed. She changed into a red string bikini the moment they checked into the hotel on Grand Cayman. She would wear little more for the remainder of their vacation. Jack was at first preoccupied with the Tommy matter, though the first sight of her in the bikini distracted him enough for him to begin to relax. The huge yacht came fully crewed, with a discreet staff that were well-practiced in staying out of their guests' way, while catering to their every whim.

They settled in, on two sun lounges, sipping cocktails, enjoying the sun. In the afternoon, they anchored near a small island, went swimming in the crystal-clear water, then sunning themselves on a beautiful white sandy beach.

They ate dinner right there on the beach, prepared by the chef, on a table with white linen attended by waiters. They were too self-conscious that first day to make love on the sand, waiting until they had returned to their cabin.

As their journey continued, they slowly lost their inhibitions, becoming more daring. They frolicked on the beaches, swam naked in the crystal-clear waters, their affection on display for all to witness. All too quickly it was over and they were back on Grand Cayman in a hotel overlooking the beach.

Cindy set up a small easel then began to paint. While she was busy, Jack rested in their room, watched television or went for long walks on the beach. When she wasn't, they spent their time exploring the island, whiling away the hours, wandering, wherever their feet carried them, with no real plans.

At night they made love with the balcony doors open, the soft warm breeze caressing their bodies as they lay on top of the sheets. After they lay in the darkness, Cindy whispered with him, until they fell asleep. She asked everything, from questions about the war, to details about his first girlfriend, losing his virginity, his childhood, family, law school. He caught the bug. Soon Jack started asking her things. He found, as the days went by, that where before he hadn't pried into her life, enjoying the mystery, he now wanted to know as much as possible about her.

She was open, sharing far more with him than she either planned or ever had shared with anyone else. Her stories were wild, intriguing. His life, in comparison, was tame, boring. She told him how, in the first year of art school, she had been pursued by a beautiful, married woman who worked as an assistant to one the teachers. How this woman had romanced her, how she had resisted at first, only eventually to succumb and be seduced, falling headfirst into an affair that had lasted for almost a year. The vivid descriptions of her interactions, the detailed emotional recount of her feelings, the eroticism ignited in his imagination after she described their love-making, was incredible. The detailed descriptions so real that he recalled them as if he had been a participant. Seeing her former younger self, in a tirade of emotions, stealing moments in cafes, alleyways and sultry hotel rooms.

Late one night, she asked him what his greatest fear was. He went quiet for the longest time. When he spoke, it was in a whisper.

'Losing you.'

The soft words gently caressed her ears. Cindy kissed him in the darkness, then they held one another for a long time. Before they fell asleep, Jack asked her, 'What's yours?'

He waited in the dark for a reply. Cindy remained silent. Too soon it was over and they were flying to Washington DC.

David Savage had spent the intervening days, doing his best to gather information. Speaking to a range of people, many of whom knew Johnny or had known of him but nobody who had been close. Johnny was remembered as the school football captain, the son of the governor but all his classmates had left. Nobody he spoke to had a bad word to say about him; the younger students held him in almost god-like esteem. Using the guise of a reporter researching an article, he trawled for information, widening his search, shifting his attention to wealthy young people on the edge of Johnny's social circle. He worked the bars and night clubs. Slowly, he started getting somewhere. Then, one evening, while sitting in a bar on Sunset Boulevarde he got lucky.

He was approached by a young man, while he sat in a booth sipping a beer. Coming straight to the point, without any small talk, the young man spoke with confidence.

'You the reporter looking for information about Johnny Hollingsworth?'

David smiled, stood up, offering his hand. The young man was tall, over six feet and had a strong grip. Looking him up and down, David noticed his short, cropped, blond hair. He looked like a marine, strong, muscly.

'Gene Fuller, pleased to meet you,' David said offering the young man a card that proclaimed him a journalist at The Tribune.

'Christoper, you can call me Chris.' The young man offered no surname. David decided not to ask.

'Okay Chris, nice to meet you. Take a seat.'

They sat down and David noticed the young man eyeing his beer.

'Can I get you something.'

'I'll take one of those.'

David signalled the waitress.

'Tell me something about yourself, Chris. How did you know Johnny?'

'We were in the same fraternity, played football together. I'm two years behind him but as you can see, what I lack in age, I make up for in size.'

David nodded. The young man made for an impressive sight, visions of him running wild on the football field were not difficult to conjure into the imagination. The waitress arrived with their beers and they paused until she left.

'So, what do you have to tell me?'

'First of all, what's in it for me?'

David eyed him carefully, Chris looked around nervously.

'Depends on what you have to tell me.'

'You see, I'm in a bit of a jam and I need some money.'

'Can't your parents help?' David was surprised. Most of the kids he had spoken to had wealthy parents. Money didn't seem to interest them.

'That's complicated,' he snarled, not appreciating the question.

'Okay keep your cool I'm only trying to help.'

Chris relaxed.

'Sorry, it's a touchy subject.'

'Sure, if what you have to tell me is interesting, credible, I might be able to throw a few bucks your way.'

It was only there for a second but David saw a glimmer in Chris' eye.

'Money first?'

'Can't do it, Chris. Come on, spill the beans. You have my word, if the information is good, I'll take care of you.'

He seemed doubtful. David pushed harder. Reaching into his pocket, he removed a bill fold wrapped in $50 and $100 bills. He made sure Chris got a good look. His eyes didn't leave the bill fold as he held it out in front of him. Carefully, he unwrapped a crisp new $50 bill and placed it on the table.

'For starters, what does that get me?'

Chris snatched it up then took a long drink of his beer.

'My girlfriend used to be Johnny's. Well, Johnny had lots of girlfriends and boy...' He paused, blushing at the mistake. David looked across the table sympathetically.

'Don't be embarrassed, you can tell me anything.'

The young man nodded, still beet red. David dropped another $50 on the table.

'It happened when I was only a freshman. It was nothing, just some horse play in his room.'

As interesting as Johnny's sexual dalliances were, it was information he didn't need to know.

'You were saying, your girlfriend?'

'Well, Johnny's main girl wasn't all that accommodating, if you know what I mean. He played the field. One night, my girl goes on a date with him to the movies. When they come out after the show, they are walking back to his car and they come across this old lady with a shopping cart, a street person. She asks for money and Johnny tells her to fuck off. My girl tells him to show some compassion and goes into her purse for some coins. He pushes the old woman away; she trips, falls, then while she is still on the ground, he kicks her a couple of times. The old woman starts to scream. He grabs my girl by the hand, forcing her to run away with him. They reach the car and he spins her around, kisses her real hard on the lips. She thought he would be mad but he's real turned on by the whole thing. Scared, she kisses him back. He opens the car door, pushes her onto the seat and right there, they do it.'

He said this in an impassionate emotionless way, as if speaking of a stranger. David was wary. It was unusual for a young man to not be more emotional when talking about someone, other than himself, having sex with his current girlfriend, even if it was something, that had happened in the days before they were together. Wary, yet he believed him. Perhaps his earlier indication towards bisexual encounters hid something deeper. He wouldn't be the first male to date or even marry a woman, while harbouring illicit desires. He looked across at the young man who was clearly not finished. This time, David dropped a $100 on the table.

'In the middle of it all, while they were doing it, he pulled her by the hair. As they went on, he became more aggressive, even violent. He told her to tell him what she had seen him do to the old woman. When she did, it drove him crazy, so much so that he finished inside her. They had always been very careful. She wasn't on the pill but he had always used protection. The inevitable happened, she became pregnant. He went into a rage, when she told him. Then he made some calls, some lawyer guy handled the whole thing, it was all taken care of.

'She was given $1000. It was the end of their relationship. The lawyer told her, it might be better if they didn't see one another again. She got the message.'

There was a pause as David took it all in. Chris eyed the money again and made another play for it.

'There's other sex and drug stuff. Johnny's quite the party animal. They once asked her to help him seduce a friend of hers into joining them in a three way.'

David smiled. He had what he wanted.

'Are there other acts of cruelty, like the one with the old woman?' he asked.

'None that she told me, but he could be rough with her, slapping her during sex, pulling her hair. She has been very open about it; he could be quite sadistic and demanding.'

'Have you ever heard anything about the time he shot himself?'

'That was an accident. He was drunk and fooling around with a gun. I didn't see it, only heard about it, some of the boys got a free vacation afterwards.'

David nodded.

'I could introduce you to my girl. She could tell you more,' said Chris.

David dropped two more $100 bills on the table.

'Tell you what, put that in your pocket. If I need to speak to you again, I'll call the frat house, are you still there?'

The boy nodded.

'Also, if you think of anything else, call the number on the card and I'll get back to you.'

They shook hands. It had turned out to be an interesting afternoon, David thought, his head consumed with the story he had just been told. Engrossed in his own thoughts, he didn't notice the slender figure watching him from the other side of the parking lot. She was still watching as Christopher exited a few moments later. She took careful mental notes, before returning to her car and quietly slipping away.

50

S HE WAS A former CIA agent, one of only a handful of female operatives. Nobody knew her real name or rather, anyone who did, was no longer around. She travelled on a diplomatic passport issued in Venezuela, an old favour bestowed by a grateful president long ago. She enjoyed the tropical climate, maintaining a house there. She was a woman of average height, was nondescript, forgettable, a one glance person who quickly blended into the crowd, easily forgotten. She had been contacted through a third party, which was her standard way of operating. It was a long assignment, one that she had only taken because the client was a regular, reliable, easy to work with, always paying on time.

She had been alerted to the presence of a man asking questions about her client's grandson. Interested, she had decided to take a look herself. Watching him all day, she had followed David Savage to the bar where he made his connection with the young man who he thought was going to be his star witness. Sitting nearby, she had heard snippets of their conversation, which in her opinion had been carelessly conducted. She had slipped out just before they left, watching them from a distance, eyeing her prey.

David, meanwhile, was considering verifying the abortion story

Chris had told him, then decided it wasn't necessary. Why would he make it up? The clinic he mentioned had a reputation for providing the service required. There was something in his demeanour, a sincerity that David's instincts told him he was telling the truth. *Maybe,* he thought, *it was also the story about the old lady that had added credibility to his story.* That was no fantasy. It tied in with what they knew about him already.

He was sitting in a coffee shop, one that had a large variety of donuts, a rare indulgence for a man who liked to remain in shape. Forcing himself to leave after eating four iced delicacies, he didn't notice the car across the street. They noticed him, as he drove away. They followed at a discreet distance. The game was beginning to heat up only David hadn't been notified that the whistle had blown.

They were unimpressed with his investigating skills. What they wanted to learn now was who he worked for. Next, he had a meeting with Jim Teal. This led to some heated debate. Why would he meet with an entertainment lawyer? Many theories were offered to explain this but, in the end, the only plausible likelihood was, it was in relation to another case.

When the assassin received her daily anonymous briefing file, she was also left confused. Although something told her otherwise, she had to admit that perhaps they were right. Who was the client? *Well,* she thought, *if nothing else, I can grab him at some point and find out.* She had learned the art of interrogation in the back streets of Saigon, her methods proving quite persuasive.

It validated Michael Lethbridge's decision to act. Trouble comes from within, he remarked. Johnny could well be the family's greatest liability. He had already decided that he would have to be sent away, somewhere remote where he could be hidden. The assassin knew who she worked for, knew a great deal about him and his family, only she had never spoken to any of them. She was summoned on a note, written on a single sheet of paper that had originated in Tokyo. All her briefings were delivered by anonymous messenger to drop locations slipped under her hotel room door in the dead of night. There was absolutely nothing to tie anything back to them. Right now, she was simply learning. Her real purpose was yet to be revealed. The people following David didn't even know about her.

Michael Lethbridge had Johnny constantly on his mind. Of all the grandchildren, Johnny was his biggest pain in the ass, an even bigger problem than his lunatic cousin, who mercifully kept a large distance. He couldn't stand the girl. He considered the money spent on keeping her away, to be some of the best he had ever spent.

Something had come over them the day they became teenagers. He had spent fortunes on shrinks, to no avail. Where the girl was just out of her fucking mind, Johnny was far more dangerous. He had been the one who needed to have things fixed; cover ups had become the accepted norm. From throwing stones through church windows, to peeping through bathroom windows, a litany of driving offences, affairs with married women, pregnant girlfriends. Was it four or six? He could no longer remember. Forcing himself on a young servant at one of their homes in Ireland, animal cruelty, now this, attacking homeless people, resulting in death, then being shot in the process.

Michael thanked God, the rumour Johnny having an incestuous affair with his lunatic cousin had been found to be untrue. These mistakes were not going away. No, it had to stop. He would fix this. It would be bloody but when it was over, that was it. Johnny would be given an ultimatum: leave for some far-flung place never to return, where he could live out his life with every luxury. *Well, he may be family, but nothing comes without sacrifice,* the old man thought.

Cindy was also very busy. She had been inundated with requests for tickets from VIPs to the opening of the Washington DC Exhibition. So many, in fact, that they had decided to hold a VIP-only pre-opening gala. Similar to the one they had held at the governor's mansion, opening the same as they had done in LA when the governor had visited. She hired the same PR firm to handle the event. They erected a huge marquee on the lawns outside the gallery.

Armando and Tommy had done an excellent job in setting up the exhibition and, as Armando's photographs had become so popular, the book already in its fourth print, they had decided to add a display of photographs, taken by him, while the artists were working and of some of the men who had given their stories. There was an endless amount of press to do and a special delegation from the National Ministry of the Arts had enjoyed a lunch before a private viewing.

There was interest from a man wanting to make a documentary and the President of Mexico had sent a personal letter through her father, asking her to bring the exhibition to Mexico City. Similar requests were arriving daily from all parts of the globe: London, Paris, Berlin, Rome. A reporter from The Times in London was coming to see what all the fuss was about.

Cindy was staying in a suite at a hotel where Jack had insisted on 24-hour security. He was worried about her.

'Things were getting out of control,' he had argued. She felt suffocated.

A limousine was at her disposal 24-hours a day. She wasn't used to this much fuss and attention and she didn't enjoy it. Armando was also playing the protector. With Jack and Tommy back in LA, he was also becoming insufferable.

The guards were always there, two permanently stationed outside her door, day and night. They followed her wherever she went. At the gallery, they faded away, yet there was always one close at hand.

They met in the living room of Jack's large Santa Monica home, sitting opposite one another, across the coffee table on the two custom extra-long lounges, parallel to the fireplace. They were all gathered: Jack and Tommy on one side, Jim Teal and David Savage on the other. Two six packs of beer and two pizzas were Jack's only attempt at catering. There was a nervousness in the air and, at first, they just drank and ate their pizza while making small talk.

After they had run out of things to say, Jack decided it was time to talk business.

'Jim what have you learned?'

Jim immediately deferred to David.

'David?'

David, used to discussing the sordid details of people's lives, put down his slice of pizza, took a swig from his beer and then ran through the events of the previous weeks.

'I made enquiries at the university, as suggested by Jim. Unfortunately, I learned very little there. Johnny's classmates have all graduated and moved on. The younger class students, in general, hold him in high esteem. I could find nobody who was present when he had his shooting accident, though it was generally known that an accident had occurred. I have so far been unable to find any evidence placing him at the scene of either incident, nor anything that points involvement by any of the students from the school or fraternity. Widening my search, I began to frequent places where he was known to hang out. I put out a cover story, that I was a reporter digging for information. This must have spread around as I was approached by a young man who knew Johnny and who is currently dating a former girlfriend of his. Johnny apparently liked to play the field. His main girlfriend wouldn't go all the way, so he sought the company of others, his interests were not confined to girls, either.' He paused letting this sink in. Jack and Tommy exchanged glances. Jim sat impassive; he was used to this kind of thing. David continued.

'The young man, Chris, was on the football team with Johnny. He also lived in the fraternity, only he is two years younger. It seems, he was only on the periphery. He did, however, hint at some sexual dalliance in his freshman year. I didn't push him on it as I didn't think it relevant. He told me a story though, that I found very interesting. It concerned an incident that happened after his now girlfriend was on a date with our loverboy, how he had assaulted an old homeless lady.'

All three men raised their eyebrows, sitting up in their seats and edging a little closer to the source, as David recounted what he had been told.

'Sound familiar?' he asked when he had finished.

They all shook their heads.

'If there had ever been any doubts, this, it would seem, confirmed Tommy's recollections and what they had learned. I can arrange a meeting with the young lady. It won't be cheap and I couldn't see the value in doing so, but if you would like I can arrange it.'

Tommy looked at Jack who was contemplating it. Tommy nodded, 'Yes please.'

Jack at first gave no indication, but Tommy's pleading look gave him the upper hand.

'Please do,' said Jack, thinking, *Well, it's only money.* David made a note.

'Chris, as I said, was not present at the shooting accident, though he knew that it occurred. He also told me that some or all of those present had received a free vacation. He did not know the details of the treatment Johnny would have received.'

This was disappointing. Jack felt it might go a long way to proving the truth, if the bullet from Tommy's gun could be matched to the one removed from Johnny, then, who knows? It was a major piece of evidence. At the same time, he also knew, it still being available for forensic analysis was a long shot.

'Do you have any opinions, David?' Jack asked, clinging at straws.

'The young woman, his former girlfriend, was treated for a gynaecology problem at a private clinic. All arranged and paid for by one of the family's lawyers. I have been wondering if he was treated there.'

They considered the suggestion.

'It's worth looking into, only he would have needed emergency care initially. All alone with the boys, in the middle of the night, wounded, panicking. I doubt any of them would have had the presence of mind to contact his lawyer for help, though he may have gone there later. As I said, check into it.'

David continued making notes. Jim teal shared a thought.

'That hospital or clinic at the university any luck there?'

David shuffled the pages in his note pad.

'No, not for lack of trying. It's really just a small clinic looking after very basic things: scraped knees. I spoke with some of the students. They had nothing of interest to say and I'm certain a shooting victim would have been big news.'

'Why not try one of the custodial staff? If there was something like that involving lots of blood, maybe they know something,' Jim added.

David felt that this was pure fantasy, yet he noted it down. After all, they were paying the bills. David had little else to offer. Jack showed him and Jim to the door then returned to face a forlorn-looking Tommy.

'Without the bullet what do we have?' asked Tommy.

'The bullet isn't everything. We have proof of his violent nature. If we can place him at the scene, that may be enough. If we have witnesses, then we don't need it. Look, it would be surprising if the bullet had not been disposed of long ago.' Jack was concerned this lack of information could trigger a negative episode in his friend and he looked to reassure him.

'Let the detective dig a little further. Who knows, this former girlfriend might prove to be our star witness.'

Tommy offered a weak smile. Out in the back yard of the house, lurking in the shadows was their own secret weapon. His name was Tank, an ex-green beret Jack had known since the war. He had been drafted in to look after them. A second team followed Jim Teal just in case. David, for now, was on his own. Jack reasoned, he could look after himself.

51

CINDY HAD HAD enough. Suffocated, she decided to give her protectors the slip. Needing his help, she recruited Armando into the conspiracy. They would sneak away together for a few hours. What harm could it do? In the end, it was easier than she thought, pretending to work in a room that opened onto the outside alley. She asked her guard to fetch her some water. As soon as he left, with Armando in tow, she made a dash for freedom, running down the alleyway and out onto the street. Turning left, they quickly made their way around the corner, hailed a cab and disappeared into the traffic.

When the guard discovered they were missing, he immediately raised the alarm. Within five minutes, everyone they could muster was scouring the streets looking for them.

Back in California, Jack was just about to turn in when there was a soft knock at the back door. It was Tank. He was wearing a look of concern that immediately worried Jack.

'That detective that was here earlier,' he started.

'Yes?' said Jack, instantly becoming alarmed.

'One of the team thought he was followed here so, counter to your instructions, I had a team shadow him and well...'

'Well, what?'

Tank went quiet.

Jack had been concerned that the enquiries David made, might be attracting attention. Worried about where this might lead, he had brought in all of this security. The others mocked him for it. Now though. He stared at Tank waiting for an answer.

The breakthrough, along with the decision to eliminate David Savage, had come earlier that afternoon. After assembling some pictures, including one of Jim Teal, they had learned that he worked for Jack, a picture of whom was easily obtainable. Johnny was shown these pictures. He remembered Jack and his friend from the gala; he had then for the first time spoken about his suspicions about Tommy after their encounter on the terrace. A search of their own image library produced a picture of Jack, Tommy and Cindy. Johnny confirmed Tommy was the man who had shot him.

The pieces came together and they held an emergency meeting with the old man, who granted permission to act immediately. He also decided that it was unfortunately necessary to tie up all the loose ends. The decision was made that David Savage would be eliminated by a team of their own men. This would, they believed, send a clear message to Jack who, in their estimation, was in charge. The assassin who had been flown in especially, would tie up the loose ends, which he considered would better suit her specialist skill set.

They had also devised another plan to get the message to Jack, one he would definitely take notice of. With everything in place, they had followed David to Jack's house, then waited patiently for him to leave. Watching him pull away from the house, they joked at how easy it was going to be. Keeping a discreet distance, they followed, stalking their prey, waiting for the moment to strike. Unknown to them, they had also been careless as they were also being followed.

Tank's men rode in silence. All former Green Berets, they were used to communicating by way of a nod or a hand signal without the need to speak. The driver, nickname Speakeasy, sensing something was about to happen, signalled to the others then sped up, overtaking the car that was following David Savage. One of the men in the backseat, Highball, reached down to the floor, retrieving an M16, pulled back the bolt and unclicked the safety.

The people in the car following David Savage, were unaware that the stakes in the game they had begun, had changed. Busy readying themselves for their own mission, they had forgotten to continuously check their surroundings. Completely oblivious to any of this, David innocently slowed down for a traffic light that had turned red, when he heard a screech of tyres as the car behind him pulled up at an angle across the back of his car. Screening him from the car behind, Highball saw the shooter emerge and was on him before he had the chance to react. He fell silently backward into the street. Speakeasy and the others were out of the car in a flash, firing into the car with precision bursts. It was over in seconds. One of the men ran to David's car, finding a man in shock. He opened the passenger door, climbed in and gave a single command.

'Drive.'

Completely on auto pilot, David did as he was told. They were closely followed by Speakeasy in the car behind. Sirens wailed in the distance as they headed for a safe house.

Jack stood open mouthed as Tank relayed the events to him. He was unable to respond. What could he say?

'That's not the worst of it,' Tank's voice continued.

Through the fog of his brain, Jack grasped at this statement. *Worst of it? What could be worse than this?* he thought. Tank's already low voice went down to a whisper.

'Cindy and her friend are missing.'

Every horror imaginable attempted to rush through the tiny window into his mind at once. As a river of ice began moving along his spine, the convulsions started and his lungs were emptied as the bile rose further, blocking any relief.

The battle had begun.

52

T HE FINAL PIECE of their plan was the kidnapping of the shyster lawyer's slut. This was necessary, not to harm her but simply to give the bitch a scare, thereby winning her over instantly to their side. If not philosophically, for they would never be friends, but so she would practically work for them, campaigning for the lawyer to drop everything and move on. Secondly, it was more obviously a show of strength, letting him know they could and would touch him in ways that his tiny mind could only imagine. They had the resources, the means and, more importantly, the will to do anything necessary so that he, a nothing, a nobody, could never stop them, could never bring them down. they, not he, held the power.

The plan for kidnapping was in place, then after observing her security, they had decided that the mission was too risky right now. They would be cautious and wait. They could hardly believe this. What an incredible gift from her. Subconsciously she had climbed onto their side of the fence.

Cindy and Armando had found a restaurant, a small place that was almost empty. The décor was comfortable, nothing fancy, small tables scattered throughout one large, square, dimly lit room that the proprietors possibly thought was romantic or maybe was considered so at some time. Potted green plants and ferns in brass pots were positioned here and there, in a style that had not been fashionable for a while. An empty bar ran along one of the walls. Feeling relaxed for the first time in days, Cindy let her guard down. After ordering, settling into a nice table and chatting happily with her lifelong friend and former lover, they waited for their food with a nice bottle of wine. Cindy filled Armando in on the vacation.

Armando couldn't help but feel the odd pang of jealousy rise, for he had never become inwardly at peace with losing her. Especially when hearing her speak excitedly about another man, regardless of his outward portrayal. This included any statements he made, especially to Jack, who he liked, though against who, he would always secretly harbour a grudge. For the truth was, he always hoped to one day be forgiven, to be able to resume his relationship with Cindy. That somehow, by accepting the blame for all that had transpired, by being a self-imposed celibate, always showing kindness and through suffering and remorse, he would gain absolution, ultimately winning her back.

Cindy would never admit it, even to herself but she did miss his touch, did miss his hands, his passion, his insatiability. He sadly, now realised that, if there once had been the smallest of chances, with this new man in her life, it was moving inextricably towards the impossible. He fantasised for a moment, about one final liaison, one final act of passion so intense, that perhaps that would win her over. Both were so engrossed in their own thoughts that neither of them noticed the woman being seated at a table near theirs. Armando took Cindy by the hand. Not romantically, more the act of a caring friend or relative.

'I'm glad you are happy,' he said not meaning it.

Outside, a van pulled up not far from the entrance to the restaurant. Cindy and Armando ordered more wine as their food arrived.

After they had been there for about an hour, Cindy started to feel guilty. Jack had made these security arrangements to keep her safe but, like a spoilt child, she had snuck away. He would be angry. Then it dawned on her that her disappearance, which would certainly have been discovered by now, would have caused a certain amount of panic. She asked the waiter to bring her a telephone; he did so immediately, plugging it into the wall next to the table.

The woman sitting near them was trying to listen without being overly obvious. Cindy phoned the gallery. She asked for her security guard. She was informed that he was not there, that he was in fact out looking for her. She was told to wait inside the restaurant, that under no circumstances was she to leave before help arrived. Suitably chastened, Cindy wondered what would happen when she returned. Again, she felt like a child, waiting outside her father's study to be punished. In a way, she hoped she would be punished, something to alleviate the feelings of guilt. The waiter returned, enquiring about dessert, but her appetite had disappeared. They sat in silence. Armando spotted a limo pulling up outside. Quickly, they stood up. Cindy paid the bill then they ventured out into the street.

The street was empty, except for a white van. The limo was stopped just beyond it. Just as they approached the long car, the door on the van sprung open. The woman who had been sitting near them in the restaurant, ran full tilt at Cindy who, off balance at the shock of the sudden action, moved out of the entrance of the open van door. The woman then attempted to force her into the van by dragging her inside. Armando grabbed Cindy's arm and a strange game of tug of war broke out with Cindy as the rope. It was frantic. With all his strength, Armando pulled her free of the woman's grip then with the momentum generated, threw her behind him.

The woman pulled a gun and a man emerged from the back of the van. Cindy hit the pavement. Armando kept himself in between the van and Cindy. The woman raised her gun. Armando shoved out his chest just as a car pulled up. It was their security. Two men jumped out, guns drawn. Two people emerged from the limo, both holding guns. The woman, who had held Cindy, and the man, who came from the back of the van, pointed their guns upwards and slowly backed away. Jumping into the van, just as the door was closing, a solitary shot rang out. Armando gripped his stomach with his right hand. Looking down, he saw it covered in blood. He fell to the ground as the van, followed by the limo, sped away.

Everything slowed down. As they descended on Armando, collapsed on the ground, Cindy threw herself over him as if to shield his body from further harm. One of her own security detail pulled her away. There was blood on her hands, on her clothes, her face. She was bundled into the front seat of the car where she sat staring through tears to the drama unfolding outside, her hands pressing on the window of the car.

'Armando! Armando!' she screamed.

Her bloodied hands left a mark on the window. The security men half carried, half dragged Armando towards the car. Together and with great difficulty, they managed to lift him up then get him into the back seat of the car. His size and proportions making it harder than it should have been. To Cindy, it looked as if they were being careless, insensitive and in the heat of the moment she lashed out, punching one of the men, the blow deflecting off one of his muscular arms, yet with enough force to make him glance in her direction.

He felt like saying, *You did this bitch. This is your fault. This mess is on you!* He was a professional though, one who knew that if anyone hung for this and someone inevitably would, it wouldn't be her. Cindy leaned through from the front, attempting to comfort Armando while one man administered aid and the other jumped into the driver's seat.

Cindy fell backwards, almost ending up on top of Armando, as the car accelerated away. The next moment, she was flung forward towards the windscreen as the driver braked heavily to turn, forcing her sit like a good girl, covered in blood and, through tears, stared out into the dark night. Armando, the boy she had known all her life, who she had once loved, was dying in the back seat of a car and it was her fault.

The security guards, both combat veterans, were well aware of the danger of stomach wounds. Each was silently placing bets on the outcome. Speed was the key. Shock would kill him if the loss of blood didn't. If he could be treated quickly, maybe, neither was willing to lay that wager.

When they reached the hospital and he was still alive, both gave a nod to his tenacity. He was far from being okay but now the odds slightly shifted in his favour. *Hang in there buddy,* one doctor screamed. *I'm losing him,* said another. He proved to be tougher than they thought; they watched as he was wheeled away. They sat with Cindy in the waiting room. They considered the location, deciding in whispers, they could protect her if anything further did happen. Something they doubted, though it was always in the back of their minds that this might be the ideal time.

Cindy wondered if she should phone Armando's parents. How could she tell them? How could she explain what happened? *What was all of this? What on earth was going on? What world had she entered?* These thoughts would haunt her in the days and months to come.

The police arrived at the hospital, two uniformed officers. They commandeered the matron's office and started asking questions. First was Cindy's security officers who, being fully licenced, having acted above the law, had nothing to worry about. Then it was Cindy's turn. A detective showed up, a tall man named Phillips, who made it plain from the outset that he didn't appreciate being dragged out of his home at night. He took over, as the victim, Cindy, would need to file a report. That could wait. He wanted answers, demanded them.

'Why would someone attempt to grab you off the street young lady?' he asked in a condescending tone, for Phillips was maybe ten years older and cared little for the feelings of the wealthy elite who visited his hometown.

'I have no idea sir,' Cindy feebly offered, not sure what to say.

Jack had told her to say nothing when speaking to the police, to call for him or another lawyer, though that was only general advice. Surely, this nice man only wanted to help.

'Listen lady, people don't just get dragged off the street by thugs. Now, are you going to co-operate, tell me what are you mixed up in?'

'I assure you, Mr Phillips, I have done nothing wrong. I have no idea. Perhaps it's connected to my fiancé's business.'

'And what business might that be, if you don't mind me asking?'

'He's a lawyer, owns his own firm.'

'And tell me, where is Mr Hotshot lawyer boy now?'

'In Las Angeles where we live.'

Detective Phillips took a pack of gum out of his pocket and offered Cindy some. When she refused, he took out a long piece, unwrapped it from its silver wrapper, then carefully placed it into his mouth.

'Look I know something ain't right here. It's no skin off my nose, you get me? Maybe you've done nothing wrong, maybe not, but these are the facts. You're here in the nation's capital, alone. You have a small army of private security guards, professionals too, while your husband, sorry fiancé, is a few thousand miles away. Your friend's in there dying from a gunshot wound to the stomach and you don't know why someone is after you. Now let me ask you one final thing, if I told that story to you, would you believe it?'

It was the breaking point. Cindy burst into tears. Phillips smiled. He had won, she would sing like a bird now, when she stopped crying, of course. He was basking in the glow when a tall, thin, solemn-looking man, dressed in a dark black suit, like an undertaker, approached the matron's office. Spotting him immediately through the glass office windows, Phillips knew he meant trouble. There was a gentle wrap on the door.

'Excuse me, my name is Wilson, attorney-at-law.' He offered Detective Phillips his card. 'This lady is my client and, as you might agree, she seems to be in an inordinate amount of distress. I respectfully ask that this meeting be postponed to a later date, so that my client may receive some much-needed medical attention.'

'She don't need any medical attention,' asserted Phillips, spoiling to enforce his authority.

In response Wilson was cordial but firm.

'I beg to differ but don't take my word for it, let's allow the doctor to decide.'

On cue, a man in a white coat, accompanied by a nurse, appeared.

'My apologies,' the doctor said, pushing his way past Wilson who, apologetically, moved out of the way. The medical team each took one of Cindy's arms.

'Come now,' the doctor said in a calm friendly voice, 'we are ready to see you, miss.'

Without another word, they led Cindy away. Phillips was unhappy. He scowled at the lawyer who stood impassive.

'She needs to file a report, make sure she comes down to the station in the morning,' said the grumpy detective.

'If the doctor allows it, of course.' Wilson remained immovable, unflappable.

Phillips attempted to stare him down.

'We can, of course, take this before a judge if you prefer but I don't think that will be necessary, do you?' said Wilson.

Detective Phillips stormed out.

Cindy's wrist had been injured during the tug o' war between Armando and her attackers. She had also twisted her ankle and there was bruising on her arm. It was all superficial. The doctor checked her for concussion and the nurse reassured her that she would be fine. She was prescribed some pain medication and some sleeping tablets, told to keep warm, eat well and take plenty of rest. The police were now guarding Armando so her own security were insisting that they return to the hotel. Cindy dug her heels in on this, while Armando stayed in the hospital, she would stay with him. A private room was organised for her and as soon as she was alone, the tears returned in floods.

She began telling herself off; she was a fool. She had brought this on herself. She tried to stop but the tears kept flowing. She sat alone on the floor of her room, wondering what on earth she would do next. Was this where it should end? Surely, she couldn't be expected to go on, not after this. After all, where was he, the love of her life? He had not even spoken to her. The cold, antiseptic tiles in her bathroom, mirrored how she now viewed her soul. The cold rose through her pores, into her blood stream, flowing around her busybody and stealing every piece of her. Would she ever paint again? Would she ever love again? Thrashing about on the ground, like someone possessed, Cindy poured herself out onto the cold floor. It was gut wrenching and necessary.

53

TANK HAD TAKEN over Jack's study. He relayed the latest bad news to an incoherent Jack as cars pulled up in the driveway, overflowing onto the street in front and opposite his house. The men discreetly positioned themselves around the property with one even taking up a position on the roof. All over the city, Tank's men left their homes, ready to report for duty. The safe house where David, the private detective, and now, Jim Teal, Jack's best litigator, were staying, was reinforced. The cars from the earlier incident had both been disposed of. David's requests to call in law enforcement were ignored; he was becoming understandably frustrated. Tank left the study and went through to the kitchen. There he found Jack and Tommy sitting in silence.

There was no real good news to share, so he simply tried to reassure them that everything would be okay, even though he had no idea if it would. Choosing his words carefully, he tried to give the impression that all was under control, while, expecting a counterattack at any moment. He could imagine, what the rest of the night might have in store, because he had been in jams like this more times than he cared to remember. The thing that bothered him this time, in particular, was not the enemy so much but the power that seemed to be behind them.

Jack was all for hiring a plane and traveling to Cindy. Tank was all for relocating everyone to a safe house, somewhere far away, He knew of a couple that were in the middle of ranches, surrounded by thousands of acres of land, available at very low rates.

Jack's mind was not functioning properly. His instincts had been correct, they had been in danger, this though, in his current state, scared him more than it reassured. As his imagination ran wild and paranoia increased, the size and reach of their enemy increased. He focused his rage on the governor, having not yet realised, who the real power was. He froze. Even though he was the one who said that rich people could get away with anything, in the back of his mind he now realised he hadn't before actually believed it, until now.

They had attempted to kill the detective he had hired, tried to kidnap Cindy and attempted to murder Armando. He stood up and ran to the kitchen sink where he vomited. This was spiralling out of control. He now realised they should have gone to the police the moment it had happened. No, the moment they became aware, plain and simple, gone to the police and let them deal with it. *Could he call them now?* he asked himself, leaning over the sink breathing heavily. No, the thought in his mind was, that time had passed, the game had begun and they had entered it. A second bout of nausea washed over him as the others, with deep concern, looked on.

<h1 style="text-align:center">54</h1>

MICHAEL LETHBRIDGE HAD been briefed on the evening's events. He had not taken it well. It was past midnight and he was sitting alone in his study, drinking whiskey and trying to come to terms with the news that they had failed completely at what he saw as a few simple tasks. Tying up all the loose ends now became critical, before the entire situation moved beyond their control.

Johnny. They should have drowned him at birth or had him locked up the moment he had shown signs of being a sadist, a sexual pervert and whatever else he was. It was poor judgement on his part and he was unsure what had made him panic. He had to kill this and quickly. The race for the White House would soon be upon them and there were many old enemies out there, who, if they caught a sniff of blood, would come running to join the fight to take them down.

How hard could it be to kill a private detective, to kidnap a young woman, hold her for a day or two, terrorise, then release her? This Jack fellow, the one whom owned this tin cup law firm, a self-proclaimed do-gooder, would have given anything for her safe return. The whole thing would have been forgotten in a few weeks. Hell, he probably would have voted for his son-in-law come polling day. Instead, everything had gone wrong. It was his fault, he was old and he trusted others to do what he had once done himself. Now, the threat was greater than ever and this Jack, this shyster lawyer, had his own private army.

Was it too late for them? Had time finally passed him by? He could take his wife, find a nice place in the tropics, spend the rest of their days in the sun, play golf and enjoy the time that they had left. Damn the rest of them, they could fend for themselves. Not that they would suffer, not with the legacy he had bestowed upon them.

Anger rose within him. Anger that lived somewhere deep inside. In an instant, his blood boiled, turning his skin red, while his fingers began to scratch. The burst of this anger was so strong, anything could happen while it lasted. Nobody was safe. He focused his anger on the people who worked for him, then on his son-in-law, then on the enemy and finally on himself, for being so weak. He raged around the room, the anger moving him, jerking him around as if performing some strangely choreographed dance. Deflated, he slumped. No, damn it! There was work to be done. This was no time for running scared; this was the time when a man like him needed to be strong, to stand up, to lead them to victory. He would show them, would show this shyster lawyer, teach him who was stronger, who had the greatest will. He would not run from this nobody. Not now, not ever!

'Mistakes have been made,' he said out loud to his private audience, 'That's how we learn. The important thing is to never let them happen again.' He would regroup, keep to their plans or devise new ones. All the evidence from their mistakes could be disposed of. That was the key: remove all witnesses, remove everything. Then, even if it all came out, how would they prove it? What could they do with innuendo? Nothing, even the shyster lawyer knew that. He thought about all that he had built over years, decades. Nothing and nobody could stop them.

55

J**ACK, AGAINST ALL** opposing advice, had convinced the others to allow him to travel to Cindy. He made this decision after they had finally been reunited on the phone. There was a change in her voice, a coolness towards him. He had not expected it and it cut him to the bone. Jack knew she blamed all of this on him and maybe she was right but he loved her. Didn't that count for something? When he had said it to her, she had not even responded, just moved to the next topic of conversation. The decision to go there was childish, irresponsible, yet he could not stop himself, feeling that if he didn't, he would definitely lose her.

Tommy was his next problem. He had no idea what to do about him. Tommy was his conscience, could he really afford to have one if the price to pay was the love of his life? If he had to choose between them, there was no doubt who would win. He would extricate himself somehow from this entire affair, grab her and run. He would make a deal with the devil, if necessary. All of his bravado had disappeared after the phone call. So long justice, farewell moral principles, he wanted his girl. His mind flexed. He thought he would cry. Could he have one without the other?

The private plane was booked. Tank had an endless number of

contacts who could provide anything, if one had the money to pay. They took four of Tank's top bodyguards with them, plus Tank, who would oversee the operation personally. Tommy was spending the next few days, while they were away, on a ranch with David Savage and Jim Teal for company. It was a compromise to gain his support for Jack's journey to DC.

In Vietnam, Jack had called "sleeping" his escape. Nobody could get you in your dreams, he would say, or could they? His dreams were now full of people dressed in black, trying to kill him, from the Viet Cong in their pyjama uniforms, to the businessmen in their suits. They were all the same, vultures clamouring for his blood.

Once it had been his sanctuary, now there was nowhere to hide.

Tank sat at the front of the plane next to Jack, nervous. F flying wasn't his thing. On the drive to the airport, he had been ready for anything, a coiled spring made of hardened steel. He only began to relax when they reached cruising altitude. In his experience, danger when flying, only existed in the first and last 30 minutes of a flight. In the middle, it was okay. He had first been deployed to Vietnam, way back in 1962, a raw kid with more courage than brains. Eight years later, he had boarded a flight in Saigon, saying goodbye to the place for the final time. In between, he had seen everything there was to see, learned everything there was to know about the country. He had gone from an optimist, who foresaw a new country built on freedom and democracy, to accepting the reality that it would be overrun eventually and that the majority of the population didn't want them there.

Tank and Jack crossed paths many times over those eight long years. Jack was more than a friend; he was a brother. He, like Tank, had made the grade as a professional soldier, a man you could count on. Tank, though, sometimes wondered where the man, he had known, had gone. Only weren't they all different now? He knew Tommy, though they had never worked together. He did not put him in the same class as Jack. Jack's success in business impressed him. He had known Jack was determined to make something of himself when he returned home and he had done so. This hiccup aside, he was doing well. Tank didn't have the heart to tell him what he really thought of the situation, of Tommy, of Cindy, of the entire mess. Didn't share with him that he had crossed a line they would never ever come back from, that the life he had before all of this was gone, that the future would need to be different. Jack would figure that out for himself, eventually, although Tank could not foresee what that next chapter would be, he would be there for Jack when he needed him the most. That, in his opinion, was the most important thing he could do.

When they landed in DC, Tank's people were there to meet them. Traveling in four nondescript cars, they cut through the empty streets of the nation's capital in the early hours.

By the time they arrived, Armando was out of the woods. Although he was still sedated in the intensive care ward, the doctors had no reason to believe he would not make a full recovery. Cindy had continued to be difficult, refusing to leave the hospital until he woke up. When Jack appeared, to his dismay, she did not run to him. She was holding a cup of water, her eyes red, gripping a cardigan with her free hand, holding it closed across her front. His heart sank. He attempted a smile, approaching cautiously. Her stare was blank.

'How is Armando?'

'You bastard, you fucking bastard.' She lunged at him and pounded his chest with her fists.

He stood passive, allowing it to happen. She continued pounding until exhausted then she burst into tears, pushing him away. She began to walk away when he grabbed her, spun her around and collapsed, sobbing into her arms but it was temporary. She fought him off, refusing to be comforted by him. Too much time had elapsed as she had been left to fight on her own for too long. Jack should have jumped on the first flight. If she meant anything to him, he would have. At first, she didn't know what to do, it was awkward. Standing stiff, she pushed every feeling that she had for him, away, avoided looking into his eyes, refusing all petitions for clemency. This did not need to happen.

Suddenly, the weakness she had felt, the vulnerability, the helplessness, was replaced with anger; anger which she unleashed upon him. He protested.

'If you love me as you say you do, then bring him back as he was, then and only then can we talk,' she spat at him.

This demand sent Jack cold. How could he fix this? This was beyond the realms of his power. What could he do?

The moment he left her room, she cried, for she loved him still, only that love was different to the early infatuation, the happy love, the joyous love. Why? Then she asked herself, could she let him go? What if he was the love of her life, her soul mate? What then? Would she never know love again? Was that what the future held? What of Armando? She had taken a similar path with him, had never forgiven him, had allowed him to painfully remain in her world, in a way to torture him, showing him, see this, you once had this, now you can never touch it again, had flaunted a stream of other lovers in front of him, watched as he sank into alcoholism, lost his power to create, lost everything, living at her mercy, fell into despair. The cruelty of it. What had she done?!

The evil, selfish way in which she had treated him she was now proposing this same fate for Jack. What of that? Jack was trying to help his friend. Jack had tried to protect her; she had run away from security she had. She refused to say it, then realised she must.

Oh God! She had said that before, also had said she hadn't forced Armando to have an affair but had she? Had she, through her actions, been somehow to blame? But this was worse, far worse. She had caused Armando to be shot. It was her decision, her fault and, deep down, *oh this was too terrible to contemplate*, deep down, she thought he deserved it. *Oh god.* With that revelation, she fell back onto the hard, cold floor weeping.

'This must end, this must end,' she cried.

Staggering to her feet, she raced through the door. She found Jack standing alongside Tank, outside the intensive care ward. They stood staring at each other. Tank walked away as they each opened their arms.

Tank was nervous. Even with the police presence at the hospital and his own people in place, he felt the risk of remaining there was simply too great. Gently, he suggested, with the help of one of the surgeons, who had operated on Armando, that they head to the hotel for some much-needed rest. Reluctantly, Cindy agreed.

Tank organised new rooms, booking out an entire floor where the only access was on foot from a secured stairway from the floor below. Stationing guards at the only access points, while rigorously checking everyone who entered, made him feel they were as safe there as they possibly could be. They reached the hotel by mid-morning and Jack and Cindy were asleep within minutes of laying down in their room. Cindy woke in the late afternoon; it was time to face up to things. She phoned her father. It took time to explain all that had happened. He promised to speak to Armando's family, also he wanted to see her and wanted to come right away. Cindy tried putting him off. How could she ever explain a situation like this one and have it sound anything other than abnormal? Calmly, he agreed to wait. In reality, he was on the phone seeking help the moment he hung up.

When he woke, Jack called Jim Teal, who was in a seriously bad mood. He too, took some calming down. He asked some difficult questions, which Jack tried his best to answer. Next, he spoke to Tommy, who was distraught, barely holding it together. They had decided to go to the police, he informed Jack. Jim would begin to organise it. Jack asked him not to. He said he would think about it. When would he return? he demanded. Jack wasn't sure. They hung up on bad terms.

He tried to talk to Cindy, only he couldn't put the words together. They sat, watching the television in silence, then Cindy stood up and went for a nap. It was a new low point; he felt the weight of it.

Cindy awoke with a start. Her mind was scrambled and not for the first time she wondered what was she doing? She and Armando were artists. How had they been drawn into this? What rubbish all this was.

She had fallen for this man, now her friend had almost been killed. She had to live under 24-hour guard. It was a fresh feeling of doubt. This was no way to live.

Everything in her being, told her to get out, to call her father back and tell him to come get her. Little did she know, he was already putting the wheels in motion. Time and time again, over the following weeks, she would go to leave, sometimes going so far as to pack a bag. She would begin to walk out the door only to change her mind. How far did she need to go to escape this? All the way to Mexico? Had it reached that point? Pack up everything then runaway? Regardless of their reconciliation, she fought daily battles with herself to stay. Pledges, statements of affection, grand proclamations meant nothing. This was a time of crisis, a fight for survival, one that Cindy was losing.

After a restless night, they awoke to the news that the doctors had decided to wake Armando up. After breakfast, they went to the hospital. As they entered the intensive care unit, Cindy's father, Eduardo, was there to meet them. Cindy hugged her father, Jack shook his hand but the reunion was subdued. Eduardo then introduced Jack to a short, non-descript man, who was shyly lurking a few feet away. It was Armando's father, Matias. Shaking hands was awkward and Jack had nothing to say. Cindy kissed Matias on the cheek. Eduardo was abrupt, in complete contrast to his demeanour the last time he and Jack had met.

'Come children, sit. We cannot see Armando for a while yet. The doctors will let us know,' said Eduardo.

The four of them sat facing one another. They were the only people in the waiting room. Tank was around, along with a few more guards, who were making themselves scarce.

'So, tell me Jack, how is it that we come to be here? Our friend, Armando, badly injured, my daughter in such a terrible state, please tell us so we can understand. What kind of life is it that you lead?'

Cindy started to explain but her father cut her off immediately.

'No, my child, now is not the time for you to talk. This is for Jack to explain. Go ahead, tell us.'

Jack did exactly that. He told the story from start to finish, leaving nothing out. It was his version of events maybe but it was the truth, nonetheless.

'Tell me Jack, what do you owe to this man, Tommy, that you would do these things for him, that you would sacrifice everything to help him?'

Jack looked Eduardo straight in the eye and said, 'My life.'

'I see, go on.'

Jack looked at Cindy. Her face was covered in tears. He closed his eyes for a moment, biting down hard. To say this was painful, not the act of being saved but the events that surrounded it. Old wounds that were deep, ones that had never healed were the most painful.

'We were caught in an ambush, a handful of men against perhaps 100 enemy soldiers. We managed to keep them at bay until help arrived. Our helicopter gunships broke them up and they started disappearing into the jungle. We had to cross a rice field to reach the extraction point. I was bringing up the rear, making sure all my men made it out. I didn't see from which direction the bullet came but it hit me like a sledgehammer, right in the chest. I took another in the right thigh. Nobody realised. They kept running for the choppers. I lay dying. I had given up, was prepared to meet death, when out of nowhere, Tommy appeared, hovering above me.

'He had realised I was missing and came to find me. It was crazy, made no sense. He picked me up and carried me out of there. And here I am. That's why I did it for him and that's why, even with everything that has happened, I would probably do it all again.' Jack took a deep breath. 'Perhaps it's too much. When I started helping him, I was a single man, with nothing or nobody to think about but myself. I realise now that I have to stop thinking like that.'

Cindy smiled through her tears.

'In saying that,' Jack continued, 'he came back for me when nobody else would, pulled me literally from my grave. He earned my help, no matter what that help is. Senor Matias, I apologise for what happened to your son. I would do anything to undo that. I hope the people who did this to him are brought to justice, it's little compensation but I will do whatever is necessary to see that that happens and, I assure you that, regardless of what happens, between us I will see that he is taken care of. I will see him back to health whatever it takes.' Jack was tired of talking, he was done. *Let the cards fall where they may,* he thought.

'Cindy, I want you to return home with me, for your own safety,' said Eduardo.

'No Papa, my place is here.' Eduardo went quiet.

A nurse entered, saving them. Eduardo and Matia followed her into the ward. Jack and Cindy were not allowed in to see Armando, something to do with restricted visitation, Cindy was disappointed and, reluctantly, they returned to the hotel. There was a message from the gallery curator. She sat on the bed, staring at it. She was at a crossroads. Her work, how could she think about her work?

56

C ONTINUING WITH THE exhibition, including its opening gala, seemed crazy, yet Jack wanted her to, was insistent. How could she? What message would this send to Armando? How could she face him and his father? His only consideration was whether they, the enemy, would use the opening in some way to gain an advantage, to attack by some means. Jack was almost certain they, whoever they were, would not come at them so openly again. Now he wanted to prove that this theory was correct. Why did that matter? He was convinced that next time they came and he felt certain they would, it would be subtle and devious. Again, why did that matter? If she did go ahead and he could not understand why she wouldn't, with no Armando available to help her, Tommy would be badly needed. Jack wanted to fly him in at once. He would arrange it, ignoring her protestations. Tommy would be able to help with the preparations for the event that was only three days away. Then they would all leave the capital the day after the exhibition opened to the public. It was after he said this that his reason for doing it all became clear to her; a thought which almost caused her to vomit. Jack only wanted to do this as a show of strength, as a direct retaliation to the attack upon them, to show the enemy that they had a strong will also, that they were not scared, would not be pushed around. He was continuing with the battle, joining it with a happy heart. Once again, marching off to war She had discovered another thing about him and through her acquiescence, discovered something about herself.

After the frosty reception the day before, it was not easy for either Cindy or Jack to return to the hospital. Cindy would have been happy for Jack to stay away, only she didn't have the heart to tell him. Unlike the day before, they were admitted at once. It was with a mixture of surprise and relief that they found Armando sitting up in bed. Cindy's father sat in the chair next to the bed watching over him.

As soon as they approached, Eduardo issued a warning to them, 'Now children, no over exciting our patient here and please, all visits are to be kept to a maximum 10 minutes.' He added, 'You should know, my darling Cindy, that the doctors told us the first words from Armando's lips, were said out of concern for you, "Is she okay?" he asked over and over.' This brought tears to Cindy, who in her vulnerable state realised more than ever that he had never stopped loving her.

Armando had no way of knowing that Cindy was questioning everything in her life, as he had decided to move on and start living his. He had experienced an epiphany while on the edge of possibly leaving this world, realising that for years he had been in a state of depression, because of their breakup, that his behaviour was self-destructive. He now vowed to put it all behind him and move on. He would open his heart. This would do more than just open the opportunities to love again; it would also reignite his creative flow.

He would return home to Mexico. He could feel it building inside of him already, the desire was fast returning. He would have left then and there if he was able. He would build a studio; not just a studio, a sanctuary, a place where he could live and work. A special place, a base from where he could re-ignite his career, more importantly, a place where he could be happy. Cindy could see a sparkle in his eye, heard a humbleness in his voice. She knew he meant what he said, that he had turned a corner with his life. She was thankful. Tears of happiness followed.

'Now,' he said to her, in a sweet, yet serious, tone, 'The time has come for us to part. Promise me you will come visit, once I have myself established. You will always be welcome.' It was goodbye, yet the door was also open. Cindy realised she had options; there was a lot of soul searching to be done.

Cindy did not say goodbye, she simply smiled through tears, tears that were real, raised a finger to her lips and kissed it. Armando did the same. They then touched them together, holding them briefly, before she turned and for now, walked away.

When the governor arrived at the gala, Jack went cold. Stiffly, he shook his hand, staring unflinchingly into the man's eyes, saw again, up close, his warm smile. Then he hesitated, this was not as expected. There was no emotion in the man's expression, no gloating or even the hint of it. Nothing but complete detachment, as if this was the most natural normal situation. What had he expected? A tyrant? A villain the presence of a mask? What? Here was a man who had ordered the execution of others, plotted to take his beloved Cindy, wanted him dead. Then it came to him, the old gangster saying 'It's not personal, only business'. Therein the difference lay. This was the thing that separated them.

Jack had been a fool. Here was a man who would do anything necessary to achieve his aims. Jack would not. Where Jack made statements like, 'I would do anything for my friend who saved my life' this man would not. And this was where his ruthlessness lay. Jack would never be like that, no matter how he stood up to them, no matter how he liked to see this as an even contest. For it could never be. He did not now, nor would he ever possess, that kind of ruthlessness.

These were the people who justified the death of innocent children, when their chemical plant poisoned water supplies or justified genocide or, oh god, defended people who were party to the death of teenage girls. Men like this did not question their decisions, did not wrestle with their conscience. Perhaps they had limits to their depravity, limits to what they could or would do and this was what was happening to them. They were in the parameters of his. And it wasn't personal: the message the Governor of California was delivering to him with his warm smile, 'Hey, I'm sorry Jack, it's nothing personal. Apologies, only you and your friends, all of the people you love, well, it's just the way things are. I'm going to have to do whatever I have to do to protect me and mine, only we are civilised. Let's enjoy this evening together then I will send murderous gangs to kill you tomorrow. Why? Because that's the way of things, because whereas you may do things to defend yourself, you would never kidnap and torture to death a member of my family, just to make a point, just to assert yourself. Only I would and I will do so to you and I'll do it, then attend the opera!'

Jim Teal had elements of this, as he realised in a crushing moment of self-awareness that they did not exist within him. Fear gripped him, in these brief few seconds, he had realised that he could never win this fight, could never, would never win it, therefore, he must somehow, end it.

The president was not able to attend but the vice president was there, Jack and Cindy were introduced to him and his wife, the second lady, by Governor Hollingsworth, as if they were dear friends, not hated enemies, because in his eyes they were not. Only business Jack, nothing more. Both of them expressed great gratitude to Cindy for her work. They were told they must accept an invitation to dine at the White House with the president when he was available, just the six of them. Jack was in amazement. Then, another thought occurred to him, here was the vice president and the man who would be president, perhaps, joking and laughing. They would have dinner together, enjoy one another's company, while secretly planning to destroy one another.

On the plane ride back to California Jack confided in Tank his deepest concerns. Tank listened carefully. One of the things that concerned Jack the most was the clean up after the attempted assassination of David Savage. The resources necessary, to make this happen, were mind blowing. There had been no mention anywhere of the shootout, not a line in the paper, not a word, No reports of any kind.

Tank's people had reported hearing sirens, multiple sirens: ambulance, police, fire brigade, yet there was no record anywhere, not even a note in a dispatcher's log. Here was an incident that had happened in public, that included a shootout with automatic weapons in the middle of the street, that resulted in multiple homicides, every emergency service department in the city, with not only the responders but hundreds of support staff. That simply did not happen, there was zero evidence remaining to support that it had ever occurred.

Tank asked, 'Does Governor Hollingsworth have enough power on his own to do that, I mean that's a hell of a lot, to ask of one man, it's as if he's changing history.'

'If Hollingsworth is not working alone then, who is he working with? His father?' Jack asked in a calm reasoning tone.

Tank considered it.

'No, he's an inn keeper. A powerful man in his realm, perhaps, but my guess would be no. That's not the world he lives in. My bet would be the banker!'

'The father-in-law?'

'Yes.'

Jack looked doubtful.

'But he's so slight, so nondescript.'

'Power doesn't come from stature,' said Tank, 'It comes from the ability to convince people, to influence others to do things. He attracts no attention, lives in the shadows. I've heard he is one of the wealthiest men in the world, that he makes Onassis look like a pauper, that the Rothschilds, look upon him with envy and...' Tank moved closer, lowering his voice, '...that he has a ruthless streak that would put Hitler to shame.'

Jack considered it. How could it be? Then his logic kicked in. If not him, then who?

Tank continued, 'Think about it. The governor's charming influence and cunning, his father-in-law's ruthlessness, connections and incredible wealth. They make the perfect team. Hollingsworth as governor can influence many things on his own. Couple that with a man whose bank holds a 500 million dollar note against the state. Suddenly, people are falling over themselves to help."

Jack could see it clearly now; he took a moment, rubbing his temples. Yes, it was entirely plausible.

'You're right, it's him. They are working together. Why are they so constrained though?'

It was an interesting question.

'Let's presume that they somehow put two and two together and uncovered Tommy's role in shooting his grandson, they eliminate David Savage, then kidnap Cindy. Why not simply assassinate you and Tommy?'

The emotionless way that Tank said this, sent a chill down Jack's spine.

'Messages. Savage and Cindy were messages to me,' Jack said. 'They figure that I have a contingency in place. If anything happens to myself or Tommy, then whatever evidence I have will be passed on to the attorney general or probably several highly placed people and the media. They can't eliminate myself or me, what they need is our silence, but why?'

Tank smiled.

'The presidential race. They have spent years getting Hollingsworth to this point. An incident like this will taint the entire family. There's no way he can run for the nation's top job if his son has murdered a veteran in such a sadistic way. That's what we are up against. Savage is lucky to be alive and Cindy's friend was unluckily wrong place wrong time.'

The more Jack considered it, the more sense it made. Here was a man who had immense power. He could never be president himself; his life had been about building an empire with all of the resources and connections that could make someone president. In his son-in-law he had found someone, who had all the qualities he lacked, who, like him, had the necessary killer instinct to go all the way to do whatever it took to succeed. Imagine what they could do together for eight years. They would be able to reshape the entire world.

Jack continued turning it over in his mind. This had been years in the making, millions of dollars had been invested, as they manoeuvred their position into the governorship of California. The old man ensured his son-in-law's tenure as governor was successful. He attracted business investment in the state through his contacts, made sure any failures disappeared, utilised his friends in the media to build an image, portraying him as the perfect leader, strong, understanding and resourceful, while running down his opposition. Then made a run for the Republican candidacy. People felt the Democrats were failing; they needed a new hero, someone who could get the country back on track. All they needed now was the endorsement. To be so close, only for something like this to derail the dream. It was too late to start over. He wasn't getting any younger.

Tank knew what Jack was thinking as the wheels ticked over in his mind. Now they just needed to stay alive long enough to find a way out.

57

JULIA HAD READ and reread some of the diaries several times. They had become dear to her, unlocking many secrets, the answers to questions which had laid hidden her entire life. It gave her a fresh perspective of her father, placed questions about her brothers and her paternity she did not wish to face but, most importantly, had given her a new respect for a man she had long looked upon with disdain for running away, abandoning his children. She was embarrassed by this former attitude now and would give anything to have known this earlier, to have done something. Anything.

One of the entries that stuck in her mind the most was an account of being overrun, then pursued, through the Dutch countryside, by a platoon of crack SS panzer troops. Terrified, expecting death at any moment, he had prayed for a miracle and been given one. To survive that, then die horribly 30 years later in his own country, broke her heart.

How strong her father must have been to lead men under such horrible conditions. Why was he and so many other men of his generation forgotten, left to die alone on the street, homeless, in such a terrible way? Why was there nowhere for the mentally ill, like her father, to go? The borderline men, the ones who were just not able to cope, why did society forget them? The ones to whom they owed so much.

Julia had returned to LA twice now, looking for answers. None were forthcoming. She walked the lonely streets as her father had done. She found it depressing. This, she had decided, would be her last visit. If the police or someone, could not provide anything this time, she would go home for good.

For Julia, unlike like her father, cowering on the battle fields of Holland, salvation was not at hand!

58

AGAINST, WHAT HE believed was, his better judgement, Jack had allowed Jim Teal to organise a meeting with the police. There were provisos: number one was, the incident involving David Savage was never to be mentioned, nor was the hiding of the gun. For the time, being it was thrown off the pier into the ocean and two was the kidnapping and shooting of Armando and all talk about Cindy, who would not be joining them.

The meeting was to strictly relate the events of the night when Tommy had shot Johnny, who he later recognised. A junior detective, Jack realised, would quickly be able to pull the case apart, let alone a seasoned veteran, but that could not be helped. He had been out-voted and, in a democracy, that was the way it went. Tank called it what it was: a declaration of war. By going on public record, they were declaring war on the governor and his family, who's retribution, he felt, would be swift.

The police captain's car entered via a small entrance at the southern end of the sprawling grounds of Michael Lethbridge's estate. In the distance, the police captain could see the main house, sitting elevated on a hill. He parked near a building that resembled a barn, guarded by two serious-looking men. Inside, his bag was checked by an equally serious-looking woman, before he was allowed through. He was then ushered into a small office where he found the most serious-looking man of them all, sitting smoking a cigar behind a desk. An envelope, stuffed with money, sat ready for him. He eyed it but did not touch. Not yet. The two men knew one another. There was little small talk. The cigar-smoking man held the title of head of security. He had worked for Lethbridge and his family for over 20 years and handled all of the issues his boss did not want to, including meetings like this one.

He got straight to the point, smiled and said, 'Well, what have you got for me?'

The police captain was nervous. He wasn't used to this kind of dealing; his conscience was giving him a hard time. The man behind the desk patiently waited.

'Today,' he stammered. 'I attended a meeting... no, an interview.' He looked around, as if checking they were alone. The man behind the desk was mildly amused. 'Where a man identified your boss' grandson as one of a group of young men who attacked a homeless man, resulting in the man's death.'

The head of security's expression was blank. He simply nodded as if what had just been said was the most normal thing in the world.

'This afternoon,' he paused, looking around again, 'another witness also identified him. The next step is to bring him in for questioning. I believe that this will happen quickly.'

The police captain had been staring at the desk. When he looked up, the smile was gone.

'Do you have these witnesses' details?'

Reaching into his top pocket, the police captain retrieved a folded piece of paper, placed it next to the envelope containing the money, then pushed it across the desk. The head of security picked it up unfolded it and read it.

'Can you delay things, perhaps make them disappear,' he said.

'Not as easily as the shooting,' the police captain responded.

The head of security eyed him cautiously.

'But it's possible?'

He reached into a drawer, taking out another envelope and placing it next to the one already on the table.

'Anything is possible, it just won't be easy.' The police captain scooped up the two envelopes, then placed them in his bag.

'We can count on you?'

'Yes, but we all have a part to play. If certain evidence was to disappear, for example, witnesses were to become lost, change their stories, even.'

'Believe me I'm onto it.'

'Very well then, I'll do what I can.'

'Do I need to worry?'

'I don't think so.'

There were no niceties, no shaking of hands. The police captain simply stood up and left. On the car journey home, he thought it over. He had already begun formulating a plan before the meeting, now he needed to flesh it out and put it into action.

As always, at times like this, he found himself looking in the rear vison mirror the entire way. The guilty feelings were never far away. By the time he turned into his driveway, the plan was clear in his mind. In the morning, he would turn it into reality.

59

THE COMMISSION HAD come through her agent in New York. It provided a healthy distraction. Cindy received a package containing three photographs, the subject of which were two girls, aged under 10, standing together, holding hands on a lawn that overlooked the ocean at sunset. One girl was slightly taller than the other. The shorter one looked slightly younger.

Cindy accepted few commissions, yet this one intrigued her as it reflected, in a small way, the biographical portraits she had painted of her childhood from memory. She chose the picture taken from behind the girls then, using the other two, changed the angle as if viewing them diagonally. It captured their faces, while showing them looking out to the ocean. There were wildflowers growing in the lawn and Cindy captured these beautifully, shading each, subtly in the afternoon light, to brilliant effect. The innocence of the children, happily playing outside, was in direct contrast to the chaos they were experiencing in their own lives.

The stress at home was unbearable. Cindy was spending more and more time in her studio. Despite her love for Jack, it was a difficult period, one that she doubted they would get through. She couldn't abandon him, not while all this was happening. She was mixed up in it all now, with no idea of what was going to happen next. It was plain, though, if she could not, they could not find a way through this. Then, one day, she would find herself heading off into the sunset, alone.

59

60

USINESS WAS BOOMING but Jack was as disconnected as he possibly could be. Others had taken over his role, apart from weekly check-ins with Maria, he had little involvement. This bred paranoia, leading to the creation of non-existent threats and scenarios in his mind.

Annie had sent through a request for him to review another case. It was for a rock band: a new client. After the success of the previous case he had advised on, she was extremely anxious to have his input. He had promised to review it. So far, he had not been able to bring himself to do so.

It wasn't for lack of trying. Jack sat in front of it, the folder sitting on the desk of his study for hours. David Savage had work to do but for obvious reasons, nobody wanted him out in the field. Instead, it fell to his partner, Henry. Henry, a former accountant, had made his name gathering evidence against errant partners in divorce cases. His meticulous approach, along with a forensic ability to trace assets, gained him a reputation for being the best at what he did, in a place that provided a seemingly endless stream of wealthy clients with adulterous partners. He and David had forged a good partnership, with Henry happily doing, what David saw as, the more boring side of investigating and chasing paper trails, while David pounded the pavement conducting field investigations. Unlucky in love, Henry had never married or even had a long-term girlfriend.

Although it really wasn't his thing, something made him accept the challenge of joining the investigation. In any case, with David out of action, there was little other choice. Carefully, he moved about the city, under strict instructions to, in no way, allow people to know what he was doing. Difficult when you were investigating an individual.

He struck gold at the clinic where the young woman had been given the abortion. There, he found a cleaner who worked the night shift. He confirmed that Johnny had also been treated there. Finding this man was a serious piece of luck because he was there when Johnny arrived late at night. Under the cover of darkness, he had arrived in an ambulance that, on the back, had the name of the hospital where he had been treated. He had helped unload Johnny and taken him to his room.

At the university hospital, David was nervous to approach anybody. Quite by accident, he had seen two women taking a smoke break just outside of a service door. He kept an eye out and noticed them again the following night. Every two hours, they would emerge with a cup of coffee in one hand and a cigarette in the other. When another two hours had passed, just like clockwork, the door opened. Only this time, only one woman came out. He climbed out of his car and approached her.

'Excuse me miss, would you have a light?'

She was a young woman, maybe 22 or 23. She had a soft, olive complexion but no accent. He could not place where she might be from. South America, he wondered. *No,* he thought, *perhaps Greece or Southern Italy.* She smiled, reaching into her pocket for a lighter and lit his cigarette for him. She looked at him but he had no story ready if she challenged him so he might have to run away.

'Busy night?' he asked, offering him his warmest smile.

'Not really, it never is. This is just a teaching hospital, we have very few interesting cases and at night it's dead.'

'Are you a nurse?'

She looked at him with eyes yearning. He guessed she was single and looking.

'Yes, at least I will be in a few months' time. What brings you here at this time of night?'

'It's classified. I could tell you only it might be dangerous.'

That had simply flowed out, only it was the truth. She smiled.

'Oh really? I bet that's what you say to all the girls.'

They exchanged a chuckle.

'So, you're a student?'

'Yes, final year.'

'If all the students were as pretty as you, back when I was in school, maybe I would have stuck around.'

Even he cringed at this pick-up line. He felt embarrassed, a dirty old man. She blushed at the compliment and forgave him for it. He quickly changed the subject.

'So, it's pretty dull around here?'

'For the most part. It has its moments, though.'

Her expression changed. She looked at him conspiratorially, lowering her voice, she moved closer to him and he could smell the nicotine on her breath.

'What will you give me for a secret?'

'A secret?'

'Yes, a secret.' Her eyes sparkled and she winked at him. He stared back at her not knowing what to say. 'Go on, be brave. Believe me, I'm worth it.' She winked again as she said this.

'Dinner and a movie of your choice, anytime you want.'

She didn't hesitate. 'Deal.'

Just then, there was a noise from inside. Someone was calling her.

'Anastasia, where are you? We're needed.'

'Just a minute,' she replied, then turned to David. 'Do you know Zevon's Deli? It's a 24-hour place?'

'I know it.'

'Meet me there in an hour.'

He looked into her eyes. They were green; they were beautiful. For a brief second, he felt a pang of guilt. *Leave this beautiful, young woman alone.* Only now he was intrigued. He would find out what she had to say then leave her alone, it might be nothing anyway.

'Okay, it was Anastasia, wasn't it?' He smiled, a little weakly, under the shadow. She smiled from hearing him say her name for the first time.

'See you there.' She smiled a final time, then dropped her cigarette, stubbed it out with her foot, then disappeared through the door.

He was there, waiting in a booth at the back of the restaurant, when she walked in. She had changed into jeans and a tight-fitting white t-shirt. Once again, she was all smiles. They ordered toasted sandwiches and coffee. They made small talk until their food was delivered, then sat nervously eating, neither wanting to take the initiative. Finally, Anastasia spoke.

'You didn't tell me your name.'

This was tricky. Should he tell her the truth? If he didn't, there was no future for them. *What future?* he wondered. Where had that come from? This was a job, plain and simple. If only she wasn't a pretty, very pretty, member of the opposite sex; one he had immediate chemistry with. People like that did not come along every day. Still, he had a job to do.

'Henry.'

'Hello Henry. Tell me, Henry, is your offer still good?'

'Yes absolutely. Only, you don't need to tell me anything.'

'A deal's a deal.'

She picked up her sandwich and he laughed.

'Next Saturday night suit?' he asked.

'Sounds like a plan. Now, where were we? Oh yes, here, shake.' She held out her hand and he took it.

There was electricity and his heart swelled. Her touch was gentle, yet explosive. He felt a tingle all the way up his arm. It seemed to flow throughout his entire body. She continued chewing.

'Now that the formalities are over, a few months ago, we had a kid come in, a real rich kid. He had been shot or shot himself or something. It was all a bit fishy. Anyway, his friends bring him in, blood pouring out from God knows where. I'm the duty nurse and I've never had anyone with more than a sprained ankle. Luckily, our resident doctor, he's ex-military, had seen this sort of thing a million times. Another nurse, older matron, one of our teachers, she joins him and they take charge. Luckily, they were there or this kid might be dead. Anyhow, couple of days later, this lawyer comes in, gives $500 cash, tells me I will need to sign a document, only I go home before signing and they never come back. Hence, I now get a free dinner and movie with a handsome man.'

He couldn't believe his ears; this was simply amazing. He looked across the table, she winked at him again.

'So, was it worth it?'

'This kid have a name?'

She leaned closer.

'Johnny Hollingsworth, the governor's son.'

They wanted proof and here it was. He couldn't believe it, only, now what? He liked this girl. Wave after wave of guilt washed over him. *A fresh dilemma,* he thought. He smiled as his suffering began.

61

TOMMY SCANNED THE news constantly: newspapers, television and even the radio was now switched on 24/7. He gritted his teeth and became tense every time a bulletin came on, but there was no news. As the days passed, he became despondent. In the beginning, it had made him chuckle, now he looked at his friend with growing concern. The delay did not surprise him, he knew how things worked, at least how they worked if fair due process was followed, though he had begun to wonder if it had been.

In cases like these, involving senior members of the public, the experienced members of the team would work on the case: the district attorney and senior prosecutors. Secrecy was imperative, after all, it was the governor's son. They would then take it to the judge. The higher, the better.

It was a state matter, so there would be no federal involvement, not yet anyway. Once they had the opinion of one, they would seek another. If they both agreed, then things would progress. A meeting of senior officials would decide Johnny's fate. Only, it was on public record, therefore they would have to proceed or face the threat of a scandal, something that could see them all in front of a judge. The DA would then personally contact Hollingsworth's legal representative.

It would be a polite cordial conversation; Johnny would be invited to attend a formal discussion.

The thought of this made Jack laugh. If Johnny was from a poor family, the police, disgusted by his crimes, would have already kicked the front door in, dragged him from the house, as violently as possible, without getting themselves into too much trouble. He would be interrogated, though his guilt already established, would make the outcome a forgone conclusion.

If he was reluctant to confess, they would then bully and harass him until he saw the error of his ways. He would then be charged and appear in front of a judge. Bail would be set beyond his means, leaving him to rot in jail until his case came to trial. Then, to conclude matters, represented by the public defender, his spirit broken, he would plead guilty and begin his 20-30-year sentence. He wouldn't be alone, though. They would have rounded up all his friends and anyone else, who had the slightest connection to what had happened, would be joining him.

They needed a lot to go in their favour. The DA would need to be strong-willed, the police, everyone needed to be united, dedicated with a sole aim, to see justice done. He had serious doubts.

Later, he was in the middle of a chat with Cindy, when an idea crossed his mind. It took root quickly and required immediate action. She saw the moment his mind left the conversation. Frowning, she dropped what she was saying. It was pointless. She watched helpless as it took hold, consuming him. *Everyone was at a crossroads*, she thought, *the time of reckoning was approaching.*

62

J ACK WAS LIKE a cat on a hot tin roof for the remainder of the day. Late in the evening, he still hadn't managed to calm or slow down. David Savage had been summoned from the safe house; he was yet to receive a report from his partner, Henry. The team, including Tank, had discussed David's visiting. Tank was against it. The private investigator was still very much a target and extremely vulnerable. The fact the case was not moving forward, wasn't lost on him. It pointed to danger.

Jack, however, was too wound up and he needed to speak to David in person, urgently, so they had gone to fetch him. Jack's plan was simple. The others couldn't see the merit in it, not at first and not after longer consideration. He wanted David to reach out to the young man who had shared the valuable information about the girlfriend who used to date Johnny. He didn't want information about Johnny though. Well, he did, but in a roundabout way, that would come later. What he wanted to learn about was his friend, the one who had been with Johnny at Cindy's gala, the one whose name none of them could remember. Jack wanted to learn as much as he could about this young man, then through him, to learn more, no, find more evidence, that incriminated Johnny.

'Could you contact him?' Jack asked David.

'Of course, do you think it's wise?'

'Why not? We can't get to the man himself, so let's try this friend of his.'

'He would be loyal. Why would he speak to us? Surely by now, all of Johnny's friends are on the lookout, have been briefed, asked to keep their mouths shut.'

'Call him now.'

'Now, it's the middle of the night.'

'He lives in a frat house, they won't care.'

David looked at the others, then shrugged. They were sitting around the desk in Jack's study. Without another word, he opened his notebook, then picked up the phone's receiver. All eyes were on him as he made the call. To everyone's surprise the phone was answered immediately.

'Hello, is Chris there?'

They watched intently only able to hear his side of the conversation.

'Yes, I'm a friend of his, friend of the family, actually.'

They strained to hear, hopeful. Instead, they watched as David went white.

'Yes, I'm very sorry. Terrible news, thank you.'

As he moved the receiver away from his ear, they heard a faint voice.

'Hello, are you there? What did you say your name was?'

He replaced the receiver. The others exchanged worried glances, while David gathered his thoughts. When he finally spoke, he did so to nobody in particular.

'The young man who spoke to me.' There was a pause. 'The young man who spoke to me.' Another longer pause. 'Well, it seems, there has been a terrible accident.'

At the mention of this, fear gripped everyone in the room. They hung on what was to come, though none present wanted to hear it. Now it was the opposition's turn to raise the ante.

63

ANASTASIA MET HIM at the restaurant, which was fine, only he had found it a little disappointing, not being able to pick her up from where she lived. She was leaving her options open, he supposed or then, he thought, maybe, as she lived on campus in a sorority, perhaps intimate relations there were not a possibility or even more likely. Maybe she wasn't as enthusiastic a member of the sexual revolution as he was. This thought brightened his mood on the drive to the restaurant.

She had chosen Romano's, a very intimate Italian seafood restaurant. Then she wanted to see the new Star Wars sequel. He had already bought the tickets to the 9 o'clock show. He was 15 minutes early and was surprised when the maître d informed him that his guest had already arrived.

She was wearing a short, red dress that hugged her body, setting his heart racing. Her smile was as sweet as he remembered and those eyes, those beautiful eyes, like two shining green emeralds, seemed to sparkle. She offered him her hand; the touch of her skin was electric. He found conversation difficult and tried to stop himself from staring, but it was hard.

Then the guilt returned. If this continued beyond tonight, how could he ever explain it. He was in a deadly panic of her asking him what he did for a living. What could he say? If he told her the truth, she would likely leave him sitting there. If he lied, he would be simply digging a deeper hole, one that he would never be able to escape from. Perhaps she wouldn't ask. He decided that he needed to control the conversation.

'Tell me more about the hospital?'

She shrugged.

'There's not much to tell. We treat students, sprains, abrasions, bad cases of the flu, pneumonia, the measles.' She paused to eat some fried shrimp, then drink some wine, continuing without looking up. 'Simple things, the odd tonsillectomy, ingrown toenails. We get some charity cases: orphanage kids with broken limbs, poor people who need a break from the world. Anything serious is transferred to county or, if they have money, one of the private clinics That's where the students end up.'

'Like the governor's son?'

'Yep, couldn't get him out of there fast enough. It was like he was never there.'

'So, nobody speaks about it?'

'Nu uh, all too scared. Neither would I if I had signed that form. You got lucky, plus I like you.'

He felt the red spreading across his face; this made her giggle. She finished the last of her shrimp then did the same to her wine. He poured her another glass.

'So, there's no trace?'

'No files, no mention, no entry in the log,' she confirmed.

'No souvenirs?' he said jokingly, adding some laughter of his own.

'Only one.'

His expression changed involuntarily and he moved forward in his seat.

'Really?'

'You bet, the bullet. The surgeon kept it, called it his good luck charm, had it turned into a necklace. We all said it was disgusting. He just laughed and said he always does it. Apparently, he still had the first one he removed from a GI in the Korean War. He wears the governor's kid's every night now, bold as brass. Swears they bring good fortune to him. Apparently, he has a heap of them.'

He sat stunned. Not knowing what to say next, all he wanted to do was get to a phone and call this in. Here it was, their literal smoking gun, if they had the bullet. The rest of dinner, the movie, all passed in a blur.

Not wanting to disappoint her, he had enthusiastically or, so he thought, made a play for her affections. In the front seat of his car, they had made out. He had pushed, more for show or so he told himself and he almost lost himself in the moment, before he was politely declined at what he once would have described as second base.

She promised to call him after dinner the following evening and agreed to another date the following Saturday. There was no getting around it now, he had to tell the others. It was late, midnight. He decided it could wait until the morning, then decided he should at least let them know he had something for them. He wove his way back to the emergency apartment he had been assigned, after their own apartment became uninhabitable after the attempt on David's life. To his surprise, the phone was picked up on the third ring, by none other than Jack himself.

'Hi Jack, it's me David.'

'David, how are you?'

'I'm well, I have news.'

'Really?' Jack's voice brightened.

'Yes, a bit of a breakthrough.'

'Better not speak over the phone, can you be ready at 7?'

'Sure.'

'Great, I'll send someone, get some sleep.'

Jack put down the receiver. David didn't know there were guards all around him in the apartments on either side and a team had been shadowing him. They had not been listening though, so they had no inkling of what he was saying or who to. They were just observing, ready for the worst. Jack desperately wanted to hear his news. He had learned to be patient, though. Instead, he climbed the stairs where he found Cindy, not as of old, waiting for him dressed in lingerie, but dressed like a boxer in sweatpants and a hooded jumper, curled up on the bed, like a coiled spring, ready to jump, then begin running in an instant. With a sad heart he climbed in on the other side.

Times, he thought, *they were definitely a-changing!*

64

THE FOLLOWING MORNING, they convened around the breakfast table in Jack's house. The mood, though tinged with fear, was still buoyant. For those who had served overseas, which was most of them, it had a familiar feeling, like the breakfast prior to a big mission. Jack's housekeeper did the cooking and they ate before she discreetly retreated and the discussion began. Cindy did not join them; she had already taken sanctuary in her studio where she would remain alone for the majority of the day. All eyes were on David this morning. He pushed aside all his feelings and delivered his report. They sat, mouths agape. It was the best piece of evidence so far. David was greeted with smiles and well wishes. The feelings didn't last for long though. A single thought of Anastasia removed them completely, bringing with them, shame, guilt and betrayal. Jack summed everything up for them.

'Not only have you found proof from two witnesses that place Johnny at each hospital, wounded on the first night, then treated on the next, the bullet is out there in the possession of the surgeon?'

'Yes correct.'

Tommy laughed.

'Case closed,' he said emphatically. Jack raised a hand.

'It's great information. Fantastic, only we still have a long way to go, until it's verified and in our possession.'

'Let's not forget about the poor young man and his girlfriend,' David added.

This immediately dampened the mood although, in many ways, David was grateful for it.

A dark chilling thought crossed Jack's mind.

'If they have begun tying up loose ends...' he tailed off not wanting to kill their hopes.

'What about this young woman?' Tank asked.

'Do we bring her in, the cleaner, also?'

Jack reasoned it.

'There's a good chance, a very good one, that they don't know about the bullet. I don't know, we owe it to her and the doctor, how do we explain it to them?'

Things were growing too quickly, fast moving beyond his control. Panic set in as he imagined the number of potential victims they needed to protect. His conscience would not tolerate this for long.

'David, your friends at the police department, have you been able to learn anything about the accident involving the young man and his girlfriend?'

By not using their names, it made it easier to speak about.

'No, not yet, it doesn't help that I can't move around.'

They all acknowledged this. Jack was dreading his next question.

'The other witness, the one they have in protection..?' Shrugs, all round. 'Realistically,' Tank started, 'we have no way of knowing whether they have begun or it's a genuine accident. What happened to the boy? I mean, we don't know the details, I wonder could the girl David met...?'

'NO,' David said forcefully, aggressively cutting off Tank mid-sentence.

Tank raised a hand, to indicate no hard feelings. The conversation was becoming heated and Jack felt his blood pressure rising. Looking at Tommy, he felt lost once again, not coping well with any of this. It was time for action, so he gathered his thoughts for a moment, then spoke, firing orders rapidly, not taking time to dwell on them, relying on the group to raise any issues and concerns.

'Tank, begin shadowing this young lady. At the first sign of anything, extract her. We have a responsibility to protect these people; same goes for the cleaner who originally tipped David off. This surgeon, what do we know about him?' Jack's question was met with silence and shrugs of shoulders again. 'David, we need you back in the field, he's yours. You will have three of Tank's men with you at all times. Please be careful. Henry, your job is to find out from your police contacts, what's happening with the case? What happened to our friend and his girlfriend? Can you do it?'

He looked up at Jack holding back the information that he was falling for Anastasia.

'Yes.'

'Please be as careful as possible and try to be discreet. Take two of Tank's people with you.'

It felt good being assertive, Jack thought. He was scared out of his wits. This was not an unfamiliar feeling. Many times, when in battle, he had felt the same way. He supposed that all officers felt like this. It was pointless keeping David locked away, Tommy also. They were close to breaking point. In a way, it was their own declaration, one from which they could quickly retreat, if necessary. Although the battle lines were blurred, Jack felt, after this morning, like they were winning.

65

THEY WERE BACK in the beautiful wood-panelled office on his father-in law's estate. It was time for another showdown of sorts. The governor felt another rebuke was headed his way and had ensured that Johnny, Rory and his trusted advisor, Randle, were all in attendance. The old man had his own people there. They were facing one another across the long coffee table, while the old man, perched on an armchair at the head, eyed them all with contempt. If a rebuke was coming, then it was coming for more than him, the governor thought. You could have heard a pin drop as the old man began.

'Gentlemen, once again I find myself having to become involved in matters that do not deserve my attention.' The old man ran a critical eye along each of the rows of uncomfortable faces, without singling out any, before continuing.

He would speak in this roundabout way, the governor thought, as always, he would never be one to directly discuss or admit intimate knowledge of any particular detail.

'As lady luck would have it, I believe that with the help of our sympathetic friends, of which I can happily count many, it may not be too late to save the day. God has shown us that he favours our work by having providence intervene on our behalf. I thank you all for your continued prayers,' He paused here to collect his thoughts. 'The expungement process has commenced. Johnny, my beloved grandson, has decided to spend some time abroad working in our offices in Europe. Rory, who I am happy to say, will officially join our family in just one month's time, will continue to work with my son-in-law, Michael, who as you all know, will begin working towards the next phase of his political career.'

All eyes turned to Rory first, then Michael, along with nods of approval.

'None of these men will have any further involvement in this matter. All, if any, communication is to be conducted through Randle, who will act with their authority and mine, for that matter. Does everybody understand?'

The message was clear. They were to be distanced as much as possible from ongoing events, while Randle was tasked with taking the risk and cleaning the mess.

'You will all report to him, until this thing is over, is that clear?'

More nods of agreement.

'Randle, I would prefer to hear no more about this. You have full resources of the family at your disposal; please ensure that this is an end to the matter.'

Randle was flattered yet also weary. It was odd that he was being put in charge and not one of the old man's people. It must be far riskier than he was aware. Still, he found himself offering a smile and a nod. When he looked back at the governor, sitting beside him, he was met with a look of concern.

'Very well then, gentlemen, if you will excuse me, I will take my leave to confer with my son-in-law, grandson and future grandson-in-law and leave you men to finalise the details. Gentlemen, come with me.'

They stood up and left Randle there, looking a little sheepish and very vulnerable. He watched as the doors were closed behind them, then looked across the table. There was Porter, one of the old man's most trusted advisors: a tough Chicago street lawyer who, legend had it, had known Al Capone, Myer Lansky and every other dubious Chicago businessman of the 20s and 30s.

There was his personal accountant, Phillips. He began life running for bookmakers, eventually finding his way into night school then somehow ended up a CPA. He had grown through the ranks and was a master at hiding money.

Then there was Emil Peters, the head of security, the most mysterious of them all. Not only was that not the one-time Golden Gloves boxing champion's name, but a warrant had once been issued for the man's arrest under it, for, of all things, murder.

Randle noticed, at once, there were no ivy leaguers in the bunch. No, these were his street heavies, his inner circle, the people he had grown up with, the ones who would get their hands dirty, out of respect or misguided loyalty or some lingering debt that could never be settled. He, an advisor to the governor, a Harvard man, was being placed in the same company as these street-smart thugs. Not only that, he was in charge of them, until one of them knifed him in the back. *Literally,* he thought. Now they were staring at him. Normally, not able to be shut up, he was lost for words. Taking a deep breath, he forced a few out.

'Well, gentlemen, it would seem that we have our work cut out for us.'

They eyed him suspiciously. The head of security reached into a briefcase with one of his meaty hands, retrieving a file. He threw it on the table. Randle left it sitting there. Porter glanced at it, motioning with his eyes. Reluctantly, Randle picked it up and opened it. Inside was a business card with a phone number written in pencil and the photo of a woman, late 30s, maybe a little older, taken at, what looked like, an airport.

'Not much in the way of a dossier.'

Porter spoke, without acknowledging the comment.

'She is known to us as Maya. The old man knows her real name, maybe, but the rest of us have never even spoken to her, never even been in the same room as her. Which is probably, no, definitely, a good thing.

'She was brought in to clean things up, tie up the loose ends. I don't know what you don't know, so I'll keep it brief. She is in town until she isn't, if you get what I mean. We contact her by coded message at different drop points around town. It's old school spy style, which gives you an idea about her background, probably more than you want, or need, to know. She has a younger assistant here with her. I haven't seen her but the boys tell me she is quite the looker.' Porter stopped talking.

After a moment or two, they began staring at him. *They speak in bigger riddles than the old man*, Randle thought.

'Is there a list?' he asked.

They looked confused. Eventually Phillips spoke this time.

'List?'

He stared back at them; it was going to be a long night.

66

T HAT IT WAS easy did not register with Maya. The only thing that mattered was, it was done. She had been supplied with the location of the safe house and the time of the shift changeover. That was all she needed. While the officers chatted in the hall, she entered the hotel room via the fire escape into the room next door, then through the adjoining door. Found the old woman, fired two shots from behind with her silenced pistol, before the old woman knew what hit her. Then was on her way before the officers had a chance to say goodbye to one another. It was clean, efficient and clinical.

When they entered, the smell of gunpowder filled the air. It was too late. After checking Elyse and confirming she was deceased, they searched for the assassin. Maya, the ghost, was gone.

67

DETECTIVE LAWRENCE WAS waiting in his office for the green light to bring in Johnny, when John Stanley's daughter arrived, unannounced. This time it was a positive meeting, as he let her know that there had been developments. Sadly, he had done so before the news of the death of their witnesses arrived. This news sent him into a rage. He read the official report in disbelief. How? Why? Who and why would they kill this harmless old woman? Then it dawned on him. He went to see the police captain to share his suspicions. He was busy but agreed to see him briefly.

'Yes detective?'

'Well Sir, it's about Elyse, the witness in the Stanley case. She has been assassinated.'

'Yes, I have been read the report. Tragic. I understand how hard you have been working on that case; you must be disappointed.'

'Sir, I want permission to bring in the young man, the governor's son. It appears to be a professional hit. There's something very fishy here, who else would have a motive to kill the old woman?'

'I don't think so. Sounds like a robbery gone bad to me. Cheap hotel, villain gained access via a fire escape, no sheer coincidence. Look, why don't you take a break? Have a couple of weeks off, you've earned it. I'll square it with the duty sergeant myself, come back fresh.'

Instinct told him to back away. *Pick your battles,* he thought.

'Yes sir, I will and thank you.'

'You'll see in a week or two, it will all have blown over. It will be just like it never happened.'

When he left the police captain's office, he had never been so scared. How did he know about the fire escape? There was no mention of it in the official report. Detective Lawrence had been there, seen it with his own eyes but the police captain, Donnelly... *my God,* he thought, *my God!*

68

J ULIA STANLEY WAS in a great mood after she left her meeting with Detective Lawrence. There was a spring in her step, a smile on her face and, for a while, the world seemed to be a better place. She hopped on a bus. She was headed for the areas her father used to frequent; she enjoyed wandering around the streets he knew and lived in. It brought her closer to him. She was walking around when she saw a sign she hadn't noticed before.

"Methodist Centre"

She wondered. They had attended a Methodist church when she was little girl. Maybe they knew her father. Since she was in such a good mood, she decided to give it a try. A nice young man at reception introduced her to a young minister who introduced himself as Johnathon. He, in turn, led her to an office where she met an older minister, whose name was Sean.

'I knew your father, knew him well. We conduct services here on Sundays and he was something of a regular. I was sorry to hear about your father.'

His kindness overwhelmed her.

'Can you tell me more about my father? What was he like?'

'I can do better than that. Come with me.'

He led her down into the basement. There was row after row of steel shelves, all stocked with all manner of items. He walked along a row then stopped and squatted down on his haunches.

'Here, these three boxes.'

Julia lifted the lid of the first box. Inside were the familiar notebooks that journaled her father's life. It was too much. She picked up one of the books, clutching it to her chest.

69

ENRY SHARED THE bad news about the death of the witness, the suspension of the case and the surprise leave of Detective Lawrence to a stunned Jack in the office of his home in Santa Monica. It called for a change in their plans. They needed to contact the surgeon urgently. Henry sighed. What would it mean for his growing relationship with Anastasia? He had shared a wonderful phone conversation with her just hours before. Still, he gave in. It had to be done. He would be exposed as a liar then that would be the end of that, plain and simple.

'Has David managed to make any headway?' asked Jack.

'Not that he has shared with me, I'll check in with him,' Henry replied.

'Go find this surgeon. You have 24 hours maybe less. Use everything at your disposal.'

Great, Henry thought, *he means Anastasia.*

When he left Jack's, he didn't know who to call first. He stopped at a payphone. Putting off the call to Anastasia, he checked in with David, who had so far gathered no information. He was terse with him and seemed frustrated. Henry paused for a moment, considering what he was about to do. He didn't want it to end, for in his mind he had already lived a lifetime with her. 'Damn it,' he said out loud, then he picked up the phone. She answered quickly, there formed a lump in his throat, the moment he heard her sweet voice.

'Hello, Anastasia?"

'Henry is that you?'

'Yes,' he responded in a whisper, 'Sorry to bother you, only I need to speak to you, it's important. Are you available to talk?'

There was a pause. The silence worried him. On the other end of the line, Anastasia was rejoicing. She wanted him to like her, really like her. This was a promising sign. Still, she played it cool, not wanting to seem overly interested.

'Are you alright? You sound troubled.'

'It's serious, I need to speak to you in person.'

'What's wrong Henry, you're scaring me?'

'I'm sorry I can't say on the phone.'

'I can come to your apartment, would that be okay?' She spoke softly; there was a demure edge to her words as if she were seducing him.

'Yes, look I am very sorry to have to bother you like this.'

'Don't be silly. It's okay, really, I'm not bothered. Give me your address.'

He felt like a heel betraying her like this, using her, this nice woman, who he had been deceiving. He felt like one of the wives or husbands who sought his help, remembering the expressions on their faces when informed that yes, they had been betrayed. This filled the time, before she arrived, with impending dread. Damn it to hell. He would just abandon David and their clients, tell this woman that he loved her, grab her and runaway somewhere with her. This noble woman, this person who had dedicated her life to caring for others. There was a knock at the door. He checked the peep hole and it was her, so he unlocked the door, then welcomed her inside. Without a word, Anastasia pulled him into her arms and they kissed passionately. She held him long after the kiss was broken. Spotting a sofa, she led him to it. They fell onto it, leaning against the back where they kissed again. Then more holding and another kiss. Then it was time to speak.

'What is it, Henry?' He was still reluctant to speak. She prompted further. 'Can't you tell me? What's stopping you?'

'This, all of this, you, the fear of what might happen.'

'The fear of what could happen? What could possibly happen, silly? Let me help you find your courage.' She closed her eyes, kissing him again.

'Ready now?' she said. Her soft skin radiated and he had dreamed of this moment, sitting here on this very sofa.

'I'm not who you think I am,' he started, 'however... how can I explain?'

She stopped him.

'That's not important, what is important is who you are now.'

She held his face as she kissed him, this time drawing him closer.

'You're a nice caring man; there is nothing you could have said or done that could change my opinion of you.'

'It was no accident that I ran into you at the hospital. I'm a private detective; I was hired to discover information about Governor Hollingsworth's son. When you gave me that information, I was so happy thought it was Christmas, only now there have been developments. People have been...' He found the next part difficult to say.

Using her index finger, she began playing with a tuft of his hair.

'People are being killed. We are all in danger, especially your surgeon friend. We need to visit him, help him.' He watched her carefully. She remained impassive, unmoved. It was odd.

'What do you need me to do?'

'We have to be careful. Do you know the surgeon well?'

'Dr Cortez is a teacher at the university, he's Hispanic. No, I mean I know him, only in the context of teacher-student. He's a nice man.'

'Does he live near the university?'

'I really don't...wait, someone mentioned he has an apartment near the university, but he lives in San Francisco. He comes down and works for three weeks then has two weeks off or something. It's flexible.'

'Is he there now?'

'I'm not certain. I didn't go in today; it's my day off. Wait, let me think. He was here last week, the week before and the week before that, yes, I think he might be?'

'We need his address.'

'A phone number?'

'No, that won't work. We need to see him in person. He'll never believe it.'

'He might not believe it, anyway.'

'He might if you're with us, someone he knows and trusts.' He was keeping the truth from her again. What they really needed was the bullet. Yes, they cared about the surgeon, as they cared about Anastasia. Well, he cared about her more than the others, but what they needed, more than anything, was that damn bullet!

'I'll find out his address, everything. Give me an hour and I'll call you. I'll come with you in the morning. We can drive up there. I think that might be safest.'

'Okay,' he said, nervous about this development. 'Can we take your car, just in case?'

'Okay, wait, I'll borrow a friend's car in case we are both being followed.'

'Good idea.'

'See, everything is going to be fine, you're so silly to have worried, Henry.'

'Aren't you scared, even in the slightest?'

'No, I find this exciting. Tell me though, why can't we just call the police? Why can't they protect Doctor Cortez?'

'We can't do that.'

'Why not?'

'It's complicated, the Police can't be involved in this.'

'Okay, now come on I know that everything is going to be fine.'

'How can you know that?'

'Because I trust you.'

He was concerned about her leaving, then remembered that Tank's people were watching out for her. Then he froze. They would know about her visiting him. Damn, he was slipping. He would have to explain it. She kissed him again, distracting him. It was sensuous and long.

For the next hour, they played like that. Twice he attempted to entice her into the bedroom, twice he was rebuffed. Patience, she insisted and he acquiesced. He must have looked sorrowful, so she unbuttoned his trousers. It was just a taste of what was to come, she promised, they would have more time. When she left, his head was swimming. Anastasia stopped at a payphone, not far from Henry's apartment.

'Hello, it's me.'

'Anastasia?' asked a female voice.

'Yes, I need your help.'

'Sure, is everything okay?'

'Better than expected. Henry, my new friend, has taken the bait. He told me everything.'

'Good work.'

'I need an address for one of the doctors at the hospital, Dr Cortez. He has an apartment near the university but I need his other address up in San Francisco and I need to borrow your car. Can you help?'

'Dr Cortez? I believe we have it on file so shouldn't be a problem. Why do you need my car?'

'They think Doctor Cortez is in danger, so they want to bring him in. They think having someone along that knows him, will help convince him to come in my car.

'I thought it was a good idea; they have been following me. I'll tell him to meet me in a parking garage. Can you arrange that also. Hopefully, I can swap without anyone realising. I won't give him the address until I see him either. No tails. We can drive up together and take care of the whole thing all at once.'

'Good thinking, I'll have the address of the doctor and the parking garage, along with the keys delivered to you tonight, ASAP.'

'Thanks.'

'Take care.'

70

RORY'S LIFE HAD been transformed. Standing in the empty house in Brentwood, he could not have been happier. The seven-bedroom, four-bathroom, newly renovated home, with the redbrick colonial façade, had caught his and Claire's eye when they were driving to visit her grandfather in Beverly Hills. He watched as Claire wandered through the downstairs now, dreaming of decorating and furniture. He remembered how they had stopped, peaking in through the windows when they found that it was empty, dreaming of a life that they wanted but could not yet afford.

Claire had continued talking about the house when they arrived at her grandparents' estate. Her grandmother had caught the bug. Before he knew it, they were in her grandfather's limousine on their way back to see it. As luck would have it, the agent had just been showing another couple around. She was only too happy to do the same for them. He watched Claire dreaming of the day he could afford to buy it for her, maybe in 10 or 15years' time, he calculated. While Claire and her grandmother explored upstairs with the agent, the old man cornered him in the kitchen.

'What do you think, young man?'

'It's very nice but there's no way we can afford it, not yet. In a few years' time though.'

The old man looked at him strangely.

'You mean, you don't want me to buy it for you?'

'No sir, I could never ask you to do that. Your family has already done so much for me, for both of us. We will buy a house in a year or so, not as nice as this one, maybe, but one day we will make it here.'

'You surprise me, young man. I suppose I shouldn't be surprised; your character is impeccable.'

It touched and wounded Rory at the same time. His character was not impeccable enough that he wouldn't be an accessory to murder or the covering up of the same. The old man placed his hand on Rory's shoulder.

'I could help you; Claire has a trust fund.'

'Yes, but we try not to use that. We've managed to save some money since we both started working. We're careful with our spending.'

'What if I loaned you the money, officially, through the bank? Let me take care of it. For now, you pay what you can afford then, over time, when your income improves, you can increase how much you pay.'

Rory looked uncertain.

'It's your decision though, I don't want to pressure you.' Just then Claire, her grandmother and the agent came back downstairs. 'Look how happy she is. Go on, make this day a special one.'

Simple as that, the house was theirs, in both their names, with a mortgage registered with the family bank. Their savings would never cover the decorating bill, let alone the furniture. They had been assured, though, that wedding presents would go a long way to helping. Rory had agreed to the arrangement only, in a way, he felt cheated. He had enjoyed building a future together. Watching their bank account slowly grow, eventually being able to buy a home they could afford. It was exciting, not knowing what was coming next.

The huge house with pool, tennis court and manicured gardens would require upkeep he could not yet afford. He stopped thinking about it.

In a few days' time he would be married, then off to a honeymoon, a gift from his new uncle, the governor. Johnny was leaving for Europe the day after the wedding. Tonight, his bachelor party, would be the last time they saw one another for who knew how long.

He had heard Johnny had taken up with a ballet dancer. They no longer spent much time together now Johnny had stopped helping his father. Chloe was still around but, apparently, he was besotted with this dancer. Rory grabbed a hold of Claire by the waist; she jumped, wrapping her legs around him. Kissing him.

'Thank you, Rory. I know how much this must have hurt. I promise I'll make it up to you. We'll pay back every cent.'

'I know and you're wrong, it doesn't hurt.'

She kissed him, appreciating the lie. Claire was wearing a short summer dress. He moved his hands down to her bottom and touched bare skin.

'Hey, you're not wearing any underwear.'

She smiled, giving him a wink. 'Let's christen this place.'

71

THE STANLEY CASE haunted Detective Lawrence. Try as he might, he couldn't expel it from his mind. The other case, the one with the couple, although equally tragic because the bodies had never been identified, didn't have the same impact on him emotionally. He had little doubt that the Hollingsworth family were behind the assassination of the witness and that his own boss, the police captain, was involved.

He should walk away, close his eyes, do what he had to do. Only, his conscience wouldn't allow it. Remembering the men who had visited the station: Jack and Tommy, he started following them. Why? He could not explain. Maybe it was because of how they had spoken about justice, how John Stanley had earned his justice on the battlefields of Europe. He recognised Henry and, putting two and two together, he figured he was investigating the case. He had nothing else to do so he began following him as well.

He was on edge. He noticed the men shadowing Henry, the ones he had seen them outside Jack's house. He guessed they were friendlies, though he remained in the shadows or so he hoped. The following morning, he followed Henry as he picked up David and then drove into a multi-storey parking garage. He parked on the street outside, as did Henry's bodyguards.

Not 10 minutes later, he watched as a yellow-coloured sedan emerged. It turned right, passing him. Strangely, at the same time, a large delivery van pulled up next to the bodyguards, obscuring their view. Detective Lawrence spotted Henry, sitting in the front passenger seat of a yellow sedan driven by a young woman. *Odd*, he thought. He also spotted a white station wagon, with a single, female occupant, pull in behind them. Quickly, he started the car and keeping his distance as he followed both cars.

As the miles passed, he started to realise they were not on a short journey. Before he knew it, they had been on the road for two hours. Remaining inconspicuous was difficult but where were they heading? He had to take a risk. He passed both of the cars and would drive as fast as he could, without attracting attention, then wait for them somewhere further up the road. If they turned off before that, so be it. It was a risk he had to take.

He drove for an hour then pulled into a gas station. Nervously, he waited. He was just about to give up when they pulled in. Ecstatic, he pulled out and resumed the journey to an unknown destination. Stopping twice more, they eventually arrived in San Francisco, back in convoy. He had no idea why they were there or what was happening. He was winging it now.

72

HENRY HAD SPENT the time between when he picked up David and they arrived at the parking garage, explaining his relationship with Anastasia. David was happy for him, though concerned.

'Don't get me wrong, I'm happy for you, I guess. You say that she's helping us?'

'I know what you think but she's a student, a decent kid. She got us the address of the doctor.'

'The surgeon.'

'Yeah.'

'You did some background, confirmed her story?'

'Relax, wait till you meet her. We're in love.'

'You called in the address?'

'Not exactly. She is going to give it to us this morning.'

'And we are meeting her at a parking garage?'

'Relax, everything is okay.'

'You aren't making it very easy to relax.'

When he saw Anastasia and Henry kiss, he was concerned. She, on the other hand, seemed overly relaxed for a 22-year-old student whose life was in danger. She had great legs that were on display. He found it disconcerting, the way she constantly touched Henry. Watching from the back seat, he observed her doing it constantly. It began to irritate him. Something wasn't right. He found himself looking for their bodyguards, panicking from time to time, when he couldn't see them.

Back at the house, Jack was sitting with Tank in the study when the phone rang. Tank picked it up. Jack couldn't hear what was being said but Tank did not look very happy, Jack heard Tank say, 'Hit the road,' before he put the receiver down. Jack looked across the desk at Tank, who was shaking his head.

'Henry and David left home this morning. My people followed them to a parking garage where they lost them. Their car is there in the parking garage but they are gone.'

Jack looked puzzled. 'Wait weren't they driving up to...?'

Tank cut him off. 'San Francisco. When David phoned in, he mentioned that Henry had arranged to get the details from that student he met.'

'Wait, does that mean we don't know where they were headed?'

'Correct.'

'That doesn't sound like David or Henry, for that matter.'

'You know, that girl has some strange behaviour for a student.'

'How do you mean?'

'Well, she hasn't been to any classes since we have been following her, she also hasn't been staying at the sorority house.'

'Where has she been staying?'

'At a hotel downtown.'

'Precaution?'

'That's what we thought. We hadn't been able to confirm it, now I'm not so certain.'

Jack thought about bringing up the fact that this was all news to him. Tank saw what he was thinking and shrugged.

'Everyone is jumping at shadows, what seems strange is the norm. We are looking in so many directions, following so many different people, my people are like springs ready to uncoil.'

Jack held up his hands, palms facing out.

'I get it. I just, I don't know, we need some luck and it seems in short supply.'

'They are on the road now, well behind the others, if they are on the road at all.'

'We need the surgeons address.'

Tank nodded in agreement. Neither man knew how they might obtain it.

73

IT WAS CINDY who came up with the idea that saw them obtain the address of the surgeon in San Francisco. The state medical board, she said, like it was nothing at all. A call to Doctor Feldman and three favours later, they had the address. Tank charted a helicopter.

Six or so hours after they had started their journey, the car, containing David and Henry, pulled up in front of a large Victorian house on a hill. Detective Lawrence drove past them, taking a position higher up on the hill. The other woman, he had been convinced was also following, had disappeared. He concluded it had been a coincidence. He waited until he saw them climb out of the car and begin walking toward the front of the house. It was time to get out of the car. He moved quickly, staying close to the buildings, when they disappeared. He almost broke into a run as his intuition pushed him. *Get a move on,* he told himself.

Knocking on the door, Anastasia led the way. They let her, thinking nothing of it. The door opened And Doctor Cortez appeared. Later, Henry would remember the look of confusion on his face as Anastasia called his name. His muddled response, his shock and their own as she pushed him inside. The recoil of the silenced weapon. They were spared from seeing the bullet hit, though they heard the sickening thud.

David went for his weapon. Henry, stunned, stood still, mouth wide open. They heard the call from behind to get down, heard another sound, another shot, only this was coming from the left. Detective Lawrence saw the woman, who had been following them, crouch and fire. She missed David but hit Henry in the shoulder, spinning him around. Detective Lawrence fired, hitting the woman. She now turned towards him. He did not know her or that she was known as Maya.

The bullet struck her on the hand. A noise from the top of the stairs alerted both David, who was laying on the stairs, and Detective Lawrence, who was moving toward them. It was muscle memory. David fired, hitting Anastasia, who was distracted by Detective Lawrence's shot, fatally in the chest. Henry screamed, reaching for her as she fell to her knees, then collapsed, falling forward. When Detective Lawrence turned to see where the other woman was, she was gone. Looking up and down the street, he could not find her. In the aftermath, there was calm. David expected sirens but there were none. Not a peep, not an onlooker. Detective Lawrence knew it was time to get going.

'Come on, my car is parked up the hill.'

The other two men nodded.

'Henry! Henry!' David yelled at Henry, who was staring blankly, holding his shoulder. He glanced at David. 'Go with this man, I'll tidy up here. Bring the car down.'

As they staggered away, the physically and emotionally drained detective and the wounded Henry, David dragged Anastasia's body back inside, then paused, made the sign of the cross and approached the body of Doctor Cortez. There was a small hole in his forehead. He checked the pulse out of habit, before reaching into his shirt and gently feeling for the necklace.

A minute later, having closed the front door, he was sitting in the detective's car as they retraced their steps. The silence in the car was temporary. Henry began to come around and recognised Detective Lawrence. He would never forgive himself for what had happened. Henry's wound had stopped bleeding. David checked it and surmised it was only a flesh wound.

They stopped at a payphone where they learned about the helicopter and where Jack learned about the shooting of the surgeon. It was little consolation that they had the bullet. A rendezvous was arranged. Henry flew back to LA with the bullet. David and Detective Lawrence then commenced the long drive home. Had they not decided to stop at the gas station for coffee, perhaps things would have been different.

Neither of them spotted Maya who, with bandaged hand, was calm and methodical.

74

LOUISE HAD SIMPLY had enough of being shut out. She could walk away. *How hard would that be?* she told herself. *Very.* If she thought Tommy was like all the others, she was lying to herself. Louise was in love. He was her soulmate, plain and simple. She could never just leave and pick up the pieces. At night, she lay awake in bed unable to sleep, yearning for his touch. That it was the middle of the night didn't stop her. She left her house and drove right up to the front of where Tommy was living. To her surprise, the lights were on. Two burly men stood guarding the entrance. Others, she noticed, were positioned around the property. One of the men looked her up and down.

'Name?'

She was taken aback by his rough manner.

'Louise, Tommy's girlfriend.'

The man spoke into a radio. He motioned for her to pass then thought better of it. Louise had rushed out of the house without getting properly dressed. She had thrown an overcoat over her nightgown, slipped into some shoes and run out the door. In truth, she had hoped to end up naked in Tommy's arms. She didn't think. The man began to frisk her.

'Open the coat please.'

She did as she was asked revealing a very sheer nightgown. The man, however, was professional. There was not even the hint of a smile or worse, a wink. He motioned her through again. In the living room, she found them, Jack and Tommy looking shocked, Jim Teal, one of Jack's lawyers, with a stern expression, Cindy in tears and Doctor Feldman acting as the comforting uncle, trying his best.

'What's happened?' she said, in a shaky voice, laden with concern.

Tommy looked up then ran to her. He found solace in her arms. She led him away to his room as he broke down. When Tommy had calmed down, he shared with her all that had been happening.

'Go to the police,' she said with conviction.

'Haven't you been listening? We've been to the police.'

Louise considered this. He was right. It was hard trying to think of a solution, when everything you had ever believed in, had been ripped away. It was as if she were becoming an orphan all over again.

'This bullet, it definitely comes from the boy?'

'A forensics expert is testing it. We will know, perhaps, as soon as tomorrow.'

'Then we broker a peace. We have something they want. We want to be left alone.'

'And justice?' he said it because it needed to be said, no other reason.

'Justice is a luxury we can ill afford,' she said. 'There is no justice, not in this world or any other. There is only hardship and suffering, for us anyway, perhaps for all but a precious few.'

Whether he wanted to believe it or not it was true.

'Let's go and tell the others.'

75

Rory's stag weekend was held in one of Johnny's family's hotels in Las Vegas. He hadn't wanted to go, only it would have been difficult, no awkward, to avoid. There was no use making protestations or imposing conditions. There would be strippers, there would be drugs, prostitutes and more. There was nothing he could do about it, so he just kept quiet. They flew out in the presidential candidate's new Learjet. It was just Rory and Johnny on the Friday afternoon. Around the country, the other guests were finishing up their work early and, on their way, to join them. They were sitting at a bar in the lounge of their two-storey penthouse.

'Don't you miss the games, Rory,' Johnny asked, sipping a beer.

'No, not in the slightest,' he replied.

'Come on, I've been thinking, what if I organised a sex game for Saturday night?'

'You can do what you like, so long as it doesn't include me.'

Johnny didn't hide his disappointment. Rory remained unmoved. He remembered Johnny's sex games. Yes, Johnny was correct, he had enjoyed them once, back when they had been harmless fun. They had been mysterious, everyone had worn masks, indulging in wild fantasies.

'Everyone plays games, Rory, I just take them to a new level,' grinned Johnny.

'Like the game we are playing now.'

'What game?'

'The one we have been playing for the past six years. The game that took you from an impoverished loser nobody, to being the husband of the niece of the President of the United States: a bright young man with a most promising future. Wasn't it reported in the Wall Street Journal, you are a millionaire at 25, with a house in Beverly Hills and an apartment on Fifth Avenue, also reported in the Vanity Fair special editorial.'

'This isn't a game, this is life.'

'Life, life is one big game.'

'No, it isn't.'

'Sure about that?'

Johnny reached into his pocket. 'Recognise this?'

He threw him something small and round, hand-made from wood, with a number roughly painted on it. Rory froze. He recognised it at once; it was the token he had drawn for his room assignment. Johnny laughed.

'You look shocked. Here, I know you don't believe me.'

He placed a notebook on the bar then pushed it towards him. Rory sat staring at it. The title on the front said, "The Rory Game". He opened it. "Chapter one - Room Assignment". He sat in shocked silence, flicking through the pages. Everything was here, from his internship to the games, to their private encounters, discussions, to his meeting of Claire, their relationship, the house, their engagement, his career, everything. But how?

'That old man wasn't cheap. Cost me $2,000 to make sure you drew the same room as me in the room assignment. He also had a dirty mind, had to promise him I wouldn't make a move on you, unless it was consensual. Wouldn't believe my motives weren't sexual.'

Rory had no answer, no reply. How could this have happened?

'Life, all of this is a game.' Johnny gestured with his right hand then picked up his glass and took a large swig. 'One big game. Don't you realise now, you're just a player in my games. I only asked you to play out of courtesy. You've been playing all this time and you will continue to play. Why fool yourself? All of this, you want all of this, more than I do, more than I ever did and don't think for a moment I'm the only one. We are all playing our own games. Claire is playing hers. She doesn't want to marry some rich, soft cock, she wants a real man self-made, someone who will worship her, fuck her brains out, do what he's told, someone ambitious and fun. She's running her own game while, at the same time, playing mine.'

This was too much. *But wait,* his mind said, *wait a minute.* All of a sudden, he realised, Johnny, in some perverse way, was right.

'What about my grandfather,' Johnny continued, 'Do you think becoming president was my father's idea? He was an arts history major with bi-sexual leanings, set to spend his life and his trust fund researching, digging for artefacts and fucking interns of both sexes. That was until my mother and grandfather got their hands on him. Everything we do: school, work careers, families.

'Families are the biggest game of all and now you are a part of it. You know, when she was 13, Claire was in love with her best friend and roommate at boarding school. True, she confided in me, then the friend fell in love with a boy. Happens. Claire was heartbroken, then she decided boys were for her also, started dating one when we were on vacation at Martha's Vineyard. Now I'm wondering how you will react should she change her mind. Don't worry, we will wait until you have been married for a few years. It's all there in the notebook.'

Very carefully and deliberately, he reached across and took it out of Rory's hands. They heard the doorbell.

'It's just a game, Rory. You might as well keep playing.'

76

THE WEDDING WAS a happy, if sedate, affair. Rory's family were not represented, only a few friends from school. Claire looked beautiful. Seeing her walk down the aisle in the long, flowing white dress, literally took his breath away. When she held his hand, he thought he might faint. The reception was at the Beverly Hills Hotel ballroom and it passed in a haze. In the years to come, when he would view the many photographs taken on that day, he would have no recollection of any of it. It was as if he was viewing strangers in the pictures. There was no connection, until he would appear.

Jim Teal had wrangled himself an invitation to what the social columns had been describing as the event of the season. He seemed to step out of nowhere when Rory had stepped outside for a moment to gather his thoughts and get some fresh air.

'Jim Teal, attorney-at-law, congratulations on your nuptials?' Rory was offered Jim's hand, one of the hundreds he had shaken that day.

'Thanks.'

'How do you feel?'

'Elated, I suppose is the standard response. To tell the truth, it's all a little overwhelming.'

'What is it they say? The wedding isn't for the bride and groom.'

He chuckled as he said this and Rory laughed. 'Tell me something, is it anything like the confusion during the little games you and your best man play? You know the ones, where some innocent party ends up dying?'

Rory's smile disappeared. A chill ran down his spine. Jim was still smiling.

'How do you…?'

'How do I know that? You and your little psychopath friend or is it lover over there, have murdered at least two people we know for sure, in some sick game. What's the death toll up to now? How many people have gramps, and daddy had knocked off for the pair of you?'

Rory tried to regain his composure but it was too late.

'I don't know.'

'Sure you do. You still have a conscience though, right? Want to go straight now that you have everything you ever wanted? But it was more than that, wasn't it? There's nothing to be ashamed of. Plenty of guys like to fool around a little in the locker room with one of their buddies. What was his name, the kid who recently got himself killed in that car wreck? The one with the driver who has never been found? He told us all about it, how you and Johnny have a special friendship, how you like it both ways. The 1980s are almost here, I'm sure that pretty young wife of yours will accept the real you.'

'I'm not like that, it was just…'

Jim cut him off. 'So, it was just a temporary infatuation, then it's okay with me pal. Not my thing, of course, but whatever floats your boat.'

'You don't understand, I…'

'Save it for the jury. I'm sure they'll find it fascinating, how one of the three of you used to go under the curtain of the four-poster bed in Johnny's room, poke out your ass, all that juicy stuff.'

'It was a game, women played it too.'

'Games, huh? Games are dangerous. I, myself, stopped playing games a long time ago.'

'What do you want?'

Jim looked at him flabbergasted.

'What do I want? What on earth do you mean? We're just a couple of guys having a chat on one man's wedding day?'

'Name your price.'

Jim was a master negotiator. This was his finest hour. He would let the young groom burn for a little longer.

'Rory, my friend, I'm insulted. I don't have a price. Didn't they teach you anything in that fancy university or was it all just these sick games?'

This prompted the reaction he had hoped for: denial. He had him now.

'What do you have anyway? This is all just gossip.'

'I want 10 minutes of your new wife's grandfather's time, here, right now. I want you there along with his son and son-in-law. You can bring anyone else you want. I'll put my case to them then they can give me a number and then, if that number is to our mutual satisfaction, me and my friends will disappear into the sunset. Capisci, kiddo?'

'Alright, where?'

'This is your show, isn't it?'

Rory took a moment to collect his thoughts.

'Go back out into the foyer, follow the corridor, you will come to a door marked groom's room, I'll meet you in there in five minutes.'

Rory turned to leave but Jim had one more thing to say.

'And don't worry, I'll keep all those shenanigans between you and Johnny to myself, unless well, you understand, they need to be disclosed.'

Rory stopped briefly then, without responding, went to find the others. They found Jim sitting at a round table surrounded by five chairs and a folder in front of him. All the men entered the room cautiously, watching the old man closely as to how to behave. Jim stood to greet them.

'Gentlemen, Jim Teal, attorney-at-law, won't you have a seat. Governor, Mr Lethbridge, Johnny and your name, Sir?'

They had brought Randle along.

'Randle, a fellow member of the bar,' the old man said.

'You are most welcome, Sir.'

Let the games begin! Jim thought.

77

The death of her protégé surprised Maya, but no matter. Two of the men responsible had paid for their interference. She kept an eye out for the third, he would present himself soon enough. In the meantime, there was work to do.

Her hand still ached from the wounding. She was careful, only taking the mildest of painkillers, small doses just to take the edge off. After all, there was work to be done. She had been given one final task, then it was time to disappear again. *Somewhere warm*, she thought, *perhaps for good this time.*

The problem was, the work she did was so exhilarating, nothing else came close to the thrill of it. She was dressed all in black, including her face paint. The house in Santa Monica was well guarded but for someone like her, not secure enough. She dropped from a tree in a neighbour's yard, landing awkwardly with a thud. Cursing under her breath, she made her way toward Cindy's studio. Jack heard the noise. He had heard that noise before and the word danger flashed through his mind. He glanced around; there were no guards nearby. He looked across towards Cindy's studio where he saw a figure moving. Reaching behind him, he retrieved his pistol and started to run.

78

'GENTLEMEN, I'LL GET straight down to business. I represent the party you have been, shall we say, in dispute with these past weeks, over the matter of your grandson there and your new, what shall we call him, grandson-in-law? Nephew-in-law? Over their murder of one, perhaps several, people, I distastefully describe as "homeless individuals".'

Randle moved to object but Jim raised his hand to stop him. A quick glance around the rest of the table he could see Johnny angry and Rory's head, bowed in shame, The governor and the old man were outraged at the mention of such an allegation.

'Let me offer some evidence before you waste my time with any kind of rebuttal, Mr Randle.'

'Just Randle will do fine. Go ahead.'

'Thank you. I just wanted to check. I'm fully authorised to make a deal here tonight. Are all the parties, able to make a decision on your side, present?'

The old man spoke, 'Randle has the power to act on our behalf.'

'Thank you for clarifying that. Randle, I call your attention to this document, let's call it exhibit A. It's a forensic report issued by an expert who does work for, among others, the FBI.' He slid the report across to Randle. 'In it, he confirms that a bullet dug from the leg of your grandson was fired from this pistol, owned and used by one of the members of the party I represent, in an effort to defend an elderly gentleman, one John Stanley, a war veteran, whom your grandson, along with your other relative over there...' Jim was deliberately denigrating Rory's status to upset him. It was unnecessary, the young man had begun to weep. '...was in the process of murdering, as part of some, psychopathic game they were playing,'

'We object, what proof do you really...' Randle started.

Jim threw the bullet onto the table; it landed with a dull thud.

'We're confident, that is, our FBI expert is confident, that the blood particles removed from that will match Johnny's blood type. Plus, we have these sworn affidavits from witnesses, the medical staff who saved Johnny's life, confirming that they did treat your grandson, that his best friend was there covered in blood, his blood. That's you, Rory, you were covered in your friend's blood, weren't you.'

Rory, in total defeat, nodded. Jim, emotionless but enjoying every moment, moved right along.

'We then have this documented evidence of your honourable sir, the governor over there who, in an attempt to cover up what had happened, by offering bribes and other incentives to, not only the other young men in attendance as accomplices to the murder of Mr Stanley, our war veteran, but to hospital and janitorial staff. We have the sworn affidavit of one, Benjamin Pierce, a former class mate of yours, boys, who you may be interested to know has decided to become a Jesuit priest and happily provided, not only a statement but details and other evidence of a trip to Mexico and a recording he made, where the good Mr Randle coached him in preparation for a possible police interview, if the need arose. Obviously, this, if it became public, could cause catastrophic damage to a man who holds high office and is seeking even higher.'

Randle, seething, offered only a smile.

'We have other evidence,' continued Jim, 'it's all here in this file, a copy of which has been secured, along with the other half of that bullet.' He motioned to where the bullet lay on the table. 'Now, are we at the point where we can begin to negotiate a settlement or would you like me to continue?'

Jim looked around the table once again. This time, their expressions were blank. *Good*, he thought, *they want this over with*.

'Do you have something in mind? Without the admission of any guilt, you understand.' Randle said feebly, knowing he was as fucked as the others.

'Well, far be it from me to state a number, as it were, for our aggrievement. I'll leave that to your good self but, number one, we would like a million dollars for the families of each victim, that includes the people you murdered in order to cover things up; five million for veterans' affairs or a similar charity, an undertaking of psychiatric treatment for these two fine, upstanding young men, a ceasefire and end to the hunting and killing of our people and anyone else on your hit list.'

'That's all?' Randle said sarcastically. 'On top of what you want, you're talking what...?' He tried to remember how many had died. It was beyond him in his current state.

'Well, there were the two victims, the witness, the two, no three you killed yesterday in Sisco, the man you wounded in DC, though he's not dead and I did say dead.'

The mention of the word brought a fresh round of sobbing from Rory.

'Well, he deserves something, let's call it $500,000, is it six or seven?' Jim continued. 'So that's 7.5, plus the donation, 12 plus your compensation? Sounds about right, what's your thoughts on that figure?'

Randle eyed him carefully; he could not help but admire.

'I mean, what's all this worth to you? The reputations of what, 10 or more people, people who now have a clear path to the oval office?'

Randle couldn't believe it. The emphasis on the number 10 was no accident.

'Wired here in 15 minutes if you don't mind.' Jim pushed a final document across the table.

A total of $22,000,000, thought Randle. He looked at Johnny with utter disdain. *You little bastard,* he thought, *you disgusting little bastard.* Still, it wasn't his money.

Jim stood, the negotiations were concluded. It was the performance of his life and these men were the only witnesses. Randle leaned forward. It wasn't necessary but he wanted to say it, wanted it to be known, that it was he who was in charge.

'Deal.'

79

MAYA LET OUT a sigh as she stepped into the room. Cindy, who was standing in front of an easel, turned around. Maya stared at the painting. It was the commission of the girls looking out to the ocean. She became lost for a moment in its beauty: the yellow and orange hues of the twilight sky dazzled her. Without realising, she took a step closer. Cindy, noticing the pistol in her left hand, cowered and moved to the side. Maya was having trouble processing what she was seeing. She couldn't kill this person, couldn't under any circumstances deny the world of such a person. No, she looked toward Cindy and smiled, turned and started back out the door. Jack saw a shadow. Pistol raised, he fired three times into the chest.

They heard the shots inside and came from everywhere. They found Cindy screaming, holding Maya who was bleeding profusely, while Jack stood horrified, still holding the pistol. Cindy thought of the first war painting she had produced: the one where Tommy held his dying friend. In a surreal moment, the portrait came vividly to life, enveloping her into the canvas. She felt the warm blood on her hands as it poured from this stranger's body, while she looked up at her, smiling serenely. Tank and Henry pulled her away as she clutched her hands to her breast. Jack tried to calm her but she pushed him away, while others tried to help

Maya. Confusion raged all around them. Jack felt the world spinning, spiralling out of control. The men tending to Maya, looked up, shaking their heads. Cindy howled, falling to her knees.

The air moved slowly around the chaos of the night.

80

Six months later.

THE YOUNG MAN, who was homeless at the time he had been approached, had been lured to the heavily wooded island with the promise of a caretaker's job, a cabin of his own, supplies and a large salary. It seemed too good to be true but, as the weeks passed by, any concerns he had melted away as he adapted to life in this new, idyllic location. He was, as yet, unaware that he was the first participant in a new game Johnny had devised. A game where he had taken his favourite elements from each of his previous games and brought them together, to form, what he liked to think would be the ultimate challenge. A test of human will and resistance, designed to bring out the true character of a person, find out what they were made of, providing the answers he longed to know. This was important work, he argued, work that must be done. He watched the young man swimming naked in the lake, growing stronger. There was a certain level of arousal as he watched but, was it sexual or anticipation of the game itself? He was interested to find out.

'Game On'

About the Author

Justin Fox is a writer who lives in Sydney, Australia at the foot of the Blue Mountains. A born lover of storytelling, he never tired of hearing the stories of others and began creating his own at a very early age. Justin's writing shows a deep understanding of emotion. Readers are given insight into his character's inner thoughts, feelings and emotions as they come to life. The stories that have been building up over a life spent living, are finally ready to come flowing out. Justin's 'desire' is to bring enjoyment to as many people as possible, by sharing his stories.

RICHFOX BOOKS Pty Ltd

www.justinfoxauthor.com